# WHEN EVERYTHING IS BLUE

LAURA LASCARSO

Published by
Laura Lascarso
www.lauralascarso.com

When Everything Is Blue

First Edition: © 2018 Dreamspinner Press

Second Edition: © 2019 Laura Lascarso

Cover Art by AngstyG

ISBN: 9781695471726

# WHEN EVERYTHING IS BLUE

# ONE

## BE COOL

Being horny and almost sixteen is the absolute worst.

Take it from me, Theodore Wooten III, resident expert in the spontaneous boner. The cause of my lovesickness: Christian Mitcham. The cure: hell if I know.

With his sun-bleached hair, warm brown eyes, and devil-may-care attitude, people gravitate to Chris like sugar ants on a soda can, me included. He's been my best friend since sixth grade when some neighborhood punks held me down on the sidewalk and tried to spit in my eyes. Chris called them off and threatened to beat their asses even though he was outnumbered and outgunned. I guess they believed in his conviction. I know I did.

"Chris is back."

My twin sister, Tabitha, rushes into my room, even though the door was mostly closed. When we moved into this apartment, the owner paid a contractor to split the master bedroom into two bedrooms, so that we could each have our own room. Tabs got the en suite bathroom, and I got the window. Considering the view overlooks Chris's property, where he can often be found strutting around shirtless in the wild, it now seems like a fair trade.

"You're supposed to knock," I grumble. My gut is a brew of excitement and nerves at the knowledge that Chris is back. My feelings toward my best friend have become more complicated over the past year or so. I'd hoped a summer apart would simplify things.

"I did knock, Theo. You just didn't hear me," says Tabs, she of the last word.

I was watching some skate videos online with my cans on. The music was loud, but not that loud. I toss my tablet on the bed, stand, and stretch, delaying the inevitable.

"Oooh, he looks good," Tabs says as she opens my window, piquing my interest even more. "Buff and tan. He's been working out."

"Probably just surfing." A cloud of swampy Florida air envelops me as I steal a glance over her shoulder. She's right. He's even more godly than two months ago. Lucky bastard doesn't even need to try. Ever since Chris turned thirteen, his muscles have been bursting out like microwave popcorn. He lifts a burger to his mouth and sprouts biceps, sits up in bed and *boom*, there are his abs. Meanwhile, I grow taller and lankier and have to deal with my mom telling me to stand up straight or I'm going to get scoliosis, which I'm pretty sure isn't how that disease works, but it's hard to argue with my mom when she thinks she's right.

My sister calls down to Chris. He's carrying a new surfboard— midnight blue, probably a gift from his dad. He glances up and lifts his free hand in a friendly wave.

My gut twists in a nausea-inducing way. The feelings are still there, the sharp knife of longing that slices down my sternum and scrambles my guts. I lift one hand in greeting and hope I'm far enough away so he can't see anything unusual on my face.

"Come down," Chris calls. "Bring your suits."

I'm already wearing my board shorts and a T-shirt. Standard summer attire. We live close enough to the beach that I can bike or skate there, even though my mom hates me going through all the traffic. Sometimes I just go to skate along the sea wall and smell the ocean. It reminds me of Chris.

The twist in my stomach coils into a hard knot of anxiety at the thought of our reunion, but it'll be weird if my sister goes and I don't. Plus, I've missed him like crazy. I got so bored this summer, I was finally able to nail a nightmare flip on my skateboard. Something to add to my college applications.

"Be right down," Tabs calls to Chris, then bounces out of my room like a happy Pikachu. My sister's always been the cheerful, outgoing one. I'm slightly sour.

I glance back out the window to find Chris still looking up at me. Of course I'll be down. As if there was ever a question. I always do what Chris tells me. And until recently, I've been happy to do it. I trust him to know what to do in just about any situation.

Me, not so much.

I trail behind Tabs across our driveways and through the gate into his backyard. He's laid out on a lawn chair, shirtless of course. His hair's gotten longer. He likes it that way, so he can tuck it behind his ears. He's got a deep summer tan, and his abs are even more ripped than when he left for summer a couple of months ago. His sunglasses are reflective so I can't see his eyes. I worry he can tell I'm checking him out, so I stare at the shrubbery instead.

"What is this, a race?" Chris rises from the lawn chair to give me our usual bro-hug. He means my height. I must have grown two inches over summer, but I didn't realize the difference until I have to lean down a little to embrace him. I catch a whiff of his hair—a mixture of sunshine, salt spray, and coconut shampoo. His skin is warm and feels good in my palms—dangerously good.

Chris hugs my sister too and asks her if she highlighted her hair. She did. He tells her he likes it, and my sister's smile cracks wide open. We have good teeth, my sister and I, bright white and straight thanks to orthodontia. Our dad's a dentist and our mom's a dental hygienist. Our smiles are the one trait people say we have in common, though they probably see a lot more of Tabs's teeth than my own.

"I wish my hair was your color naturally." Tabs tugs at Chris's golden locks playfully, which draws another deep chuckle from him. I study the flecks of quartz in the concrete and try to ignore the fact that my sister is flirting with my best friend. And she's doing a really good job of it.

"How have the waves been?" Chris asks, drawing me back into the conversation. He never lets me stray too far.

"A couple tropical depressions came through and kicked up the surf. We got a few good days down at the pier. Probably nothing like an average swell in Cali, though."

Chris shrugs. "It was all right. Nothing too special. I kind of missed it here."

He looks at me then with his mile-long gaze, and I wonder if he's saying that he missed me or if it's just my lovesick imagination trying to bridge the gap between friendship and something else.

"It was pretty boring." I glance out at the chemically blue water. The summer has been drab and gray without Chris. Feels like the sun is just now breaking through.

"Learn any new tricks?" he asks, meaning skateboarding. I don't usually surf too much without him.

"Yeah, a nightmare flip."

"No way."

"Yeah, landed primo a few times and almost sliced my balls in half." I stop at the mention of my balls, feeling my whole face flame up, which is stupid because we've probably talked about our balls a million times before, so why is it so weird now?

"Ew, Theo, gross. No one wants to hear about your junk," my sister says, saving me.

Chris chuckles. "Can't wait to see it. The flip, that is."

I feel intensely hot under the heft of his stare, like my body might spontaneously combust. Instead of saying something else weird, I drop my towel on a chair and take off my shirt, then dive into the water and start doing laps. I spent a lot of time swimming laps in Chris's pool over the summer. I like being submerged.

When Chris and I met, he was in seventh grade and I was in sixth. At the time my mom, my sister, and I had just moved into the garden-er's cottage next door because my parents had recently separated. I told Chris they were getting back together—I was so sure of it. But I've realized since then we were only my dad's starter family.

Chris told me about his own parents' divorce and then, when it happened to me later that year, he was there to talk me through it. I've never met another person I connected with like that. It felt special from the beginning.

Kismet.

And then last year, I started noticing things more—Chris's muscles for one, the texture of his skin—warm and golden like honey —the pucker of his lips when he's thinking, his hands. His smell. I started imagining what it might be like to kiss him, and when we'd happen to touch, it made my body go completely bonkers. It got to the point where I couldn't be in the same room with him without getting a hard-on. Then he left for California for the summer, and I hoped the feelings would pass.

But they haven't, and I'm scared they won't.

After about twenty laps, I climb out of the pool feeling a little more relaxed. There are snacks on one of the tables, probably brought out by Paloma, their housekeeper. I towel myself off and check out the spread. Chris lowers his sunglasses and looks me up and down, not even trying to hide it. I don't know if it's out of competition or appreciation.

"Been working out?" he asks in that bro-code way.

I flex my barely there biceps as a joke, but they're not as puny as I remember. "Just swimming and mowing lawns. Got a jobby job." I grab a grilled cheese sandwich off a plate. Paloma must have made it special for me, knowing they're my favorite. There's also cut celery and carrots for Tabs, who it seems is always on a diet, and chicken wings for Chris. He loves bar food—the greasier the better. He should weigh five hundred pounds, but he's doesn't. He's perfect. Le sigh.

"Who you working for?" Chris asks. Beads of sweat have collected on his bare chest, drawing my eyes to the growing patch of rangy brown hair between his chiseled pecs. And, yeah, there it goes again.

There must be some kind of pill I could take—the anti-Viagra—for when you want your dick to be cool.

"Theo?"

"A patient at my mom's office," I answer, glancing anywhere but at him. "Jack Lawson. Owns Lawson's Lawns. He needed someone who can speak Spanish to the crew."

My mom's Puerto Rican, and she and I mostly spoke Spanish in the house while Tabs and I were growing up. Tabs understands it, but she hardly ever speaks it. She's always trying to fit in, telling us to "act normal," whatever that means. Half the people in South Florida speak Spanish, so it's not even that uncommon.

"Saving up for college?" Chris asks.

I grin at that. Chris is always telling me not to worry about college, that I'll get a scholarship with my grades and his parents will probably have to pay extra to get a university to take him. He's always trying to even things out between us so that money isn't an issue— him having it and me not. Even though my dad's a dentist and comes from money, he's working on his fifth kid with his third wife, which means the child support well is drying up fast.

"I'm trying to buy a car," I remind him.

"What do you need a car for?" His sandy eyebrows draw together, giving him a stern appearance. He looks put out by it. He's been giving me rides since he got his license last year. Sometimes I feel like I'm taking advantage of his generosity, and I don't like it.

"You know, to get around. I'm getting my license soon."

"I thought I was your ride."

A bit of melted cheese gets stuck in my throat and I have a little coughing fit. Chris jumps up and slaps my back, though I'm not sure it helps. I recover pretty quickly but not before noticing the hesitation of his hand, his warm palm against my cold skin and a slight, reassuring rub that sends the exact wrong message to my dick.

"You going to let me drive your car, Theo?" Tabs calls, hitting me like an anvil to the head.

"Not without a license." My sister has shown no interest in learning to drive. She only got her learner's permit because my mom made her, and she hardly ever practices. I don't understand how she can be so reliant on others. I hate asking people for things.

"You're still going to ride with me to school, though, right?" Chris says, moistening his lips with his tongue, drawing my attention to the pink that stands out against his tanned skin. His jaw is smooth. No more soft, downy hair. He must have started shaving this summer. Makes me think I should too.

I shrug. "Or, you could ride with me."

He looks pleased with the suggestion. "Hopefully you've gotten better at driving this summer."

"Like you're the expert, Curby."

He throws his shirt at me and I throw it back, but not before catching a whiff of it. Ack. Sensory overload. I claim the lawn chair on the other side of my sister. Physical distance helps. I close my eyes and try to envision the perfect wave instead of imagining what Chris looks like naked. Unfortunately it morphs into what Chris would look like surfing the perfect wave while naked, so then I imagine my fingernails being pulled from their nail beds because only thoughts of physical torture seem to work in these situations.

Tabs sits up, hands the sunscreen to Chris, and asks him to do her back. Without waiting for a reply, she angles toward him and sweeps up her ponytail. Like it's nothing.

I tell them I have to use the bathroom so I won't have to watch the rub-a-thon. Inside, I say hello to Paloma and ask about her mother, who's still recovering from a recent illness. They're from the Dominican Republic, and I think she likes speaking Spanish to me. We catch up for a bit. Then I hang out for a while in the bathroom, wash my hands meticulously, and count to a hundred until I'm sure the sunscreening is over.

When I come back, they've traded places and Tabs is doing Chris's shoulders. I can tell she's enjoying it. Really working it in there with the palm of her hand and taking her time. Who wouldn't? All that warm, teasing skin.... I don't want to watch, but I can't seem to look away, so I stand there trapped with a crampy feeling in my balls.

"You need sunscreen?" Chris asks.

I turn fifty shades of red and stammer, "No, I'm good." The last thing I want is to sprout a hard-on while Chris rubs my back. Jesus, I hope this is just some weird hormonal thing. I'd take acne and voice cracks over impromptu erections any day.

"Brown people burn too," Tabs says, our mother's constant reminder.

"I'll be all right," I say tightly.

The three of us lounge around in the shallow end, soaking up the sun and our last few days of freedom before school starts. My sister gossips about what went on while Chris was away visiting his dad in California, which couples from school have broken up and who's gotten back together, who's cheated or been cheated on. Who's pregnant or on drugs or in rehab. I tune her out and quietly float on a raft until I hear her start talking about our birthday.

"Guess who's turning sixteen soon?" she says to Chris.

"Ummm, Theo?" he says with a smile on his face.

She punches his arm playfully. "And me."

"Really, I thought you were at least seventeen by now."

She shakes her head and laughs. It echoes across the water, and my twin-sense tells me she's working up to something. My ears perk up.

"So, I was thinking...," she says in that nasally voice she gets with my dad whenever she wants something.

"What were you thinking?" Chris asks, playing along.

"I was thinking maybe I could have my birthday party here." She motions with her manicured hands at the pool and surrounding veranda.

"No," I call from my inflatable island in the deep end. I hate it when she asks our dad for things. Asking Chris is, like, a million times worse.

Chris ignores me and says, "Will there be a lot of hot chicks here?"

I roll my eyes and groan at his predictability.

"A ton," she says with this huge smile on her face, and I already know he's going to give in to her. Everyone does. My sister's a master at getting her way.

"Will you plan it without any help from me?" he asks.

"Of course I will." She claps her hands together.

"Will you help clean up?"

"A thousand times yes!"

"One last question." He glances over at me. "Will I be invited to this party?"

She laughs and strategically places one hand on his bare shoulder. Seeing her touch him like that gets me all moody and pissed. I hate feeling that way toward Chris. And my sister too. I wish I could stop it, or even better, rewind my biology back to when I didn't have these feelings at all.

"You'll be my guest of honor, Christian Mitcham," she says dramatically.

Chris waggles his eyebrows at me. "And what about birthday boy over there, is he invited?"

Tabs turns and lowers her sunglasses, stares at me like I'm the mutant tail she just can't seem to shake. "I guess so. It's his birthday too."

"I'm not going," I announce. I hate birthday parties, especially joint ones with Tabs. I'm always on edge because she's so uptight about me not making her look bad.

"You have to go, Theo," Chris whines in a high-pitched voice and splashes me. "It's your sweet sixteen."

A car horn interrupts my everlasting groan.

"Oh, that's Lizbeth," my sister says, climbing up the stairs and quickly toweling off. She dons a slinky sundress over her bikini and grabs her bag. "Going shopping at the Gardens. Want to come with?" She directs the question at Chris, not me. My sister rarely asks me to do things with her and her friends. I'm too weird, she says. I don't talk enough and when I do, I say strange things.

"I'll stay here and catch up with Theo." Chris smiles warmly at her. He has this amazing quality of making you feel special just with a smile.

"See ya, Tabs," I call.

"Yeah," she responds and saunters off with this swishy walk she does when she thinks somebody might be watching. She has a nice little body, and she knows it. Her sandals go *clack-clack-clack* on the concrete, and then she's gone.

"Same old Tabs," Chris says with a chuckle.

"Yep," I agree, though I don't find it at all amusing. She could have at least asked me about her birthday plans before springing it on Chris. I'd have said no—hell, no—which is probably why she didn't. Maybe too I feel a little possessive over Chris. She has a ton of friends already. Does she have to add Chris to her collection?

"A party could be fun," he says, trying to warm me up to it.

"I'll be up there." I point to my bedroom window.

"Like hell you will. If I have to put up with Tabs's friends, you do too."

I groan again even though I think Chris and Tabitha have both become immune to my resistance. The only thing I want to do on my birthday is go down to the DMV and get my license, then drive down A1A in my mom's car with the windows down, unless I have my own car by then. I've got a few thousand saved up from a lifetime of being cheap, along with my pay from summer work. A car means freedom, independence, and not having to rely on Chris or my mom to cart my ass around town all the time.

Chris turns on me then with a mischievous grin, crosses the pool in two strides, and upsets my float, dumping me into the cold water. It's a bit of a shock to the system. Even more so when he wraps one muscular arm around my neck and dunks me under just to show me he still can.

I come up with a full-body shiver and shake the water from my hair. "Had to get that out, huh?" I ask, hardly even annoyed.

"Got to make sure you still know who's boss." He punches my shoulder lightly.

*Boss* is my nickname for him, whenever he's being pushy or trying hard to get his way, which is most of the time.

"So, what have you been up to?" Chris asks. "You hardly texted me at all this summer."

He's right about that. Mainly because it just made me miss him more. I did send him a few pictures, mostly of the beach and the waves, since that's always been his favorite view.

"Nothing too exciting happened while you were gone. Didn't seem like much worth mentioning."

He scowls like he doesn't believe me, though he should know nothing fun ever happens when he's not around.

"I got a new board. Want to see it?" Chris has a lot of toys, but he gets super excited about his boards.

"I'm surprised you held out this long."

"I figured Tabs wouldn't be into it. Not the way you would."

"Yeah, sure."

We climb out of the pool and towel off. I follow Chris over to one of their outdoor sheds where he keeps his half-dozen surfboards, all quality-made, on wooden racks. If the boards don't stand up to the test, Chris trades or sells them, which means his collection is always evolving to suit his style of surfing.

The floor is a concrete slab and the couple of dusty windows light the shed in a buttery yellow haze. I can't see the color and design as well as if we were outside, so I run my hand along the edge of the board where it straddles two sawhorses. It's a shortboard with a slightly upturned nose. The epoxy resin is smooth as glass, not a drop of wax on it. It's probably never even been floated before.

"You haven't used it yet," I remark. Usually Chris takes them out his first day, or he arranges to test drive them before buying.

"This weekend. Taking a trip to Sebastian before school starts. You coming?"

I have nothing planned other than working with my lawn crew, which I can probably get covered for the weekend, but it's hard enough keeping my junk in check when we're alone. I don't want the pressure of being around his ultrahetero friends or watching him make out with his squad of surfer girls.

"I don't know, Boss. School starts on Monday."

"Whaaat?" he whines and I shrug like *What can I do about it?*

"Come on, T. I really want you to come with me. We haven't hung out all summer."

"I know, but...." I drift off, not knowing how to finish that thought without telling him the real reason—it's too damn hard to be constantly tempted with something you can't have.

"I'll give you Lady Macbeth." Chris grins slyly, sweetening the pot. Lady Macbeth is my favorite of his collection, a longboard made by a local guy named Casper. We named her that because we're convinced she's suicidal. On good days that board can sail. On bad ones she drops me on my ass. I can relate to her temperament.

"I always get Lady Macbeth."

"To have." He crosses his arms over his broad chest, accentuating the swell of his biceps and the meat of his pecs.

Chris is always giving me stuff. Before I got too tall, he used to give me his old clothes. My bike used to be his, too, and a couple of my skateboards. He's too generous, especially to me.

"That board's worth, like, $500. Not including sentimental value."

"It's practically yours anyway. I never ride it."

"So you're telling me you want me to store it in my garage," I say to mess with him. I don't want him to think I'm using him for his stuff, part of why I started working this summer. To give back.

"No," he says, getting a little flustered. It doesn't happen often, but I do enjoy seeing Mr. Calm, Cool, and Collected squirm. "You can still store it here. You probably should. Don't want to make the others jealous."

"Ha," I say as my eyes land on the ridgeline of his collarbone and the gold chain that rests there with a shark's tooth attached. I found it way back when on the beach and gave it to him—biggest tooth we'd ever seen. Chris had it made into a necklace. The tooth belongs to a great white, he always tells people when they ask, the same shark that chomps on surfers up and down the coast. Not us, though. By wearing its tooth, it shows the sharks we're one of them. Like most surfers, Chris is a bit superstitious.

I turn away so he won't see my face and pretend to inspect Lady Macbeth. "She's pretty dinged up, though."

"You little shit." He shoves me lightly. "You're the one who dinged her."

I smile. He's so protective of his boards. "If I take her off your hands, she might not answer to you anymore."

"She never did. I'd have sold her if it weren't for you." He lays his hand on the board's edge and gives her an affectionate little squeeze. His ruddy golden hand with his sun-bleached nails, next to mine, so close they're practically touching. Chris is always just an inch too far away.

"So, you'll come to Sebastian with me?"

Is it my imagination, or is there some unspoken plea in his voice? I don't know how I'm going to survive the weekend with him, much less my entire sophomore year. Lots of cold showers. But like most things with Chris, I don't have the willpower to say no.

"Yeah, I'll come. But I get shotgun." I always get shotgun unless there's a girl in the car. Hopefully he's not bringing a girl with us.

"Damn, Theo, I go away for a summer and you've turned into a shark."

I shake my head and nudge him lightly with my shoulder, my bare skin brushing against his. I glance over, and even though I can't see them in this light, I know that's where he collects his freckles, on the tops of his shoulders. I've spent way too much time memorizing them, but it's partly his fault for never wearing a damn shirt.

"You know you always get what you want in the end," I tell him. As if there was ever a question.

He smiles with an arrogance that only adds to his appeal. "Don't make me work too hard."

That deep, gravelly voice gets me every time. Feels like my heart is being rubbed over a cheese grater. I remind myself to breathe, then make up an excuse about something I need to do at home and walk back out of the shed with his fumes still in my nostrils and his voice humming in my head.

Our summer apart hasn't changed a thing. If anything, it's only gotten worse. I'm still hopelessly infatuated with my best friend.

My *straight* best friend.

## TWO

## AM I BEING PUNKED?

On Saturday we load up Chris's Volvo station wagon in the purple light of predawn and head north on A1A, which means the trip will take a little longer, but the views are prettier and we can watch the sun come up over the water. Chris has me check Surfline on the way to see what the waves look like. The man-made jetty at Sebastian Inlet creates perfect swells on a good day, great for cutbacks and aerial tricks. When a storm blows through, it's totally rocking, and all the surf rats congregate in a few tiny pockets of surf. This weekend it shouldn't be too crowded, though, which is how I prefer it. People, ugh. Exhausting.

"Three to five feet, rolling. Low tide's at 7:00 p.m.," I tell him.

"Perfect for the longboard."

"Yeah, not too shabby."

"You surf much this summer?"

"Eh, mostly skateboarded. You?"

"Had a couple good days up at this place called Salt Creek. Water's pretty there but so cold. Had to wear a wet suit."

"Bet you hated that." Chris would probably surf naked if it was legal.

"Yeah, couldn't show off my abs." He rubs his belly with one hand, lifting his shirt a little to offer me a glimpse. I chuckle at his vanity. His abs are amazing—all grooved and chiseled all the way down to his dips, which he's always showing off because he wears his board shorts super low on his hips. So tempting. And he doesn't even have to work at it. Dick.

"I met a girl," he says then, a little quieter.

I go still at the mention of a girl—my fugue state.

"On the beach," Chris continues. "We messed around some one night when we were at a party."

"Oh yeah?" I manage to choke out like I'm interested, though I'd rather not hear about it. I've seen Chris make out with girls before, and it's not my favorite pastime. I'm not sure if he wants me to ask about her. I usually don't have to, which is part of the problem.

"How about you?" he says after a moment. "Hook up with anyone this summer?"

"Nope." I've never lied to Chris, except for my growing attraction to him. I've thought about coming clean, but that would change everything. Not that he'd care if I like guys, but he might care that I like him. Talk about awkward. Things would be way too weird between us. Losing him as a friend would be the absolute worst.

"No one?" he says. "Seems like girls are always asking me about you."

I make some noise in the back of my throat that suggests I don't believe him.

"For real. I was talking to Ryanne last night. She asked me if you were coming out today."

First question: why was he talking to Ryanne? Second question: why did my name come up at all? I chew on my lower lip and stare out the window, wondering if this can get any more difficult. The silence seems to suck all the air out of the car.

"Ryanne's an older woman, you know," he teases. "You want me to say something to her?"

"No," I say too quickly. Ryanne is cool but as I've said, not exactly my type.

"I know you're shy and all...." He glances over at me with brotherly affection, eyes searching mine. Being shy is the least of my problems.

"Don't say anything," I say again, and then with a little less intensity, "I'm not looking for a girlfriend." Technically true. Alone is my default setting. I'm fine with it.

He shakes his head like he's disappointed. "Handsome guy like you. The girls wouldn't know what hit them."

I manage a weak smile and mumble something in agreement while thinking *The only person I ever want is you.*

*Dumbass.*

THERE ARE A FEW SURF RATS ALREADY OUT ON THE BEACH WHEN WE arrive. The sun is still low on the horizon, a melting blob of butter in the sky. The waves are rolling in like a pack of excited puppies, and the beach has a freshness that only a new day can bring. This spot we're at, Monster Hole, is mostly surfers who know how to take care of the beach, so there's no litter or trash anywhere. We know some of the people already. Surfers are a tribe of nomads in the sense that they're usually chasing the same waves up and down the coast. Whenever there's a hurricane or tropical depression, we end up crowded in the same campsites and cheap hotels, getting drunk on whatever we can get the locals to buy for us. Chris is a favorite among the girls. I bet he'll have some cute blonde on his lap by the end of the night.

And I'll be doing everything I can to ignore it.

We unload our boards and greet the few surfers who've already gathered. After getting an update on the day's surf report, we paddle out to test the waves. The water's still a little chilly, but the sun is coming up fast, spreading its warmth like a hug from a fat, happy god. Lady Macbeth gives me a hard time, or maybe it's me who's rusty. I spend more time underwater than I do on the board, but after a couple hours, the waves calm down and smooth out so I'm able to catch longer rides.

Every so often I glance over to see Chris cutting it up on his new board. They've become fast friends, which means now he'll have to name her. He's a powerful surfer. And fearless. When photographers come out, all the cameras angle toward him to capture his perfect blend of style and charisma. At the moment he's working on his alley-oop, trying to get as much air as he can while still finishing on his board. His muscular legs pump the board for max speed, and he lifts off the waves like a surf angel before bouncing back down and being swallowed up by whitewater.

My stomach starts to rumble, so I come out to the shore for a spell. Ryanne is there as promised, and we say hello. Her eyes kind of linger on my chest, and I wonder if she likes what she sees. I never know what to do with that. Should I look at her boobs or something to return the favor? More often than not, I look at my feet.

"Haven't seen you around much this summer," Ryanne says with an easy smile. Not like she's flirting, just being conversational, which I appreciate. I suck at small talk.

"Yeah, I got a job. Saving up for a car and all." I run a hand through my wet hair and try to tame it down a little.

"What kind of car are you looking for?" She squints up at me, shading her eyes from the sun.

"Something that's good on gas and not too expensive. And doesn't need fixing." I'm a little embarrassed to admit it, but I tell her, "I don't know much about cars."

"Me neither. Does it need to fit your board?"

"Nah, I've got Chris for that. Skating's more my thing anyway."

She nods. "I'll keep an eye out for you."

"Thanks. I'd appreciate it." I glance around, looking for Chris.

"He's over there talking to Kelli." She points. Chris is farther down the beach with one of his groupies, Kelli Keyhoe. Kelli goes to our school and is one of Chris's regular make-out buddies. She's a junior like Chris and Ryanne. Blonde and beautiful with what the guys call a banging body, Kelli's doing all the moves I've seen my sister use—hair toss, bared neck, laughing at shit that probably isn't that funny. Guys like that, I guess.

What do gay guys like? I have no idea. I've never seen two guys flirt with each other before. Do they even flirt? They must, right? I could really use a few gay rom-coms to guide me. Not that it would help much. I couldn't flirt to save my life.

I turn back to Ryanne. "I'm going to get some food. You want anything?"

"I can give you a ride. You can check out my Subaru."

"I was just going to take my skateboard."

"Oh, okay." She frowns a little, and I don't want to be rude, so I add, "But a ride would be great if you're up for it."

She agrees, and we walk over to Chris to get his order. He sees Ryanne with me and raises his eyebrows like this is my big chance to hook up with a real, live girl. I have to suppress a massive eye roll because if he only knew. I put on a shirt and wrap my towel around my waist before climbing into Ryanne's Subaru, so I won't drip on her upholstery. She brought a board with her to surf, which is cool. Most of the surfer chicks just come to lay out and flirt with the guys. Ryanne can hold her own out there in the surf. And she's easy to talk to.

While we pick up subs, Ryanne vents to me about her sister who graduated last year and thinks she's hot shit. I've seen her around school. Fast crowd, into those expensive drugs. I can relate to Ryanne's struggle. Tabs has that same desire to be accepted and popular, at whatever cost. I worry about Tabs and her friends getting into pills or coke. Seems like they'd try some stupid shit just to look cool. Addiction runs in our family.

"She's completely off the rails," Ryanne tells me. "Sometimes she'll disappear for a couple days and we'll get a call to come pick her up from some rando's house, totally wrecked and out of her mind. It's killing my parents."

I commiserate with her while we wait for the food. I tell her about my mom, who had to deal with the same thing with my dad, getting calls in the middle of the night to come pick him up from whatever bar he'd gotten shit-faced at, then having to fight with him to come home in front of everyone else, dealing with his sulky, woe-is-me attitude the next day. I can remember her actually apologizing to him for not being more understanding. What madness. My dad's an expert gaslighter.

"That's bullshit," Ryanne says, and I wholeheartedly agree.

When we get back to the beach, we all dig into our subs. Chris tries to give me money for the food, but I tell him to keep it for gas. "I'm a working man now." To get out of an awkward argument, I grab my board and head back out.

The winds have picked up and the waves are coming in faster now, rolling a little higher, breaking with more force. I love how the waves can turn on you so quickly. And the summer storms in Florida —they're the best. I love to watch the clouds roll in like the four horsemen of the apocalypse, the lightning tearing through the black sky like it's splitting it in two. The way the winds make the palm trees bend to their will with so much power and ferocity. And then the whole thing blows over like it never happened and the sun breaks through again.

I feel the undertow tugging at my legs as I paddle out to where the water's beginning to curl. I let a few good ones pass by, then jump on a beastly bomb, biggest one I've seen all day. I turn my board away, catching it at just the right angle. But when I'm about to pop up, Lady Macbeth gets caught on the wind and turns up hard. Her nose goes completely vertical and dumps me into a swirly that sucks me in deep. The dump is such a surprise that it knocks the wind out of me and I don't grab enough air before going under. My legs are trapped in the undertow, making it impossible to climb to the surface.

I get rag-dolled by the wave, try to grapple my way out of it, and end up getting buried in deeper while the waves still pound me. My lungs are burning, and for a moment I can't tell which way is up. I sweep with my arms and scissor my legs, kicking as hard as I can. Finally the pressure relents and I'm able to claw my way to the surface. Just as I breach the waves, two massive hands grab hold of my shoulders and yank me the rest of the way out. Chris is treading water right in front of me with a terrified look on his face.

"Shit, Theo. What took you so long?"

The alarm on his face makes me wonder how long I was under. I glance around for my board and see that Ryanne has trapped it way down the beach. It must have come untethered from my ankle in the swirly.

"You okay?" he asks and shakes my shoulders a bit.

"Should have waited half an hour before swimming," I say weakly, still breathless and dizzy from lack of oxygen.

He pushes me away and barks a harsh laugh. "Jesus. You're such an asshole. You sure you're all right?"

"Yeah, caught me by surprise is all."

We swim back toward the shore—Chris keeps me at his bow—and catch up with Ryanne and my board. I thank her for retrieving it.

"That board's a crazy bitch," Chris says, spitting into the shallows as we wade out. "You need to give her a rest."

"Can't. She's mine now. Got to tame her."

"Well, take five for my sake. I almost shit my pants."

I laugh, which is more like a gurgle, then have a little coughing spell. I must have taken on some water while I was under. Chris thumps my back, and I'm not sure it helps, but it does improve my spirits. Once on the beach, I wrap myself in a towel and lie down in the warm sand. Between waking up at 5:00 a.m. and the near-drowning, I'm pretty pooped. I pass out there on the beach and wake up hours later to find our spot mostly deserted and the sun starting to set.

"Morning, sunshine," Chris says. He's sitting next to me, cheeks ruddy from the sun, hair stiff from the salt water but still with that cherubic curl at the ends. The freckles on his shoulders stand out more, like connect-the-dots. Is it strange that I want to lick the salt crust from his skin? Yeah, a little bit.

"Where's the party at?" I ask, sitting up and rubbing my eyes. That's the routine. Surf till dark, then link up at wherever the beach rats are holed up for the weekend and drink. Or in my case, watch other people drink. My dad's a high-functioning alcoholic, so I'm not too keen to go there, even recreationally.

"I was thinking we could grab dinner and turn in early." He

stretches his arms and yawns. I resist the temptation to check him out. I also feel a little bad since I slept the afternoon away. He could have drowned on my watch. "That okay with you?" he asks when I don't respond.

"Yeah, it's fine."

"Unless you and Ryanne had plans...."

"We don't."

"All right, then. I picked lunch. You pick dinner."

We grab a pizza and bring it back with us to where we're camping. I set up the tent and Chris makes the fire. It's kind of our routine. We go in for another round of pizza, then sit around and poke at the fire for a while. Chris is quiet, on the verge of moody, which is rare for him. He's usually the conversationalist. I ask him what's up.

"Nothing." He rubs his bloodshot eyes. "Just tired, I guess."

"I'm ready when you are." I'm not tired, but Chris won't turn in until I do. He always has something to prove.

"Yeah, okay."

We each piss in the bushes and brush our teeth, dump some sand into the fire to put it out. I change out of my board shorts into some dry athletic shorts and a clean T-shirt. I don't smell too bad, thanks to the salt water, so I skip the shower.

Inside the tent I expect Chris to pass out right away, but he doesn't. I can tell by his breathing and the way he keeps glancing over at me to see if I'm asleep. It used to be a thing between us, whoever fell asleep first got punked in increasingly bizarre ways—toothpaste mustache, words written on your forehead, Vagisil in your hand. We haven't done that in a while, so I don't think that's what's keeping him up. But honestly, a part of me still worries I'll wake up tomorrow morning missing an eyebrow.

"Can't sleep?" I ask.

"No."

"Thinking about ways to punk me?"

He chuckles. "Now I am."

We're each sprawled out on top of our sleeping bags because it's hot as hell in here, even with the fly off. I can smell him inside the tent, rising up like heat from the pavement. Salt spray and sunscreen and something sharp and manly. So tangy I can almost taste it. The scent of him is so familiar, even while the desires it triggers are not.

"That girl I was telling you about earlier," he says, picking up the conversation right where we left it. It's something he does; he'll start a conversation, then drop it for hours or sometimes days, until he's ready to share more.

"Yeah, what about her?" I'd rather not know about Chris's exploits, but this must be something he needs to get off his chest, and what kind of best friend am I if I don't let him?

"We were at this party, in some back room. It was dark and we were on the couch. There were other people around, but it wasn't like they were paying attention. We were making out and she, like, wanted me to finger her. Right there."

I suck in a deep breath and let it out slowly. When Chris left for summer, he was a virgin, as far as I knew. Maybe not anymore. How do I feel about it? Doesn't matter. He needs his best friend right now.

"So did you?" I ask.

"Yeah."

"How was it?" I'm mildly curious myself.

"Mmmm...." Chris has a habit of humming while he gathers his thoughts, also while he's eating. I don't think he even knows he's doing it. "It was... squishy."

I laugh out loud. I can't help it. "Squishy?"

"Yeah, like a jellyfish."

"Did it sting you?" I chuckle again.

"No," he practically shouts. "It just had that... consistency, you know?"

"I *don't* know, but that's a pretty good description."

He's quiet for a moment and then he goes, "She wanted to blow me."

I feel my eyebrows crawl to the top of my forehead. Chris has no concept of TMI, at least not with me. "Did you let her?"

"No, but man, she wanted to," he says again.

I don't know too many guys who would turn down a blowjob.

That's, like, the thing at our school. Guys are always talking about who gave them a blowjob that weekend and how it rated with the rest. It makes me feel bad for the girls at our school, how meaningless and one-sided the guys make it seem.

"Why didn't you?" I ask.

"I don't know. I just met her, like, the day before. Felt... empty or something."

I say nothing, just imagine my best friend with a girl, his fingers all up in her jellyfish, her offering up a blowjob and him turning her down, even though it probably would have been easier to go with it. I'm kind of proud of him. And jealous of her that it was even a possibility he entertained. If Chris wants a blowjob, I'd totally take one for the team, but I'm guessing that's not what he has in mind.

"You would have let her?" he asks, like he might have done something wrong.

"No, I mean, I don't know. No one's ever offered. But, in your situation, I probably would have done the same thing."

"Yeah?"

"Yeah."

We're quiet after that. Chris is so open and honest. It makes me want to give something back, but whenever I think about expressing myself to him, my stomach gets all tied up in knots and my mouth cements shut and my brain screams *no, no, noooo.*

"Wow," Chris says.

"What?"

He chuckles.

"What?" I ask again, feeling paranoid that he somehow read my mind.

"I am so hard right now."

My breath hitches and my head swivels toward him. His eyes are aimed at his crotch, the tent that's formed in his basketball shorts, the shiny material pitched in the middle like a beacon. I've seen his dick before in passing, but not when it was hard. Never on display.

"So hard it, like, hurts," Chris says and curls his shoulders a little, like the sensation is uncomfortable.

My fingers dig into the fabric of my sleeping bag while my eyes travel to the tip of his tent, where his hard-on strains against the material, down the slope of his shorts to the waistband, the exposed skin, and the narrow trail of hair that leads to the hard lines of his abs.

"Take a look at this," he says and pulls down the waistband of his shorts so his dick pops up into full view, a little paler than the rest of him but just as hearty. Thick and meaty with a slight curve to it. Even in the dark, I can make out the swollen vein branching along his shaft. The head nods like a small man in a wide-brimmed hat, and a little drop of dew has collected at the tip. My heart races and my throat goes dry as my own cock starts to pitch and froth inside my shorts.

Does he know what he's doing to me right now?

Instead of putting it away, Chris grabs hold of it and gives it a long leisurely tug, like he knows I'm watching. My eyes are transfixed on the motion of his hand over his cock, so casually confident, and the soft, shushing sound it makes in the quiet tent. When I glance up at him, he's already looking at me, looking inside me, seeing the jumble of emotions I still haven't sorted through—desire, friendship, trust, and fear all mixed together in a riot of indecision.

"Feel how hard it is," he says and slowly moves his hand away.

I lick my lips and question him with my eyes. Is he for real right now? He wants me to touch his dick? Like, with my hand?

Chris nods, so slight I almost miss it in the dark. I don't know what else to do. He's the boss in this two-man show. I swallow down my nerves, reach over, and grab hold. All five fingers wrap around his thick cock. It's alive. Pulsing and warm, so smooth and ready. A real show-off, just like the rest of him. Chris closes his hand over mine and moves it up and down like it's the most natural thing in the world. He curls inward a little bit, shuts his eyes, and moans, and I don't need to guess what he wants me to do next.

He slowly moves his hand away and raises his hips off the ground to give me a better angle. I grip him tighter, rolling my hand up and down in a rhythm I've used on myself countless times, teasing the head with my thumb. Chris groans and puckers his lips. His eyebrows draw together and he gasps like he's in pain, but I know he's not. Sweat droplets collect at his temple, and I focus on his Adam's apple bobbing in his throat, nodding at me to keep on.

"Yeah," he utters from somewhere deep down as my palm rides him. "Oh shit, Theo," he exclaims, so I pump faster, gliding up and down his shaft while his face contorts into one I've never seen before. I jerk him off until he erupts, his warm goo spilling over my knuckles and into his curly light brown pubes. I pull my hand away, staring at it in disbelief. Not knowing what else to do, I wipe it on my shirt. The smell of him is everywhere, his skin and sweat and cum. My shirt is stuck to me from the dampness of my own exertion. My hands are shaking. Mind racing and breathless, I feel like I'm trapped in that swirly all over again.

"Let me do you," Chris says, sitting up in the tent. He's tucked his junk back into his shorts and his eyes have a drowsy, dreamy look. His mouth still hangs open, pearly pink lips shining with spit. I know he hasn't been drinking, so this must mean he really wants to? I lean back on my elbows, and he reaches inside my shorts for my own throbbing junk, tugs at it until it's at peak mass. It doesn't take much.

"I guess it's true what they say about tall guys," he remarks, and I have to hide my smile. Yeah, my junk's pretty big.

I watch him work me over, still struck dumb with disbelief and unable to process that this is really happening. Chris handles me with such ease, like it's the most normal thing in the world. His tongue edges out the corner of his mouth and curls on the side as he jerks me off with a look of deep concentration on his face. No one has ever touched me like this before, and even though it's Chris, my best friend, my *straight* best friend, it feels natural and right and *sofuckingawesome*.

The sensation builds until I'm bucking my hips in rhythm with his hand. A ragged growl erupts from my throat as seismic tremors roll through me in quick succession. My mind explodes, my body convulses, and my dick shoots out stars like the Milky Way. I don't even see where my spunk lands. Maybe the next galaxy over.

"Damn, Theo," Chris says and leans back, chuckling. "Been saving up for that, huh?"

"Ha," I utter, a little disoriented, a little delirious, clawing my way back into this new reality where my best friend touches my junk. Is Chris *gay*? My heart still pounds in my throat and a thin sheen of sweat covers my body and upper lip. I clench my teeth because I'm afraid to say anything that will break the spell. Chris lays back and spreads his arms, ruffles my hair, and generally takes up way more than his fair share of the tent. I listen to his breathing and wait for him to say something. Anything. *Any day now.* I count his breaths until at last, I risk a glance over and see that he's already fallen asleep.

I take a few deep breaths, trying to settle my nerves, then adjust my boys, who are still reeling in shock. I drag my hand across my shirt to find Chris's cum trail has dried into a thin crust, proving I didn't just dream it. Finally I roll over onto my stomach with the smell of him soaking into my pores, wondering what the hell just happened.

This changes everything.

# THREE

# NOPE

I don't wake up to breakfast in bed. Not even the smells of coffee and bacon.

I wake up alone. And there's a chill in the air. It sends a shiver through me and gives me a strange sense of unease.

The sun is just starting to bleed through the trees when I crawl out of the tent. I take the opportunity to change out of my jismed shirt into a clean long-sleeve that used to belong to Chris. I actually love wearing his old clothes, mainly because they remind me of something we did together while he wore them. I take a leak in the bushes, then poke at the coals of our fire with a stick. I consider restarting it, even though it's Chris's domain, when he finally shows up with a beach towel thrown over his shoulder, clean clothes, and wet hair. He usually never showers on our beach trips, says the ocean is all he needs.

I haven't rehearsed what I'll say to him. I'm trusting him to know what to do, since he initiated things last night. I study him as he comes closer, searching for some indication of where we stand. He looks a little nervous, embarrassed even, and keeps glancing away. I clear my throat while my guts do a Riverdance. His smile seems way too forced, like I could peel it right off his face. I'm balanced on the balls of my feet in anticipation when Chris finally opens his mouth and says, "I'm thinking donuts."

I run a hand through my hair and stare at my bare feet, which have been getting a lot of attention lately. He's thinking donuts. How am I supposed to answer that?

"Yeah, okay."

That settles it, I guess. We pack up the tent, and I notice the shirt he was wearing last night has disappeared. It seems along with it went any memory of what happened. Is it possible he was so tired he forgot? I couldn't forget it if I tried. And I don't want to. It was pretty awesome, I thought. Getting each other off like that? Way better than flying solo. Who knew a hand job could feel so good? And the fact that I care for him—right up there with my mother and sister—makes it all the more meaningful. But maybe he's ashamed of it, or of us.

We finish loading our camping equipment into the back of his car. I'm trying to think of a smooth way to bring it up when Chris turns to me and says, "Last night was crazy, right?"

He says it like we'd both gotten wasted and hit on each other's moms or something. Neither of us was drunk, and it didn't seem that crazy to me, more like, I don't know, *amazing*? But maybe he's worried it will screw up our friendship, which would suck royally. Or it was just a one-off for him. He's clearly uncomfortable about it, so there's nothing I can do but go along.

"Yeah, crazy," I echo.

"I was just messing around. You know that, right?"

*Messing around* is guy speak for *it meant nothing*. I've seen countless guys tell girls that same thing when they come calling Monday morning after a party over the weekend.

He must regret it, which makes me regret it as well.

"Yeah, sure," I mumble, then make my way blindly to the front seat, wishing I could sit in the back instead, because all I want is to curl up into a ball and teleport to literally *anywhere else*.

At Monster Hole we surf on opposite sides of the swells. Chris keeps his distance on the beach too. Maybe he's scared my dick might jump out of my pants and into his hand. He also makes sure to double his quota of flirting with the babes, proving to me or maybe himself his überheterosexuality.

Nothing says *screw you* like having a bunch of hot chicks draped all over you like Mardi Gras beads.

By the end of the day, I just want to go home, crawl into bed, and forget this weekend ever happened. Ryanne tells me about a skateboard competition coming up that I might be interested in going to, either as a spectator or a competitor. I ask her if she wants to check it out together since it was her idea. She says yes, so we exchange numbers.

On the car ride home, I pretend to be asleep so I won't sulk the whole way or make it more awkward than it already is. About halfway home, Chris clears his throat. Super loud. Like everything else he does, it commands my attention.

"Theo," he says.

I keep my eyes closed. I've already committed to it.

"Theo," he says again, louder, and then, "Come on, Theo, I know you're not sleeping."

I sigh and stretch and slowly open my eyes so he might wonder if I was sleeping or not. I don't say anything. I don't know what to say.

"I don't want it to be weird between us," he says.

He's already tried blowing me off, so what else is there to talk about? If he wants to pretend like it didn't happen, I will too.

"Why would it be weird?" I say like a shit. Maybe I am a bad friend.

He shoots me a look like *Don't be an ass*. Chastened, I sit up a little straighter and stare at my hands.

"Last night was just a weird mood," he says with purpose. Like he's trying to convince himself of it.

"I think we covered this already," I say sourly.

"No, I covered it. You haven't said a word."

I suck in my bottom lip and stare at the dashboard with my arms crossed. Ugh, the feelings. So many goddamned feelings, all swirling inside me like an undertow. None of the things I want to say to him feel safe. Chris has an agenda—he always does—so why is he trying to make me go first?

"What do you want me to say, Chris?" I finally ask.

"I want you to say it doesn't change anything."

I glance out the window, at the purple dusk blanketing the water and tucking it in for bed. I've relied on Chris for so much over the years. This summer when he was gone, I felt the loss of him deeply. It kind of scared me how much a part of my identity he's become. How often I look to him for approval, acceptance, and a shoulder to lean on. I love him as a friend and more, but I would never do anything to jeopardize our friendship.

"It doesn't change anything," I repeat.

"You believe that?"

No, but it seems he wants everything to stay the same, so what choice do I have?

"I guess so," I mutter.

He sighs, frustrated with me. For what, I have no idea. My lines aren't convincing enough. *Once more, with passion....*

"Look, Theo, I'm sorry," he says.

Now he's apologizing? He must think it was a huge fucking mistake.

"Whatever, Chris. We were horny. I'm sure other dudes have done it before without the world ending."

"I'm really—"

"Don't apologize," I cut him off.

He stares at the road. I've been too harsh. He's trying to make things right between us. Even if it's having the opposite effect, he's doing his best.

"It's cool," I say. "It was a stupid mistake. So let's forget it ever happened."

"You think it was a mistake?" He glances over at me. The fear and uncertainty in his eyes look strange on him. My best friend, who would take on ten bullies, tackle a twenty-foot wave without a second thought, punch a shark in the gill, is scared. Whatever his feelings, I'm not about to ruin five years of friendship just to prove a point.

"Yeah, it was a mistake."

He nods slowly, then settles back into driving, visibly relieved. He's off the hook.

# FOUR

## ENTER ASSHOLE DAVE

I start my sophomore year with a bad attitude. I blame it on the weather—hot, humid, and overcast, the trifecta of shitty for Florida climate. It's like being trapped in somebody's armpit. I meet Chris at the top of his driveway on the first day of school and climb into his Volvo with minimal chit-chat. I'm not a morning person and also, it's still a little weird after the weekend we just had. On the way to school, Chris tells me about a video he saw online of some kids surfing through the flooded streets of Miami during a king tide while tethered to the back bumper of a jeep.

"Urban skurfing," Chris says. "Next time there's a storm, we're totally doing it."

"It's a terrible idea," I say to him. "I'm in." It's a running joke between us whenever Chris comes up with one of his crazy stunts. This, at least, coaxes a smile from him. Besides, it does sound like fun.

"You talk to your dad lately?" Chris asks. He and his dad are pretty tight. Chris usually spends his summers in California, where they surf and camp and climb mountains and do all that father-son bonding you see in Patagonia catalogs—probably even work in a little game of catch here and there.

"Not since Easter," I tell him.

"He hasn't called?"

Chris is an only child, the apple of everyone's eyes, including his stepdad, Jay. Two sets of awesome parents for one kid. And Paloma, who dotes on him as well. Chris doesn't know what it's like to have to compete with a bubbly twin sister and younger, cuter models.

"He talks to me through Tabitha," I tell him. "There's another baby on the way. A boy."

"Wow. That makes five, huh?"

I nod. My dad is prolific. I'll give him that.

"Still," Chris says. "He could call you once in a while. Say what's up and all."

"I'd have to get a cavity for that to happen."

Chris shakes his head, trying not to smile. "That is so messed up, Theo."

"Yeah, especially since he's not even my dentist anymore."

We share a hard, bitter chuckle at that. Kind of feels like ice-cold air on the lungs. My dad's a real deadbeat, something I've gotten used to over the years. I don't like to dwell on it because then I get pissed off. Or I get sad and start feeling sorry for myself, which is way worse.

Chris and I arrive at school a few minutes early to claim our lockers, the same ones we had last year in Hibiscus Hall—the four quadrants of our school are named after flowers instead of cardinal directions. Like we can be duped by the naming of things as easily as tourists. For whatever reason Hib Hall, as it's more commonly known, is where the "popular" kids hang out. I don't really care about the cool factor, but it is centrally located, which is convenient. Chris's surfer friends all have lockers there, along with some of the skater punks—my colleagues. Our circles overlap.

We say what's up to Corbin, Jake, and Tomás, part of our inner circle who are milling around our section of lockers. Chris finds his locker from last year, and I'm about to claim the one next to his, but there's someone blocking my way.

New kid. T-shirt stretched tight over broad shoulders. He's putting his stuff into my old locker. I'm about to ask him to trade when the new kid stops and stares down the hallway, lets out a wolf whistle.

"Hot damn," he says. I follow his gaze and see that it's none other than my sister who's attracted his attention. She's sporting a dress-code violation short skirt and high heels, doing her swishy walk down the hallway, turning heads and setting loins afire. She knows exactly what she's doing.

"That is one hot tamale," the new kid bellows loud enough for everyone around us to hear. "Wouldn't mind taking her over one knee."

"Don't talk about her like that," I say instinctively, getting all up in the kid's face so I know he hears me. He's wide like Chris but a little chubby in the gut. Artfully buzzed hair like he just got it cut, and a little bit of acne on his face. He looks amused. I want to knock the smarmy smirk right off his face.

"That's his sister," Corbin says by way of explanation.

"Aye, Papi," the new kid says to me, picking up on my ethnicity, I'm guessing. His eyes go wide like he's testing me to see what I'll do next.

"Shut the fuck up and move your shit to another locker," Chris says before I have the chance to respond.

"Why?" the new kid says to him. "I don't see your name on it."

Chris doesn't argue with him, just reaches inside the locker and yanks everything out so it spills onto the floor—books, papers, folders. Chris unhinges the lock, clicks it shut, and bowls it down the hallway. It gets lost in the shuffle of feet. Corbin shakes his head, a knowing little smile on his face. Jake and Tomás pause their conversation to see what will happen next.

"Welcome to Sabal Palm High, asshole," Chris says in his deep, scary, man voice. It would intimidate me if I didn't know him like I do. "Now get the fuck out of our way."

The kid looks between Chris and me. His smile widens. He leans down and opens the locker beneath mine.

"Have it your way," he says to me. "You can be on top for now."

Those words, *on top*, and the way he says it, the way he looks at me like I'm an easy target. He knows. He knows *everything*. And he's putting it right there on display for everyone to hear. Fuck.

I jam my backpack into my locker, then stuff my skateboard on top of it, thinking to get out of there as quickly as possible. I don't want to even look at Chris because it will reveal something about me I don't want him to see. The kid just watches me, arms crossed, like he's enjoying the show.

"You skate?" he says to me like we're friends. I ignore him, fumbling with my lock. I haven't used it in three months, and I've forgotten the hang of it. "I'm new here," the kid says. "Maybe you could show me where the good skate spots are around town."

"Don't talk to him," Chris says to the new kid, still staring him down and standing broadside to further intimidate him. Chris hasn't even bothered to put his stuff away.

"Why? Is he your bitch?"

Everyone goes silent for a second, the whole hallway it seems, the whole city of West Palm proper. Then Chris lunges at him, slams him back against the locker with his forearm locked under the kid's chin, like he could break his windpipe if he felt like it. I jump out of the way. I've never seen Chris pull a move like that before. Meanwhile our crew all make *ooh* and *ahh* noises, the musical prelude to an ass beating.

"Watch your mouth," Chris hisses. Now the kid looks rattled.

"Everything all right here?" a teacher barks, storming up to us, knowing full well everything is *not* all right. Chris has a reputation for being a good kid, though, which is why the teacher gives him the chance to back down.

Chris releases the kid and backs off, but not too far. Chris's posture tells me he's ready to fight, itching for it. Chris gets this crazy look in his eyes when he's about to go off—his nostrils flare and his face flushes, his muscles get all beastly looking. I swear he grows an inch or two. He has that look now. Meanwhile I'm motionless and tense, which is my reaction to conflict—I freeze up and become generally useless.

The new kid twists his neck as though stretching it. "I was just introducing myself. My name's Dave." He holds out his hand to me. I can't believe the size of this kid's cojones. I glare at him and finish with my locker, then walk away without another word to that asshole.

"See you after class, Papi," Dave calls, and I flip him off, not caring if the teacher's still there. I hate guys like that. Guys who get off on making other people feel small, like the world isn't big enough for all of us to fit comfortably. I hate feeling weak and looking weak, especially in front of Chris.

Of course, Chris didn't have to go Hulk mode on him either. Makes me wonder if Chris reacted so strongly because of the insinuation we were gay. I don't know what the hell to do with that.

Regardless, I can't have Chris always sticking his neck out for me. I've got to start fighting my own battles. Being more independent. I'm not his bitch or anyone else's. Maybe I do have something to prove after all.

Standing up to an asshole like Dave is a good place to start.

I THOUGHT ASSHOLE DAVE WOULD TAKE THE HINT AND MOVE HIS locker somewhere else, but he seems determined to stick it out. A couple of days into school and he's practically one of us, telling jokes and talking shit with the best of them. His mouth is foul, and the only good thing I can say about him is that he doesn't talk to or about my sister again, at least not while I'm around.

Instead he's all up in my business, asking me questions about my skateboard, my hair, where I'm from, what's for lunch in the cafeteria that day, where my next class is, and if he can walk with me there. It's kind of insane. I try to ignore him, but sometimes his shit is just too much. He only pesters me when Chris isn't around, which means he thinks I'm an easy mark. Which sucks.

"The guys say you're Puerto Rican, but I've never seen a *boricua* with blue eyes," Dave says to me on Wednesday between second and third period. "You sure you're not adopted?"

"Do you know how ignorant you sound right now?" I say, unable to ignore his idiocy any longer and doubly irritated that he's asking people about me.

"He speaks," Dave exclaims and claps his hands together like he's discovered a new element. "I knew it. So, what's your name?"

I don't answer, and he continues his assholery.

"Say something to me in Spanish, Papi."

"No."

"Por favor?"

"Fuck you."

"Seriously, man. I'm in Spanish III. I'm practically fluent. Try me."

"Eres un imbécil."

"You're a...."

"Asshole," I finish for him.

He laughs, a real gut shaker. I'm so glad I can amuse him. He slaps my back, and I yank my shoulder away.

"Don't touch me."

"Lo siento," he says, and it almost seems like he means it. I finish trading out my books, go to shut my locker, and Dave reaches up and grabs the door to stop me. "We should hang out sometime. You can help me with my Español."

I glance over at him. The smile is gone and he looks sincere, but it's hard to say either way. I still can't believe he has the balls to mess with me. I'm being bullied by the fucking new guy.

"Why are you messing with me, man?" I ask.

"What?" His eyes widen. "I'm not messing with you."

"Yes, you are."

"Tú eres muy guapo, Papi."

He knows just what to say to get under my skin. I shove him off my locker, slam it shut, and walk away. I don't like Dave's vibe. He reminds me of those kids who held me down and tried to spit in my face because I talked funny. Like he's trying to push me into revealing something I don't want to. And why? To have something to hold over my head? To expose me? To fuck with me? I don't know what to do in this situation. I just want it to stop.

And what if Asshole Dave says something to Chris? Or goads Chris into a fight just to get at me?

Better to just avoid my locker altogether.

"WHERE WERE YOU AT LUNCH?" CHRIS ASKS ME THAT FRIDAY AFTER school on the car ride home. Dave's been hanging around with our lunch crew, so I took my board down to the abandoned gas station on the corner and practiced my grinds. One good thing to come out of the Great Recession is there are a lot more empty buildings and vacant lots for skaters to shred. That's what the older generation of skate rats says—sticking it to the man has never been so easy.

"I had some stuff to make up," I lie. I don't want Chris to ask me why I was off on my own. He's always trying to include me in his social circle, and he takes it personally when I opt out.

"It's the first week of school," Chris argues. He doesn't believe me. I'm not going to go into it about Dave, so I just stare out the window and hope he'll give up.

He turns up the music—a local punk band. Did I mention he has great taste in music too? I glance over to find him bobbing his head along to the beat, and I figure that must be the end of it. Chris pulls into his driveway and shuts off the engine.

"Thanks for the ride," I tell him while grabbing my skateboard and backpack.

"Hold up," he says before I can bounce. He lays one hand on my arm and leaves it there, like he's claiming it for his own.

I freeze but keep my stuff in my hands. He looks upset, and it probably has something to do with the way I've been acting. All distant and mopey.

"You've been ditching me all week. Don't think I haven't noticed."

This heart-to-heart is exactly what I wanted to avoid, in avoiding him. Chris has a way of getting at the truth of the matter. I set my backpack and board down at my feet. How do I make him feel better about it without telling him about Dave's bullshit? And what if he brings up Sebastian?

"I've just been busy," I say.

"With what?"

"I don't know. School?"

He sighs and shakes his head like he's disappointed in me, something I can't stand, to think that I've displeased him. "That's bullshit, but whatever. You working this weekend?"

"Yeah. Both days."

"What are you doing this afternoon?"

I mentally review my empty calendar. "Nothing."

"Let's go down to BOA."

BOA—Bank of America—is one of our prime skate spots and my favorite. Chris knows it too. I don't really feel like being forced to act normal in front of him, but if I bail, it will only make him try harder and probably hurt his feelings as well. Making him feel bad is, like, twice the pain for me.

"Let me change and I'll meet you back here in an hour," I say.

He nods. "See you then."

An hour or so later, we ride our skateboards down to BOA since it's not too far from where we live. The sea breeze is up, and it feels nice in my hair and billowing up my shirt. The Florida heat can make you feel like you're trapped in a sweaty plastic bubble for, like, six months out of the year, so any breeze is practically Arctic by comparison. When we arrive at the bank, there are a few kids already out. The BOA closed down a while back, and the property has been for sale ever since. Cops hardly ever patrol it, and so long as we don't break any windows or litter too much, no one seems to mind.

"Asshole Dave's here," Chris says to me. I don't know which of us came up with the name, but it stuck.

I scan the parking lot, and at the same time, Dave spots me. He doesn't give me that trademark smirk, though, just nods and goes back to whatever he was doing. Maybe he won't give me such a hard time with Chris around. It's pretty damn annoying that this kid is showing up at my neighborhood skate holes where I've been coming for years. Who the hell invited him anyway?

I grab my board and take to the concrete walkways surrounding the building. It's a two-story structure with nice, smooth concrete and a good variety of curbs, rails, and stairs. There's a loading ramp in the back and a wheelchair access out front. The way it's laid out, you can skate the whole thing without ever getting off your board. I start at the top, sweeping through the drive-thru ATMs and using the curbs to practice my nosegrinds, front tailslides, and a few backside slappies, then up the loading ramp, executing some 360s and kickflips along the way. When I'm warmed up, I do a couple of nightmare flips on the upper level to show off my new trick, then pull off a 50-50 grind down the handicap rail and land that pretty decently.

A crowd gathers, and the guys start calling out tricks. Some of them I do; some I don't. A few of them pull out their phones to film me. I'm not much of a show pony, but I'll try any trick once, even if the bros are all hating on it. And if I like it, I'll practice until I've perfected it.

I'm having a good day, feeling pretty confident, so I decide to go balls to the wall. I skate around the front of the building to the top floor, where there's a huge sprawling staircase leading down to the parking lot. Instead of grinding the rail, I do a varial kickflip in the air. I'm airborne for longer than seems humanly possible and stick it on the lower level. It's the best kind of rush. Fear and adrenaline and relief at not busting my ass in front of everyone. The guys all clap and whistle and list all the ways I murdered that trick. One kid keeps saying "What the fuck" over and over, with more passion each time.

Okay, maybe I am a bit of a show-off.

Chris laughs and punches my arm and calls me Killer, one of his nicknames for me. The attention is a little much, so I tell them I'll be back and ride next door to where there's a 7-Eleven. I say *what's up* to Justin who works there, used to go to our school, and sometimes comes out to skate with us.

"You've gotten pretty good," Justin says when I lay the drinks on the counter, Gatorade for me and a Mountain Dew for Chris. Even though I told him it shrinks your balls, he still drinks it. I guess he has the ballage to spare.

"Thanks, man. I had some time on my hands this summer." I guess Justin was watching us from inside the 7-Eleven.

"You have a lot of...." He pauses and seems to be searching for the right word. "Grace? You move well on the board. A lot of skaters look like they're trying to take a shit while skating, but you make it look easy."

"Like taking an actual shit," I joke.

He smiles and looks a little bashful. It's kind of cute. "Yeah, if everything's working right, I guess. You skate pretty, if that makes it any better."

"I appreciate it," I tell him with a smile. I'm always saying weird shit or intending to say one thing when something else slips out, so I cut Justin some slack.

I pay him for the drinks and return to the parking lot, where Chris is grinding the curbs. Chris skates like he surfs—all power and strength, but the pavement isn't nearly as flexible or forgiving as a wave. You have to relax your ankles a lot more to maneuver a skateboard, which is hard for him. Sometimes it takes a light touch.

I watch him for a few minutes, recalling how I was the one to show him how to ollie in middle school, and the only reason he stuck with it was to prove to me that he could do it too. That's probably the only reason I got so good at skateboarding—to have something I was better at than him. Then I notice his tongue poking out in concentration, and it reminds me of the other night in the tent when his focus was on getting me off.

Abort, abort, abort.

"You laid waste to that bank, Papi," Dave says to me like a bruh. He's broken away from his group of friends to join me where I stand, apart from the others.

"Don't call me that." Like a cloud passing in front of the sun, my mood instantly sours.

"Maybe you could tell me your name so I won't have to."

"You know my name."

"I want you to tell me."

"Theo Wooten."

"Dave Ackerman." He puts out his hand and instead of shaking it, I take a drink of my Gatorade. He gestures like he's slicking back his hair to play off the rebuff.

"I feel like we got off on the wrong foot," he continues. "In my defense, I didn't know she was your sister."

"Is this going to be one of those things where you pick on me until I try to fight you?"

He backs away, but not very far. "I hope not. I don't want to fight you. I know you and your friends call me Asshole Dave, but I'm really not trying to be an asshole."

"You must be a natural at it, then."

That shuts him up. I finish my drink, toss the bottle in a nearby trashcan, and drop my board on the pavement to deliver Chris his Mountain Dew while it's still cold.

Dave grabs my arm. "We should hang out," he says again.

I shrug him off me, kick up my board and look at him for the first time, thinking up a way to tell him off, but he's not smirking anymore. His eyes search mine, and his expression looks almost... vulnerable. Why in the world would Asshole Dave want to hang out with me, other than to torment me?

"Why?" I ask.

He glances away like he's nervous or maybe trying to make sure no one's around, clears his throat, and says all secretively, "Because I think you're hot?"

It takes me a few seconds to process, my disbelief registering a beat too late. "You are so full of shit."

He grabs my arm again, then seems to realize his misstep and quickly lets go. "I swear I'm not. Pull out your phone. Enter in these seven numbers. They're next week's winning Lotto numbers."

"There are only six Lotto numbers."

"The seventh is for good luck."

Now I'm confused. Asshole Dave is really trying to give me his number? He thinks I'm hot? Is he, like, gay or something? Bi? From all the trash he talks in the hallway, it seems like there's a different honey on his jock every weekend.

"Are you hitting on me?" I'm more curious than angry.

He nods, his face somber as a funeral. "I've been hitting on you all week. I guess my Spanish isn't as good as I thought."

That's a revelation. "I thought you were just being racist. Calling me Papi and shit."

"I say stupid shit sometimes. A lot of the time. Anyway, I'm risking a beatdown right now from your boyfriend just to give you my number."

I glance over at Chris, who's taken a break from skating and is watching us with interest.

"He's not my boyfriend," I say, trying to hide any feelings I might have about it.

"Does he know that?"

Because it's none of Dave's damn business and I want to quit this conversation before Chris sniffs us out, I pull out my phone, and Dave gives me his number. I don't have to call him. I could just let his number sit in there, uncalled, forever. If he is interested in me, that's one way to mess with him.

"I'll be around all weekend," Dave says. The smirk is back, and even though I don't want to admit it, even to myself, Asshole Dave is kind of growing on me.

Or maybe I'm just that desperate.

"What did Asshole Dave want?" Chris asks. We're stopped at a taco truck on our way back home from BOA. Chris is putting back five tacos to my two.

I'm not really sure what Asshole Dave wants, but I'm curious enough to find out. Whether it's bogus or not, Chris doesn't need to know about it.

"He has some decks he's trying to sell," I tell him. That's two lies I've told Chris today, a new record.

"I didn't know you were looking for a new deck."

"You know how it is. I'm never *not* looking."

"You should let me buy you one for your birthday."

I smile at that and also feel a little bad for lying to him. He's so damn thoughtful. "I'll let you know if I see something I like."

"You were really shredding it out there. You could probably go pro, you know?"

I shake my head. "I doubt it."

"Seriously, Theo."

Chris talks to me like a proud parent sometimes. Feels a little dangerous to believe him, like when your mom tells you you're the most handsome boy ever.

"Might take all the fun out of it, if it were, like, a job," I say.

Chris scowls at that. "Yeah, skateboarding for a living, what a drag. Mowing lawns is so much more fun."

"Mowing lawns is just to get my foot in the door. Maybe I'll take over Lawson's Lawns one day." He shakes his head, and I smile. It's really not the worst job in the world. I like being outside, and there's a lot of satisfaction in taking a rangy, overgrown lawn and making it look neat and tidy. I don't even mind the chore of picking all the dead petals from the flowers for our more affluent clientele. I'm kind of a neat freak in that way.

"You'd better aim higher than that, Killer." Chris reaches over and messes up my hair so that I have to finger comb it to get it out of my eyes. I pretend to be irritated even though I secretly love it.

We used to talk all the time about what we were going to do when we grow up. Chris wanted to swim with sharks on camera. Then, for a spell, he wanted to own a resort in Costa Rica that catered to surfers. I told him surfers are broke or else too cheap to pay for a room, and Chris argued that he'd go for the older crowd, surfers with families, and make it an all-inclusive destination vacation. I could never settle on something, so Chris decided I was going to be a pot farmer in California, because I'm the only one of our friends who can resist smoking the product. Chris said he'd run the store, appropriately named Potheads, and we'd recruit

some of the other guys to help with harvesting and baked goods
—*value-added products*. Chris practically had a business plan laid
out for it.

But we haven't talked about it lately, maybe because neither of us
wants to grow up. The thought of being an adult is pretty terrifying.
I'm still figuring out how to be a teenager.

"How about you?" I ask him. "You going to be a pro surfer, or is
Potheads still the plan?"

He chuckles. "Maybe. But if Potheads doesn't work out, I was
thinking I'd go into finance like my dad."

From what I understand, Chris's dad shuffles rich people's cash
from one money-making venture to another and makes a killing
doing it.

"Sounds boring." And not very much in keeping with Chris's
larger-than-life personality.

"Good money, though. You know how I like nice things." He
smiles his thousand-watt smile, the one I cave to every time.

I try to imagine it. Corporate Chris in a business suit, closing the
deal with his firm handshake. Weekender Chris with his classic good
looks, wearing a polo shirt and loafers with no socks, golfing with his
colleagues, a blonde wife waiting for him at home with a few
towheaded shorties running around. Neckties and minivans and
weekend barbecues. The American dream, man.

Kind of makes me sad as hell. I'm not sure there's any way I fit in
there.

"Just don't start wearing Crocs," I tell him.

He laughs and shakes his head. "Where do you come up with this
shit?"

We finish eating and head back home. There's this spot on the
sidewalk between our driveways where we always say goodbye. I'm
about to tell him I had a good time or something even stranger when
his phone rings. Chris pulls it out of his pocket and glances at it. "Kelli," he says simply.

Kelli Keyhoe, the blonde wife in Corporate Chris's American
dream.

"Go get her, tiger," I tell Chris with a fist-bump, the bro-est form of affection I can muster, and one that I secretly hate.

"Yeah," he says, distracted, and turns away to go answer it.

I watch Chris navigate the landscaped path up to his house. There is no hope for Chris and me. We're friends and that's all we'll ever be. I've got to get that through my thick skull. I will beat the *just friends* drum until the feelings have been forced back into that deep, dark cave where they belong. A cave so deep and twisted, a spelunker would get lost and perish before ever discovering those forbidden thoughts.

# FIVE

## GAME ON

That night I decide to text Dave. We don't text for long and it's nothing scandalous, just a *Hey, what's up, how's it going?* He tries to get me to send a picture of myself, but I politely decline—who knows what he'd do with it. We do make plans to get together over the weekend.

I work until about three on Saturday, and when I get home to shower and change, I can hear Chris and Tabs out by his pool, likely going over plans for the birthday party I didn't agree to. I glance out the window to see them deep in discussion. My sister can get pretty serious about party planning. Chris catches me looking down and waves. I lift one hand. He motions for me to come down, and I turn away from the window like I didn't see him.

I'm not up for watching my sister flirt with Chris under the guise of planning a birthday party, not that it's her intention, and not that I blame her for it. It's actually pretty clever. Still not something I want to take part in.

I text Dave while I'm changing, just a simple *Theo here.* He replies almost immediately with an address. I text him back.

*Drug deal?*

*My place. Come over.*

Dave doesn't live too far away, within skating distance. I won't have to ask my mom for a ride, which makes things a whole lot simpler. Our apartment is set up so the living quarters are upstairs and the downstairs is a big garage. Our landlord is one of the dentists at my mom's work who gives her a deal on rent. We couldn't afford this neighborhood otherwise. My mom wanted us to be in a good school zone, and she got used to living in this area after being with my dad. There are more Spanish-speakers in this section of West Palm, and I think it reminds my mom of home.

I go out through the garage door and cut through the side yard of the main house so Chris won't see me in the driveway. I hop on my skateboard, zoning out to the steady *tick-tick-tick* of the wheels rolling over the cracks in the sidewalk.

One of the things I like about skateboarding is that it's slow enough to see what's going on, but fast enough that you don't have to be drawn into the drama if you don't want to be. I see so much crazy shit while skateboarding, all the gritty, unpleasant things about living in a city, but also some really great things too—people spontaneously dancing or laughing, lovers wrapped around each other in embrace, a parent holding on to their kid's hand. It's such a nice, simple thing to do, grab someone else's hand and hold on. So many people are content to ride around in their cars with the windows up, air conditioning on, pretending there isn't a whole needful, lonely world out there. When I get a car, I'll still skateboard wherever I can. I don't want to become so indifferent.

On my way to Dave's, I pass by Saint Ann's, where my great-uncle Theo lives. I consider stopping in to visit him, but I haven't seen him since Easter, and I worry he might not even recognize me. Still, I'm pretty sure my dad isn't visiting him, which means no one is. And that sucks.

Next time.

I hop off at Dave's address, already sweaty from the ride. He lives in a tiny house behind a slightly bigger house. Both are smaller and shabbier than our gardener's cottage. The window-unit air conditioner hums with industry, and I question again what the hell I'm doing here outside his door when yesterday afternoon I hated his guts. Seems weird that my opinion of him could shift so rapidly. I sniff inside my shirt and decide it's not too foul, then lift my hand to knock, but before my knuckles make contact, the door swings open.

"Theo," Dave says with a smirk that pulls a little higher on one side, like it's caught on a fishing line. He's way too cocky for his own good.

"Those lotto numbers were bunk," I tell him. His smile widens along with the door as he gestures grandly for me to enter. The inside looks like a garage that's been converted into an efficiency apartment. Pretty basic, with unpainted cinderblock walls and a little kitchen area in the same room, a table for eating, and an adjoining bath.

"You live here by yourself?"

"Yup."

In one way it's pretty awesome. In another way, it seems lonely as hell.

"Where are your parents?"

"Charlotte. I was getting too hard to handle, so they sent me here." He makes air quotes around the *too hard to handle* part.

"That sucks." I frown, feeling bad for him that he's basically been banished to Florida, probably not the worst place to be sent, but still.

He shrugs. "My aunt hasn't started charging me rent yet. Could be a lot worse."

I glance around his bachelor pad. It's kind of dark and dank, a slight funk in the air, though it does look like he tried to clean up before I arrived. The floor is a mishmash of old carpets laid over the concrete, still bare in some places. One window has the air conditioning unit balanced in it, and on the other, instead of a curtain, has a sheet tacked up rather sloppily. There's also a beat-up leather couch situated in front of an old flat-screen TV and game controls.

"You want to play FIFA?" he asks. It looks like he has a game on pause.

"Yeah, sure."

We do that for a while, and it's not too weird. Dave does most of the talking, telling me about his parents, who weren't too keen on him dating guys and didn't want his "deviant lifestyle" to influence his little brothers. He doesn't say it outright, but they basically kicked him out for being gay, which is shitty.

"So, what are you, like, bi?" I ask.

"Eh, I'm pretty gay. I've only messed around with one girl, and it didn't really do it for me."

That seems weird, considering all the smack talk around our lockers. "What about all those stories you tell?"

"All true." He tilts his head and scores a goal on me because I'm not really paying attention to the game. "Just, it was dudes, not chicks."

That kind of blows my mind as I recall some of his stories. He's done all that with dudes?

"You must have been really popular in Charlotte."

He chuckles at that. "With a certain crowd."

"Why don't you just come out with it?" I ask, though I probably shouldn't judge because I'm not exactly *out with it* myself.

"New school. New people. Just trying to fit in, you know? Who wants to be the fat gay kid right out of the gates?"

I glance over at him. "You're not fat. A little husky, maybe."

He laughs with his head thrown back. He's got a pretty decent laugh. Like his whole body gets into it. Makes me want to make him laugh again.

"How about you?" Dave asks. "What's up with you and Mitcham?"

I turn my gaze back to the TV screen. At least I don't have to lie about it. "We're friends—best friends—since middle school."

"You think he's straight?"

"Pretty sure."

*Except there was this one time....*

Dave cocks his head. "I think my gaydar needs a tune-up. All the guys around here look gay to me, but I think it's just because it's Florida and everyone's naked all the time."

I smile at that. And the way he says Florida, like "Flaaarida."

"It's pronounced *Florida*. Otherwise you sound like a tourist."

"Thanks for the tip. Seriously, though, why does no one around here wear a shirt or shoes?"

I never really noticed it before, but people around here do dress pretty skimpy. It's funny to think about how we might be viewed by outsiders. "Because it's hot as hell and the beach is always right there?"

"I saw this guy the other day wearing a pink tank top—tight too—and I thought for sure he was gay. I was about to move on him, and then this chick comes up and they start making out. I was like, whaaat?"

I chuckle at that, then wonder about Dave's gaydar. I'm not sure I have one, because everyone seems straight to me, except a couple of guys at my school who make it known. That's one of the disadvantages of being low-key about it. If no one knows, then it's pretty impossible to find each other.

"What about me?" I ask, straightening up a bit. "Do I look gay to you?"

Dave pauses the game to glance over, tilts his head, and studies me. Even though I asked for it, his attention still makes me squirm.

"Your smile," he says at last.

"My smile?" That seems completely irrelevant. And people always tell me Tabs has the same smile, so how does that even play out?

"Your smile is too...." Dave seems to be choosing his words carefully. "Eager."

"What? My smile is too *eager*? I'm, like, the least friendly person I know."

"I don't disagree. But there was something about the way you and Mitcham played off each other. I thought there might be something there. Then, when I found out there wasn't, I was, like, game on."

"Game on, huh?" Maybe I'm not as covert with my feelings as I thought. Or Chris is the densest straight kid on the block. I also wonder what it means to "look" gay. The whole gay/straight thing is so confusing to me. A secret handshake would be so much easier.

"So, do you just hit on whatever guy you think is hot and hope that you're right?" I ask him. "Seems ballsy to me."

Dave seems to ponder the question. It's kind of personal. I'm basically asking him to let me take a peek at his playbook. "There are a few factors that go into it."

"What are they?" This is truly fascinating stuff.

"One, hotness. Two, likeliness to beat my ass. Three, level of attraction."

I suppose personality and intelligence don't factor much into Dave's equation. I'm also not sure that hotness and level of attraction are all that different.

"Have you ever gotten your ass beat?"

"Yeah, but not too bad. Even straight guys like a good blowjob."

Poof. Mind blown. Straight guys getting blowjobs from other dudes? That's, like, a thing? Then I start wondering if what happened between Chris and me was just because he was horny and I happened to be there. That's a truly depressing thought, but it would fit with what happened the morning after. Ugh, to think Chris would use me like that. Or we would use each other. It puts a whole different spin on it.

Our game ends, and Dave tosses the controller on the floor, swivels toward me.

"All this talk about blowjobs is making me thirsty. Want a drink?"

I manage to choke out a garbled response as my cheeks flame up just in case my embarrassment somehow slipped by him. From the smirk on his face, I'm guessing it didn't.

"Yeah, sure."

Dave grabs me a Gatorade from his minifridge, my favorite flavor, and tosses it to me. I wonder if he stocked up on my account or if it's just a coincidence. I don't ask.

"I could cut your hair if you want," he says casually.

I run a hand through my hair. I haven't cut it all summer, and it's gotten kind of long and shaggy. Chris usually buzzes it for me, but it's been awhile.

"I don't know if I should trust you with my hair."

Dave pulls out his phone and scrolls through his pictures, shows me a few dudes with cool-looking hair. "I cut hair back home. It's how

I made extra money, but I'll do yours for free. Make sure I've still got it."

I'm amazed Dave has this little-known talent. Men's hair. I kind of want to test out his skills, and I can always buzz it off later if I don't like it.

"Yeah, sure. Why not?"

He opens the back door and drags a chair outside to a concrete slab in the middle of a scraggly yard. The grass, or rather weeds, are all rangy and anemic-looking. I've become a bit of a yard snob since becoming a lawn maintenance technician. I can tell when a yard is neglected. Maybe I could return the favor by trimming up his weed patch.

I sit down on the chair, and he brings out a silky black cape, drapes it around my shoulders, and fastens it under my chin with a hair clip. "Should have seen my setup back home," Dave says. "I had the mirror and the swivel chair. Lights. My tunes set up in the garage."

It sounds like he had a good thing going. It helps to have a skill you can make money from. Maybe because we've never had much, I spend a lot of time thinking about how to make money and hang on to it. Chris is the complete opposite. It slips through his fingers like water, to the point where I'm, like, *Dude, do you really need that?*

"I'll come by and mow your lawn for you sometime this week," I tell Dave.

He glances around as though just noticing he has a yard, and nods.

"So, do you have a couple cuts to choose from, or are you all Edward Scissorhands with it?" I ask.

He smiles. "I'm pretty avant-garde. We're in the renaissance of men's hair. Sky's the limit."

I laugh. Dave says some weird shit, kind of like me. Except he doesn't seem to second-guess everything he says. Just rolls with it.

"But this being your first time, I'll narrow down the playing field. You want the Ronaldo, the Neymar, or the Lamela?"

"Why are you only naming Latin dudes?" I'm still not convinced he's not a racist.

"Ronaldo is Portuguese. And they're all hot men with great hair, though I can do a pretty good Beckham too."

I shake my head. "I don't know, man. You're the expert. Surprise me."

He grabs my chin, and I flinch. He pulls back his hand. "Jumpy fella, aren't you?"

I don't know why, but I'm not used to a lot of touching. We're not that affectionate with one another in my family. My mom'll kiss my cheek every once in a while. My dad, when I see him, will give me a manly thump on the back to jumpstart my heart. Chris is the only person I've ever really been affectionate with.

"Do you mind?" he asks, holding out his hand.

"No, it's fine."

He places his thumb at the bottom of my chin and turns my head from side to side, sizing me up. He fastens the hair on the top of my head, uses his clippers attached to an extension cord to shave the sides, then works his scissors over the top. I listen to the insects buzzing around the yard and the steady *snip, snip* of the scissors. Dave asks me some questions about my family so I give him our setup, how my parents met in Puerto Rico when my dad was in dental school, then they moved here to start his own practice. I skip over the part where he cheated on my mom but tell him they got divorced and my dad's been pretty absent ever since.

"You and your sister get along?" Dave asks.

"Mostly. We used to be closer, but then she got popular and forgot about the rest of us."

"That happens sometimes." Dave fists a clump of my hair and says, "You have great hair. So thick and shiny. You take supplements?"

I laugh. What a weird question. "No."

"Lucky. I'm giving you the early years Lamela, back when he played for Roma. A little treat for myself."

I grin because he's such a strange bird. "You play soccer?"

"No, but I'm a soccer enthusiast, if you know what I mean," he says, eyebrows wagging.

I definitely do, though I never looked twice at the guys on my soccer teams. I played for school last year but decided not to do it again. Too much testosterone. Some of the guys are super competitive, which takes the fun out of it. And it was pretty much my whole life my freshman year, including last summer for conditioning. It's a lot of time to spend with a group of people you don't really fit in with.

Dave uses a straight razor to cut my sideburns, then asks if I've started shaving. "Not yet," I say, a little embarrassed because I don't exactly know how. I mean, there are YouTube videos, I'm sure, but it's a little intimidating your first time. I don't want to, like, slice my lip off.

"Come inside. I'll show you how." He pulls off the cape with a flourish and shakes it out. He even has a little brush he uses to dust the loose hairs off my shoulders. "Mind if I take a picture?"

I shrug, and he pulls out his phone, snaps off a picture before I even realize he's done it.

"Damn, you're a good-looking kid. I'm saving that one for later." He winks and gives me a lecherous grin. My neck heats up because I'm not used to the attention to my looks or having dudes tell me I'm hot. Not that I mind. It's just... different.

I follow Dave inside to the bathroom, where he flicks on the light. I check myself out in the vanity mirror. My hair does look pretty tight.

"You can part it this way too," he says and combs it over the top. "I gave you a hard part, in case you want to use some product to slick it down for when you're feeling a little more Dapper Dan."

"Thanks, man." I inspect it from a few different angles, wondering what Chris will have to say about it. And my skater punk friends. They tend to rip on anything that looks the slightest bit manufactured.

"You might want to take your shirt off for this," Dave says and busies himself with switching out the razor on his blade, one of those old-school reusable ones made of metal. He lines up his instruments on the bathroom counter like a surgeon. I pull my shirt over my shoulders, and even though it's a little weird having Dave right there in the tiny bathroom with me, it's not so terribly uncomfortable.

"I guess this is something I should be doing with my dad, huh?"

Dave shrugs. "Us lost boys got to stick together."

I think about that for a minute, then about Dave, the philosopher-slash-barber with a strategy for deciding which guys he's going to hit on. I could learn a lot from him.

In order to show me proper technique, Dave lathers up his own face and I do mine. He uses a straight razor to shave himself, which is pretty badass. I get the old-timey razor. I mimic his strokes on my own face while he gives me pointers on how to angle the blade. Judging from my upper lip, I probably should have started doing this a few months ago.

When we're finished, he hands me a towel to wipe off the excess shaving cream. I'm not really that into myself, but I do look pretty damn spiffy.

"Man-eater," he says, and we both grin at that. My phone buzzes. It's my mom asking where I am because dinner's ready. I didn't realize how late it's gotten.

"I feel like I owe you a tip," I tell him.

"Next time," he says with a twinkle in his eyes. My neck heats up again because I have some idea of what he has in mind.

I pull my shirt back on over my head and straighten it out. It feels a little unbalanced between us, like he's done this really nice thing for me and I haven't done anything for him.

"Sorry about calling you Asshole Dave," I say.

"It's okay," he says. "Sometimes I am an asshole. You free tomorrow? You should come by again."

We make plans to meet up tomorrow after I get off work, and I skate home as quickly as I can. With the weekdays being so hectic for my mom and sister, weekends are when the three of us make a point to have dinner together. I get home and climb the stairs to find they've already started eating without me. Chris too. He eats over so often, he even has his own seat at the table. Chris glances up from his food, catches me in his piercing gaze, then drops his fork. It clatters to the ground, and I duck into the kitchen to get him a new one. As I hand it to him, he stares at me with the singular focus that only he has. I feel my cheeks getting warm.

"Where have you been?" Mom asks.

"At a friend's house."

"You cut your hair," Chris says, giving me the five-point inspection.

"Yeah, Dave did it for me. He could cut yours too, if you want."

"Asshole Dave?" Chris asks, then apologizes to my mother for his language.

"Why do you call him Asshole Dave?" Mom asks.

"We don't anymore," I say and look pointedly at Chris. My mom doesn't know much about my personal life, and I prefer it that way, especially with all the *feelings* I've been having lately. The expression in Chris's eyes is stony. He obviously doesn't like that Dave and I were hanging out, especially since I've been blowing him off.

"It looks good, Theo," Tabs says. "About time for a new look."

I sit down to join them. Arroz con pollo. I haven't eaten much all day for all the work I've done. I devour two platefuls, and my mom congratulates me like I'm a toddler. She's always trying to get me to eat more.

After dinner Chris and I go into my room to play video games. Neither of us suggests it. It's just something we always do. Most of the games are his anyway, and the system used to be his. I think he likes giving me his toys because he knows he can still come over and play with them when he wants. The only game I ever play without him is the Sims, and it's more like a coping strategy. A while back we made avatars of ourselves, and I spent the summer making them do corny stuff like bake a cake together or go for a drive, give our dog Mike a bath. It's pathetic, I know, but it did ease my loneliness a little.

The funk I've been sensing from Chris all night continues, even though I try to ignore it. It comes out in his grunts and sighs, getting frustrated in the game when normally he'd laugh it off. I'm about to ask him what's up when he blurts out, "So, you were hanging out with Asshole Dave all afternoon?"

"Call him Dave."

Chris looks pained by that, like I've been disloyal to him. "See any decks you like?"

I wonder what he's talking about, then remember the excuse I told him for getting Dave's number. "Nah, not really."

There's a break in the game, and Chris's eyes center on my face. He squints a little. "Did you start shaving?"

My face flames up. Not that he's trying, but he makes me feel so stupid and childish sometimes.

"Yeah," I say like it's nothing.

"Did Dave do it for you?" he asks in a low rumble.

"He showed me how."

Chris gets quiet then, brooding. I can feel his irritation reaching out to me like tentacles, lifting the hairs on my arms and the back of my neck. It puts me on edge.

"I could have showed you," he says sullenly.

I glance over and see that he's really hurt by it. His lower lip juts out in an adorable pout, *perfect for sucking on*, I think, then scold myself for the mental slip. I don't know why I didn't think to ask him. Just, we're so close—too close, it seems—and our relationship is so confusing already. I'm trying to simplify things. Strictly bros.

"It just happened. He cut my hair and then it was like, whatever, you know?"

"Yeah. Whatever." Chris grumbles.

"Sorry," I say, not exactly sure what I'm apologizing for.

Chris breathes out a long, bullish sigh. *What's his problem?* He's always hanging out with other people—other girls—doing God knows what, and I don't give him the third degree.

"How's Kelli?" I ask to remind him of the score and the fact that he's, you know, straight.

His head snaps in my direction, and he practically glares at me. Honestly, it stings.

"She's fine," he growls.

We play in silence for another ten minutes, and then Chris stands abruptly. "I'm heading out," he says.

"Hot date?"

"Not quite," he says testily and strides out of my room without looking back. I hear him say goodbye to my sister and my mom, and then the front door opens and shuts. I turn off my light and go to the window to watch him stalk across our driveways and into his house. I hate it when Chris is mad at me, and even though he has nothing to be angry about, it feels like my fault. Or like he's making it my fault.

Maybe this has nothing to do with Dave, specifically, and everything to do with the fact that Chris suspects I might be into dudes. Is he worried I'm going to ruin his rep? Knock his cool factor down a few pegs? The thought of that being his problem makes me kind of pissed.

Would Chris ditch me if he found out I was gay? I hope not, but there's no way to know unless I tell him, and I'm not even ready to face that myself.

I turn off the TV, brush my teeth, and climb into bed, thinking about Dave, seeing if I can get hard, but my thoughts keep drifting back to Chris, that night in Sebastian, the look on his face, the smell of him, the way I felt cocooned inside the tent with him like he and I were the whole world and nothing outside even mattered. The release I achieve on my own is an echo of the one Chris gave me, and I find myself feeling a little bitter I need him for that too.

# SIX

# AS BEYONCÉ WOULD SAY, WATERMELON

I pick up some hair gel on my way home from work on Sunday. I feel a little stupid doing it, and it's probably not worth the money, but I want to look nice when I go over to Dave's, even if all we do is play video games.

When Dave opens the door to his apartment, I can tell from the curl in his upper lip he likes what I've done with it. "Aye, Papi," he says like an asshole, almost ruining it but not quite because I'm getting used to Dave's particular brand of humor. When a guy is into you and makes it known, you make some allowances.

I go inside and cross the room, not knowing what to do with myself, which happens quite often. My mom says it's because I'm growing so fast, but to be truthful, I've never felt comfortable in my skin unless I'm doing something like skating or playing soccer or mowing lawns, something to take my mind off my own bumbling awkwardness.

It feels so small in here, just the two of us. Like a fishbowl. I glance toward the couch, but I don't really want to play video games. Then the bed, which is, like, way too intimidating. I start doubting myself, thinking I shouldn't have come at all. Dave seems to sense my anxiety because he offers me a drink. I tell him I'm not thirsty.

"You want to play video games?" he asks. I stare at him, unable to form the words. I shake my head instead. "Okay." He takes a step toward me, and I shift nervously from one foot to the other. He tilts his head and narrows his eyes, studying me like an algebraic equation.

"You've never done this before," he says, a statement, not a question.

I shake my head again and glance toward the door. I don't want to leave, but this is awkward as hell. What changed since yesterday? Dave tells me to have a seat on the couch and make myself comfortable. He puts on some music, not anything romantic either. Hip-hop. Not too soft, not too loud.

He plops down on the couch next to me, yawns, and puts his arm behind my back like we're on a date at the movies. He's trying to loosen me up by making me laugh, but the joke falls flat. My sense of humor is buried somewhere beneath all the nerves and whatever I had for lunch that afternoon.

"So, how about those Dolphins?" he asks, and I shake my head.

"I don't follow football."

"That was just my opener. You want to mess around?"

I shrug. Meanwhile, my junk starts acting up at the prospect and my pits start sweating something fierce. Dave glances at my crotch, then nods like he's figured something out. "Take off your shirt," he says. I take a deep breath, sit up, and pull my shirt over my shoulders, feeling a little self-conscious because I've got some muscles but I'm by no means buff. I'm hoping my deodorant did its job today. The air conditioner clicks on, and the cold air sends a shiver down my spine.

"Yeah," Dave says like he approves and gestures at my pants. "Unbutton."

It's easier when he tells me what to do, less room for me to over-think or second-guess myself. He stares at me—up, down, and back again, moistens his lips with his tongue, and reaches into his pants.

"Show me what you've got," he says while pulling out his own.

I stroke myself a few times with a trembling hand, wishing I had more confidence or that my body would just take over for me in situations like this. Regardless, I can see Dave getting turned on by it, which turns me on. It's different from how it is with Chris. Chris can walk into a room and I'm hard. With Dave, it's more like I'm turned on by thinking about what he wants. The anticipation.

Dave moves closer to me on the couch and takes off his shirt. He's got a nice chest, hairy too, which I like. He's not that cut, but there's a solidness to his physique I appreciate. And he seems very comfortable with this dance, which eases my mind a bit.

"What are you into?" he asks, and I freeze. "Never mind." He squints and assesses me, like I'm on a job interview and he's trying to determine if I'm a hard worker or a slacker, whether or not he's going to take the chance on me. I want to offer him some bit of assurance, but I'm pretty unqualified for the job.

"You ever had a blowjob before?" he asks.

I shake my head and try to swallow, remembering when Chris told me about that girl who offered to give him one and he turned her down. Now I'm in that same situation.

"You interested?"

It's not much different from when he offered to cut my hair. Strangely, it reminds me that I still need to mow his grass.

"Yeah," I say, because my prick is already twitching at the thought of it.

Dave buttons up, tells me to lean back and relax. Like when he cut my hair and taught me how to shave, there's some preparation. He gets a pillow, for instance, and a condom, then gets comfortable on his knees in front of me. I feel really exposed as he looks me over, like he could make one wisecrack and ruin everything, but he doesn't. He rubs me up and down a few times, not rough, but not too gently either. Kind of like it's a regular old job and he's done it a million times before. Strangely, his efficiency helps me relax a little. I lean back and close my eyes, gripping the couch cushions with both hands like it's Space Mountain and I'm twelve years old, knowing there's all this hype to the ride without knowing the ride itself.

Then Dave starts doing things with his mouth that feel really, really good. Like that roller coaster, my whole body is going for the ride. He's drawing all these sensations out of me I could never accomplish by myself, making me utter things in a voice I've never heard before—*yeah, come on, right there, fuck yeah.* My hips lift off the couch as my dick goes deeper inside his mouth. His lips smack as he moans, and it sounds so wet and nasty and I want to ram it farther down his throat, but I don't. No wonder the guys at school are always going on about it. Just when I'm about to cum, he slides me out, strips off the condom, and finishes me off with his fist. My dick explodes, and I think of that guy who used to smash watermelons with a hammer. All the red meat going everywhere, landing on people's faces. I'm not very tidy.

"Goooooooal," Dave says, and I chuckle, though it sounds more like I'm being strangled. I've been holding on to the couch for dear life the whole time, so when he backs away, I have to take a few deep breaths and uncoil myself like a snake.

Dave goes to the bathroom for a minute, comes back with a towel, and tosses it to me.

"Well?" he asks. "How was it?"

"Damn," I utter, catching my breath. My dick is still raw and throbbing and exposed to the cold air conditioner. I put it away before it starts to look sad and dejected, thinking what most guys have probably thought at some point in their lives: if I could do that for myself, I'd never leave my bedroom.

"You're welcome," Dave says, and his self-satisfied smirk is back. I finish buttoning my pants and glance over at him, hoping he'll tell me what happens next.

"You want to give it a try?" he asks with a teasing smile.

Like I said before, I'm a person who likes to return the favor. I settle down on my knees in front of him, appreciating the forethought of the pillow. Dave tells me what to do every step of the way. It's not much different from when he taught me how to shave.

Dave's a good teacher.

SEVEN

# HOW BIG IS A CENTAUR'S JUNK?

My arrangement with Dave is unusual. Even I, with my limited experience, know that. We slip into a kind of routine. I come over to his place in the afternoons. We mess around some, then settle in to play video games or watch TV. Sometimes he smokes pot, and I listen to him tell stories about his friends in North Carolina. He seems homesick, and he's always showing me pictures on his phone of people he used to hang out with and his little brothers. Not his parents, though. I don't think they got along too well, even before he came out.

Neither of us are too concerned with putting a label on what we have going. Nor do we let on to the rest of our friends that we're seeing each other on the side. After a couple weeks of hooking up, we're at school one day when Dave starts telling this story to our friends about a girl who once jacked him off so hard that he came in her eye and she was practically blind for a few hours. He really gets into it, shouting and miming out the scene. Everyone thinks it's hilarious, except for me, because I'm the "girl" it happened to.

Chris shakes his head and says to me, "I don't believe half the shit that asshole says."

"Me neither," I say, while wishing Dave would shut the hell up. He should know better than to tell that story. It makes me feel like a tool, not to mention that if Chris found out it was me, I'd be completely humiliated.

Later on, when no one else is around, Dave asks me if I'm coming over that afternoon. I tell him I've got stuff to do. I don't want to give him any more material.

He keeps bugging me about it while I load up my backpack with what I need for that night. My academic classes are all AP and honors. Other than a lot of homework and some studying, the classes aren't that hard, but I do need to keep up with it if I want to make that scholarship money rain down.

"Is it because of what I said earlier?" Dave asks.

I shrug and don't meet his eyes. I'm not the best at feelings or speaking the words necessary to express them.

"Papi," he says, the name he uses whenever he's teasing me, or in moments like these, to get my hackles up.

"Don't call me that." I'm not in the mood for his mouth.

"It was just so damn funny, I couldn't help it."

"I don't want you telling other people my business," I practically growl.

"Yeah, I got that impression already," he says with less humor.

It pisses me off that he hasn't already apologized and I have to explain to him why what he did was shitty. "How would you feel if I shared completely personal things about you and you had to stand around and listen to everyone laugh about it?"

He crosses his arms and stares at me. "And you wouldn't want Mitcham to find out, right?"

"The fuck is that supposed to mean?" I glance around to make sure no one can hear us. I feel like a whiny bitch, but damn if I don't expect some things to stay private.

He sighs. "Nothing. Forget I said it."

"This is about your mouth," I remind him.

"Yeah, I know. Listen, I'm an asshole. It won't happen again, okay? Come over today. I'll make it up to you."

I glance up and down the hallway. Ryanne catches my eye and

waves. I wave back. I wonder if anyone else could guess at the topic of our conversation. Do we look like we're having a lovers' quarrel? Then I think, what if Dave decides to tell people he's gay or that we've been hooking up? I'm not even completely sure I'm gay. The guys at our school who are out seem so sure about it. Maybe I'm not gay enough. Like, a seven out of ten on the gayometer. Ugh, my mind is spinning and I can't make it stop. There are all these consequences to what Dave and I are doing that I really don't want to deal with.

"Theo?" Dave asks because I still haven't answered him.

"I don't know," I say, which is the best I can muster without giving in completely. Dave is good with his hands and his mouth. And even when he's being an asshole, he's still kind of funny. I have fun when we're together, and it feels *really* good. It's nice to be wanted.

Chris comes up then, and Dave acts like we were talking about football, which is a dead giveaway because other than playing Madden with Chris from time to time, I don't keep up with football and Dave knows that.

"Go, Dolphins," Dave says like a smartass. He once went on a ten-minute diatribe about how bad the Dolphins suck, detailing just about every awful season they've had for the past two decades. I'm not a huge fan, but still, you don't rip on the Dolphins to someone from South Florida. It's poor form.

Chris glares at Dave until he bows slightly and walks away. Chris has been chilly with me lately, both of us going out of our way to be extra polite, which is a sure sign that something's wrong. We walk out together to the student parking lot, and I try to shake off the conversation I just had with Dave.

"Your birthday's next weekend," Chris says. "The party's coming together, in case you're wondering."

My sister and he both seem a little put out that I haven't been involved with the planning, even though I told them from the start I'm not into it.

"I should probably practice my driving before Friday." The party's on Saturday, but our actual birthday's the day before. I want to pass my driving test on the first go-round.

"We can practice now if you want."

"Yeah?"

"Sure. I don't have anything else going on."

Even though it's technically illegal, Chris is the one who's taken me out driving most of the time. My mom works a lot, and she's tired when she gets home and just wants to relax. She also scares easily and sets me on edge when I'm driving.

"Sounds good," I tell him. I pull out my phone to text Dave that I won't be able to meet up with him. He responds by telling me I'm an *imbécil*.

"Who's that?" Chris asks.

I glance over and because I don't want to lie, I tell him, "no one," which is probably worse.

Chris frowns but doesn't say anything more about it. He drives us out of the school parking lot, then pulls over and lets me take the wheel. I was nervous at first driving his car, but he's good about helping me relax. He doesn't get pissed at me when I make mistakes. I clipped a mailbox once taking a turn too close, and he just laughed his ass off.

We're on the bridge going over the intercoastal to the beaches. Windows down, hair blowing in the breeze. Perfect, until Chris ruins it by saying, "You and Dave have been hanging out a lot."

I think back to the story Dave shared earlier that day. I haven't said a word about Dave to Chris. And at school Dave and I hardly even talk to each other, so where is Chris getting his information?

"How do you know?"

"Find My Friends."

We installed that app when I first got my cell phone a couple of years back. I checked it a few times when Chris was in California, just to see how far away he was, but I haven't looked at it since then. Kind of strange that he has. And how does he know where Dave lives?

"I asked him if he had any decks for sale," Chris says, then waits for me to respond. When I don't, he says, "He didn't."

"You ask him to cut your hair too?" I don't like Chris checking up on me, especially when I have something to hide.

"Why are you lying to me?"

"About Dave selling decks?"

"About everything."

We exit off the bridge, and I pull over into a beach access and park the car, grab my stuff from the back seat, including my deck. I so don't want to have this conversation with him. Chris has a way of getting me to spill my guts.

"What the hell, Theo?" Chris grabs hold of my arm and squeezes. He's strong. Even though I'm pissed, I kind of like it. I never back away or flinch when Chris touches me. I like his grip. So messed up, I know.

"We used to tell each other everything," he says. "Now you act like you don't even know me."

"It's not that." Chris takes everything so personal. I dump my stuff on my lap. The car's still running, so I turn it off.

"What is it, then? Are you mad at me?"

"No."

"Because of what happened in—"

"No," I interrupt him. Chris can't have it both ways. He can't have me as his ever-faithful lap dog and expect me to just sit around and watch him hold court with every hot babe that struts through Sabal Palm High. It's not fair. I'm friggin' lonely. Dave is there, and he's into me. He's not Chris, but he's not nothing either.

"Maybe I'm too dependent on you, you know?" I say to him. "Like, for the past five years, it's just been you and me. And I do whatever you tell me to."

"You don't do whatever I tell you."

I give him a look. We both know Chris gets his way more often than not.

"So, Dave is like, Chris 2.0?" He winces as though the thought physically pains him. As if.

"No, he's not. Dave is just a guy I hang out with. He's funny and we... get along. You can't be the only person in my life. You have your surf friends and your family and your girlfriends and I... I just have you."

I swallow the lump in my throat. I hate getting emotional in front of him. Makes me feel like such a baby. Chris stares at me. He no longer looks angry; he looks hurt. His gaze drifts out to the water. His lower lip juts out, tempting me still. What would Chris do if I just leaned over and pulled him in for a big, fat kiss? With tongue. Probably freak out.

"You can drive us home," Chris says, completely deflated and still not looking at me. He cleans a patch of dust off the dashboard with his finger in a slow spiral. "I'm sorry for giving you shit. You can hang out with whoever you want. I won't bother you about it again."

I want to say something to make him feel better, but I don't know what, so I toss my stuff in the back and take the shortest route home, trying to concentrate on the road and not on Chris, who stares out the window the whole way with his arms crossed in front of his chest, looking sad as hell.

The exact thing I wanted to avoid is happening—I'm losing my best friend.

I CAVE AND END UP GOING OVER TO DAVE'S THAT SAME AFTERNOON. I'M too needy, a ping-pong ball being batted back and forth between Dave and Chris. Like my self-esteem is tied to one or the other, and I cling to the one who can provide me with some sense of reassurance. It's lame on so many levels.

In any case, Dave is happy to see me. Usually we hang out on the couch and play video games, which usually segues into other things. Today it's different, though. I'm not feeling it. I'm too stressed about Chris and how we left things. I hate that there's friction between us. I wonder if he's looking me up on his phone right now. I should take myself off the app, but at the same time, I kind of like that he's semi-stalking me, and how messed up is that?

"What's up?" Dave asks, retreating to his half of the couch, perhaps noticing that I'm only half-present (and half-aroused). The other thing about Dave and me is we never kiss. And our touching seems very focused on getting each other off and not necessarily connection. The things I want to do with Chris, I don't want to do with Dave. Is it possible to only be gay for one guy?

"I don't know what's wrong with me," I tell him. "I'm in a funk."

Dave grabs his bong and packs it. The couch is small, more the size of a love seat, and Dave sits in the middle of it with his legs spread wide so his knee rests against mine, kind of territorial. Chris does that too, takes up the maximum amount of space, even when he's sleeping. In some ways they're a lot alike. Alpha males.

Dave offers me the first hit like always, even though I've never taken him up on it. I shake my head. "Hugs not drugs, man."

Dave lights the bong, sucks up the column of smoke as his cheeks hollow out all the way—it's very phallic. It sounds like sucking through a straw in a mostly empty glass. His cheeks puff out as he holds it in, then releases a cloud of heady smoke that makes my eyes water a little. Chris went through a pot-smoking phase last year, but he hasn't done it much lately. He says all it does is give him the munchies and make him lazy. I tried it once when we were in Sebastian on a surf trip, at one of the older surf rat's shithole apartment, and I ended up holding my knees and rocking in a corner, thinking I was dying because my heart sounded too fast and my breathing too slow. Chris talked me down, and I felt bad for ruining both our nights. Later he said I probably just smoked too much, or the shit was too dank. Still, I haven't tried it since.

I don't mind it when other people smoke, though. No one gets violent, just goofy. When Dave smokes he gets a faint smile on his face, laughs at whatever I say, and wants to talk deeply about things that probably don't deserve that much attention. It's kind of funny.

"When did you know you were gay?" I ask Dave.

He scratches his head and purses his lips like he's trying to recall it. His eyes are red and glassy, and I wonder if he's high already.

"Third grade? I tried to kiss another boy in class. On the lips. Peter Bowers—he had the cutest freckles. He wasn't down with it, though, and it turned into this whole thing with our parents and the school. Counseling. I went underground after that. Didn't try it again until middle school."

"So you've always known?"

He nods. "More or less. I don't think I knew the name for it until middle school. Then it was all 'fag' this and 'fag' that. Where I'm from isn't as laid-back about it as it is here. I hid it for a while." Dave takes another hit, holds it in until his face turns red and his eyes start to water. "How about you?" he asks. The words come out with a cloud of smoke, and I think of that caterpillar in *Alice in Wonderland*. *Whoooo are yoooou?*

"I don't know when it started." I've always checked out guys, but never for too long. Seems dangerous. I check out girls too, for that matter, in a more scientific way. I like to study people—the way they move and interact with one other. Chris is the first guy I've really been able to study up close, the first guy I've imagined naked and fantasized about on purpose. Well, that's not completely true, now that I think about it. I've had fleeting thoughts about underwear models and athletes. Or, like, the weatherman on WXTV, Casanova Guerra. Something about his voice. Partly it's the name, and also how he always seems to know what's coming. Like, the chance of rain or if hurricane is going to hit us or pass by. He's so reassuring about it too. *So, board up your windows and stock up on sandbags, West Palm. It's better to be prepared for the worst and hope for the best.*

I tell Dave about my crush on Casanova Guerra and what it might be like to have sex with a weatherman, how he'd narrate the whole thing in that calming, even-keeled voice. "Ninety percent chance of an orgasm this afternoon, with the possibility of light flooding. Don't forget to pack your raincoat."

Dave cracks up at that, and we take turns making weather predictions that sound like a bad porno flick. It's kind of hot. Then I ask him, "Have you ever had sex with a dude?"

He looks at me with a halfway serious expression. "Anal?" I nod. "No, but I'm game if you are. Might be a good way to see if you really are gay or if you've been faking it this whole time."

At that I sober up instantly. I probably shouldn't have put it on the table. It was more a survey than a proposition. "I don't think I'm ready for that." Not to mention it involves at least one of our assholes getting pounded, which I've heard can be painful at first. Something tells me between Dave and I, I'd be the one getting the raw ass.

I'd do it for Chris, though, if that's what he wanted. I'd pretty much go either way for him. Sigh.

"Saving yourself?" Dave asks.

I narrow my eyes at him, annoyed at how easily it seems he can read my mind. "For what?"

"Not what. Who."

I know *who* he means. I fiddle with the controller where it lays abandoned on the couch between us. "Chris is straight," I say, though I'm having my doubts. Maybe I should just ask him, but what if he is straight? Then I've just challenged his masculinity or something. And me asking kind of reveals myself, doesn't it? Outside of him telling me himself, there's no easy way to find out.

"We should come out together," Dave says. "I could ask you out to Homecoming in a really over-the-top way. Spray paint the BOA with a proclamation of gay love. Rainbows and unicorns and centaurs with really big junk. The works."

I laugh at the thought of it. My rep would be forever ruined among the skater punks. It shouldn't matter, but they might not take me seriously if they knew I was gay. I also haven't thought about what it would mean to be out at Sabal Palm High. I'd just as soon keep it under wraps.

"I don't think so, Dave."

"You don't want people to know you're gay or that we've been messing around?"

"Neither," I say before realizing how awful it sounds. His face goes slack. "It's not personal."

"Feels personal."

I study him, wondering if I've really hurt his feelings or if he's just using this as a way to manipulate me into giving him a blowjob. Dave's pretty crafty that way. "You don't even like me."

His face screws up and he leans toward me in a slightly aggressive way. "Why would you say that?"

He's always teasing me about stuff, making fun of the things I do or say, and it seems pretty obvious that we're using each other for sexual favors. Companionship too, but that comes second.

"Why don't you think I like you?" he persists.

"I don't know." I glance around, feeling super uncomfortable. It's kind of like the first week of school, when he claimed he was "hitting on me," and I thought he was just being an asshole. But maybe it's me who's not fully invested in the feelings department of our relationship.

"It's not for the lawn maintenance part of it," Dave says, "though Becca told me to do whatever it takes to keep you happy."

His yard does look pretty tight. I even planted some leftover impatiens to make him and his aunt matching garden beds next to their front doors. When I don't respond, he continues.

"I'd totally be your boyfriend, Theo, if you weren't so hung up on Mitcham."

I lean forward and stare at my hands, ashamed of my own impossible desires and how transparent they are. By being silent, I basically just acknowledged I'm using him. Dave wants to be in a committed relationship, like boyfriend-boyfriend, and I just want sex without any complications or responsibility.

Jesus, maybe I am like my father after all.

"I'm trying to get over him," I tell Dave, which is the honest-to-God truth.

"So let me help." Dave sets down his bong and lays a proprietary hand on my thigh. He waggles his eyebrows at me. Maybe it's guilt or maybe it's my libido, but I totally crumble, and we end up giving each other what we mutually agree are the best blowjobs of our lives, which for me is much higher praise because Dave is something of a blowjob connoisseur.

And that's why Dave and I work. Because every situation that could potentially end badly turns into another opportunity for Dave to get me to pull my pants down and vice versa.

Somewhere inside me I know it's not going to last, but I'm willing to ride it out for the time being. And maybe that's me being selfish, but for the moments when we're together, Dave makes me forget about Chris and all the things I can't have with him, and in my situation, that's really the best I can hope for.

# EIGHT

# DINNER WITH DAD

"Did you get my text?"

I walk through the door that same afternoon and find my sister standing at the kitchen counter, nursing a Diet Coke and decapitating carrot sticks with her big white teeth.

"No, what?"

"Dad wants to take us out to dinner tonight."

I groan.

"It's for our birthday, Theo. He said he has a surprise for us. Maybe it's... a new car!" She makes her voice sound like a game show host and wiggles her fingers. I smile. She used to be funny like that. We used to crack each other up before she started caring so much about being cool. Now it's rare for her to risk acting silly.

"I doubt it's a new car, Tabs."

She shrugs. "A girl can dream, can't she?"

"You don't even drive."

"It's not about the car, Theo. It's the thought that counts."

"I don't want him buying us stuff."

"Well, I do."

"Just because he buys you stuff doesn't make up for him being a shitty father," I say with a rush of anger that takes me by surprise and leaves me with a prickly heat on the back of my neck.

She glares at me, her lower lip jutting out like it used to right before she'd start wailing to our mom to tell on me for being mean or hitting her, usually because she hit me first. I feel bad for saying it, not because it isn't true but because I don't want to hurt her feelings. My sister still has some faith left in my dad. I should let her hold on to it as long as she can.

"He'll be here in forty-five minutes. Don't be an asshole tonight and screw it up for me," she says tartly and takes her Diet Coke downstairs with her, slamming the door on her way out. Outside my bedroom window, I see her cross over to Chris's house. His front door opens and she disappears inside. Before the door shuts, Chris pops his head out and glances up to my window. I feel caught and slowly back away, pretending I wasn't already looking for him.

I quickly shower, then survey my closet to find something to wear because whenever we go out to dinner with my dad, it's always to some ridiculously fancy place where the servers all fall over themselves to kiss your ass. I'd rather my dad put that money toward helping my mom with the bills, but he likes flaunting his wealth in front of us. At least, that's how it seems to me.

I pick out the shirt I wore the last time I saw my dad. It was Easter, when my grandmother came down from New York and wanted all her grandchildren in the same place at once. My dad hosted a luncheon at his McMansion in Todesta, this weird Stepford planned community. His wife, Susan, was running around like crazy, trying to make sure everything was up to whatever impossible standard he'd set. I mostly kicked back and chilled with my great-uncle Theo, my namesake, who'd been sprung from the home for the day.

Uncle Theo has dementia, but even before that, he was a salty old bastard. At the party, he kept asking me to bring him more potato salad and whistling at the women when they walked by. Then, when my grandmother said it was time to go, Uncle Theo pitched a fit and called her a cocksucker.

Cocksucker.

He said it with such gusto that a little spittle came out and dotted his chin. I tried to persuade him to go quietly with a tub of potato salad, and he turned on me too. Called me a cocksucker. Like, in his eighty-plus years of living, that was the worst insult he could come up with. Chris cracked up when I told him that story, and we each took turns saying it like my Uncle Theo. *Cocksucker.*

I really should go visit Uncle Theo in the home, take him some of that potato salad he likes. Talk about being lonely. I hope they just take me out back and shoot me when I get too old. I don't ever want to end up in a home, alone, slowly losing my mind and forgetting the names of the people I once loved.

I button up the one nice collared shirt I own. It's way too small, tight along the back so I can't pull my arms forward all the way. The cuffs only make it halfway down my forearms, but I don't have time to go somewhere to get another one. I roll up the sleeves, grab my tie, and head out to the kitchen to see if my mom can knot it for me.

My mom sees me and tries to hide a smile behind her dainty little hand. My mom and sister are cute little things, and I take after my dad—tall and gangly and slightly awkward, though I'm pretty slim, whereas my dad has been packing a little extra poundage around the middle lately.

"Theo, you can't wear that," she says, shaking her head with sympathy. She feels sorry for me, either because I'm growing faster than she can keep me in clothes or because I'm the idiot who didn't realize it.

I glance down. "Is it really that noticeable?"

"You look like you're twelve years old. Lift up your arms." I do, and the shirt comes up above my navel.

"Go put on something else."

I go back to my room and ransack my closet, but all I come up with is a faded striped shirt that looks like it's been worn about a million times before. I come out with it on. This time it's my sister who gives me shit.

"You've *got* to be kidding me," she says all snottily. She's wearing this slinky black number that makes her look about thirty-five years old. Makeup, straightened hair. Man, her boobs have really grown too.

"Go borrow something from Chris," she says dismissively.

"No." The last thing I want to do is go over there and ask for a favor.

"Dad's going to be here any minute," she huffs. "There's no way he's going to let you go out with us dressed like that."

She's right. I pull off my shirt and throw it on the table, run back to my room for an undershirt and tie, then jog downstairs and over to Chris's house. Maybe he won't be home. Then I can say I did everything I could to make it happen. Maybe I can skip dinner with my dad altogether.

I knock twice, and Chris answers the door almost immediately.

"Hey." He looks me up and down and seems to pick up on my urgency.

"Can I—"

"Yeah, of course." He opens the door wide and leads me upstairs to his suite of rooms, which includes a bedroom, a game room, a palatial bathroom, and a walk-in closet that's about the size of my bedroom. I follow him into the closet, and he surveys his collection of menswear. I don't bother looking. I'll take whatever he gives me.

He pulls a blue shirt off the hanger and hands it to me. "This one's a little big on me," he says. "Matches your eyes."

It does match my eyes, almost exactly. It's kind of weird that he noticed, but I appreciate his efficiency. I toss the tie on the bed and pull the shirt on, buttoning it up as fast as I can, including the cuffs. I tuck it into my pants and redo my belt, glance up in the mirror. It fits. ¡Genial!

"Damn, Theo," he says. "When'd you get so handsome?"

That sets off a burning sensation deep in my belly that radiates outward, a telegram to the enemy line. I imagine a block of ice around my crotch, deep-freezing everything within it. I chalk up his comment to him messing with me because it's dangerous to read into things like that.

I loop the tie around my collar with shaking hands and fumble it because I've only worn a tie a half-dozen times in my life. I know my dad's about to pull up to the curb any minute, and I want to look like I have my shit together even though I feel like the opposite.

"Stop," Chris says. "You'll strangle yourself." He comes over and carefully unravels my tie. I go still—fugue state—just staring at him, my upper lip sweating a little because he's so close I can smell him, taste him. I inhale deeper even though I know I shouldn't, and it sets my every nerve on edge. His tongue is doing that little pokey thing out the side of his mouth as he knots my tie. *Please, not now*, I tell my junk, which doesn't seem to care that I'm begging. These pants are thin, and with terror I realize a huge hard-on has been erected in Chris's name. There's no hiding it. I bend my knees a little and curl inward so I don't sexually assault him, praying he doesn't have the sense to look down.

"There," he says, patting my shoulders. His gaze flickers to my mouth, and I wipe the beaded sweat from my upper lip. Our eyes meet, and it feels different—time slows and gravity presses down on us more urgently. It's like we're meeting again for the first time. *Does he see me differently now? Does he want me too?* I still my breath so as not to spook him, but he only flashes his cocky grin and turns me toward the mirror.

"Not bad, huh?" he says as if to defuse the situation.

"Yeah, not bad." I clear my throat and tamp down the disappointment threatening to consume me. He's right, though, I do look pretty hot. Maybe that was all it was between us, a friendly appreciation. I'd totally get with myself, I think, and then laugh on the inside because I already have, many times over.

"Thanks, Chris." I sigh a little and feel like I'm never able to express my gratitude to him. He's gotten me out of so many jams. Then, because I don't want my feelings to erupt like my uncontrollable boner, I get back to business. "Is this one of those shirts that needs to be dry-cleaned?" A lot of his nicer clothes have all these rules for washing. I keep throwing his old clothes into our dryer, and they come out looking like doll clothes.

"Machine wash. You can keep this one."

"I'll bring it back tomorrow, clean."

"Fine," he says, not wanting to argue with me about it.

I tell him goodbye and gallop down the stairs, exit his house just as my dad is pulling up to our driveway. He honks the horn because he's said before he doesn't want to deal with my mother, which I guess means knocking on the door and greeting her like a decent human being.

Tabs struts down our driveway like it's a catwalk and claims the front seat of his Tahoe without question. I climb into the back. Dad reaches back to shake my hand, and I do it with what I hope is the right amount of pressure, even though it's kind of weird to greet him after months of no contact with a handshake. Tabs kisses his cheek and calls him Daddy. It's like she's a grown woman at home, but when we get around my dad, she turns back into this little girl. Then I think, I'm probably not the only one who's emotionally stunted because of his neglect. I make up my mind to do whatever I can to make the night go smoothly. Tabs deserves this.

Tabs keeps up the conversation on the way to the restaurant, thankfully. I sit in the back with my long legs stretched out, letting the cool air-conditioned air wash over me, and think about Chris tying my tie for me and all the other strangely intimate things we do for each other and wonder if that's normal or if there might be something more behind it. It's a constant cycle of reflection and self-doubt, which keeps my head spinning like a weather vane in a storm. I imagine a conversation between Chris and me would go something like this:

Me: Hey there, buddy, remember that time we jacked each other off?

Chris, suspiciously: Yeah, what about it?

Me: That was amazing, and I'd like to do that with you on the regular because, guess what, I'm gay and not only that, I'm in love with you and I have been for a while now.

Chris: I'm not gay.

Me:....

Chris: Why would you even think that? Do I seem gay to you? Wait, you like me? No, love me? What the....

"Pretty quiet back there," my dad says, glancing at me in the rearview mirror.

"Just enjoying the ride," I respond lightly. I've got to get Chris out of my head. Hypnosis? Electroshock therapy? Lobotomy?

We arrive at the restaurant, and a valet takes the car. Dad tips him with a crisp bill, and I think, what a waste of money, because there's a parking spot literally ten feet away. He could have paid me the money to park his car for him. Dad comments on my height now that we're standing shoulder to shoulder. He's pretty tall and I've finally caught up with him, which I guess makes me pretty tall as well. Everything is changing—my body, my emotions, my sanity. I wish it would all just slow the hell down and let me catch my breath.

"You two must have been busy this summer," Dad says, trying to excuse his absence in our lives for the past six months, acknowledging without acknowledging how long it's been since we last saw him. I would let that shit hang over us like a silent, brooding storm cloud, but not Tabs. As if on cue, she immediately starts filling him in on everything she's been up to while I duck my head and follow them inside.

The restaurant is swanky and artfully lit, with high-end furniture and attractive servers. A model-looking hostess leads us to our table, and a server brings us waters almost immediately. Tabs fills the silence with idle chatter—maybe she's nervous too. My dad orders a Coke instead of a drink, which is good. One of the rules of his visitation is that he doesn't drink when we're with him. My mom is strict about that.

"So, Theo," Dad says rapping the table in front of me with his knuckles to get my attention, an irritating habit of his. "Your sister tells me you got a job."

"Yeah, mowing lawns on the weekends." Me and my squad, tearing up the neighborhood. Edging the shit out of Palm Beach's lawns and keeping everyone legit with their HOA's.

"Manual labor, huh?" The tone of his voice isn't one of admiration for an honest day's work, more like distaste. "You know, I could have gotten you a job at my office."

Working for my dad sounds like one long, drawn-out panic attack. The few times I've been to his office, it's this whole dog-and-pony show where my dad puts his arm around me and jokes around like we're best buds in front of all his employees. *How about those Dolphins, son?* It's the reason I stopped going to him to have my teeth cleaned—it felt fake as hell.

"It's cool, Dad. I like being outside."

"You've gotten pretty dark," he says, like it's a bad thing. My dad's a little racist. So are my grandmother and Uncle Theo, for that matter. I'm not sure what he thought might happen when he impregnated a Puerto Rican. Maybe that his Aryan genes would be that powerful.

"The sun will do that," I say.

"You could wear a long-sleeve shirt and a hat," he says, like it's a brilliant solution no one has ever thought of before. I'm tempted to tell him only middle-aged white dudes do that, but I hold my tongue.

My sister cuts in. "Theo's saving up to buy a car." I nudge her under the table. She kicks me back harder with the pointy toe of her shoe. Right in the shin. I hate it when she volunteers information about me to him. She's probably angling for him to one-up me, which he does.

"A car, huh? How much you got saved?"

"A couple thousand," I say like it's no big deal, secretly proud that I've been able to amass that much cash on my own. Like a boss.

"I can ask Susan about the Range Rover," he says, rubbing his chin thoughtfully.

My sister practically bounces out of her seat. "Really, Daddy?" she whines like a puppy. "*Ohmygod*, that would be *sooo amazing.*"

"How about it, Theo?" My dad levels his gaze at me, and it seems like a test. He wants the same reaction from me. In some weird way, it's like he needs to be needed. I think about all the things he should have been there for—teaching me how to ride a bike, how to drive a car, telling me what an erection is, which Chris had to do. *What the hell is this?* I asked Chris one day because I thought my dick was broken, and Chris explained it to me, without even laughing or making me feel stupid about it.

My dad stares at me, waiting for a response, and I feel trapped.

"That's really generous of you Dad, but I'll probably get a junker."

"Too good for the Range Rover?" he asks snidely.

"No, I just want to do this on my own." I also don't want to owe him anything. There's no such thing as no-strings-attached with my father.

His eyebrows raise, and he frowns so that his chin puckers. "Maybe you could talk to your mother about your child support, then. Wouldn't mind getting that monkey off my back."

I swallow down my rising tide of anger and study the design on the silverware. My mother hasn't had it easy since their divorce. After being cheated on and discarded like yesterday's headlines, she had to battle my dad's army of lawyers for child support. Her English wasn't exactly perfect at the time, which my dad took advantage of. Then it was the constant badgering over the years from my dad, trying to make my mom feel like a freeloader when she works harder than anyone I know. And for all that he's put her through, she never says a bad word about him, always defends him, which is a hell of a lot more than he's ever done for her.

What was it he used to call me? Oh yeah, *mama's boy*. And that was before the divorce.

Our server arrives then to take our order, and I'm thankful for the distraction. After the server leaves, my dad switches the topic to sports.

"How's soccer going?" he asks. Soccer is the one thing he used to show an interest in. He never came to my practices—that was my mom—but he'd come to my games. He was the dad on the sidelines yelling at the refs and telling the coach how to do his job. But near the end of middle school, Dad's participation in our lives dropped off dramatically, which for me included soccer.

"I decided not to go out for the team. I'm more into skateboarding now."

He squints at me. "Skateboarding? That's hardly a sport."

I rub my forehead; a headache's coming on. Maybe he'll ask me if I have a girlfriend next. *No, Dad, but I'm getting really good at giving head.* I can't even imagine coming out to my dad. What a nightmare.

"That's too bad about soccer," he says. "I was looking forward to going to a few of your games this year."

I started almost every game last year. My dad didn't make it to one of them. Chris did, though. I almost smile at that, thinking how I could always count on him to show up, even if my dad didn't. My dad stares at me, perhaps waiting for me to apologize or tell him I'll go out for the team, but I do neither. I gave up trying to impress him a while ago.

"I'm trying out for the dance team, Daddy," my sister says, trying to fill the silence. I feel bad for her. Needing his approval like that, wanting his attention bad enough to make everything nice for him. "You and Theo could come to one of our basketball games."

Dad frowns. "I'll have to check my schedule." My sister and I exchange a look. We both know what that means.

My sister, God bless her, tries again. "I saw on Facebook that the baby's a boy. Have you and Susan picked out a name yet?"

Dad fiddles with his tie. "William," he says without meeting my eyes. William is my dad's name. I got named after my great-uncle and his uncle before him. For whatever reason, the Theodores in our family don't spawn. But I wasn't named after my dad, which is strange, being firstborn and all. Maybe his heart was never in it to begin with. My sister looks at me with sympathy, which is worse. So much worse.

"When's the baby due?" my sister asks with a little less enthusiasm.

"Sometime in December," he says, and all I can think is, I hope he does a better job with this one, for the kid's sake.

My sister asks more baby-related questions, most of which my dad can't answer because he doesn't have a clue, which only makes me worry for William IV, to think my dad could potentially screw him up too. I hope Susan can keep my dad's alcoholism and wandering eye in check. My dad has a bad case of white male privilege, worsened by the fact that he grew up with money, which has given him the impression that whatever he wants in life, he can just reach out and take it, regardless of who else's life he's screwing with.

Maybe it's better that my dad didn't raise me. I've seen what that looks like on guys my age. Some of the guys on the soccer team have it. Huge assholes. The kind of asshole who fakes a foul, then picks a fight with the player on the other team when it doesn't get called. The kind of asshole who would rather be red-carded than back down, then throws a hissy fit on the sidelines because he can't play and it's all someone else's fault.

It's why I switched to skateboarding. Skaters are a kind of asshole I can deal with, hating on shit because they don't have enough confidence in themselves. Most of them skate to be alone with others and have a problem with authority. All of them seem to have a high threshold for pain. Get in where you fit in.

The server delivers our meal. I ordered salmon, even though my appetite is nada. I would have ordered a grilled cheese if I thought my dad wouldn't have a fit about it.

"You still hanging out with that neighbor of yours?" Dad asks me, slicing into his rare steak and taking a big, bloody bite.

"Chris. Yeah."

"Now that's one strange kid."

"He's not strange." That's the last word I'd used to describe Chris. If anything, I'm the strange one.

My dad continues, "You think he might be...." He lowers his head so that it accentuates his double chin, draws his eyebrows together a little, and scrunches up his nose like he's smelling someone's farts.

"Might be what?" I ask, feeling hostile and aggressive without even knowing what he's talking about. My dad can talk shit about me all he wants, but he better leave Chris out of it.

"You know...." Dad leans in closer. "Gay?"

I'm stunned silent. The way he says it, like it's so repugnant he can't even say the word. In a parallel universe, someone is laughing their ass off at my situation. But all I want is to find the nearest body of water and drown myself in it.

My sister answers before I can, "Oh my God, Daddy, *noooo*. Definitely not. He's got, like, a million girlfriends."

Dad shrugs, a little smirk on his face. He thinks it's funny. "You never know," he says while masticating his meat. "Kids these days."

I stand up suddenly, dropping my napkin onto the floor.

"Enough," I declare to the entire restaurant. I practically shout it from the rafters.

"What's your problem?" Dad asks.

I glance at my sister, who's giving me a death stare like I'd better not screw this up. I stride away from the table as fast as I can without actually running, make my way blindly to the bathroom, grapple for the sink faucet, and splash some cold water on my face, getting water on my shirtfront and not giving a shit except to wonder if it will stain Chris's shirt.

"Fuck," I mutter at my reflection. I'm going to puke. And I'm all dizzy and shit, my stomach cramping into the size of a golf ball. So much rage buzzing through me, I feel like a lunatic. I definitely can't go back out there. I come out of the bathroom and look for another way out of the restaurant so I don't have to pass by them. Seems the only way out is through the kitchen. I push through the swinging door, keeping my head down. The staff is too polite to stop me, just kindly tell me I'm going the wrong way. I find the back door and pass through it, loosening my tie along the way. I don't know how the hell to get it unknotted, so I just end up ripping it off my head and shoving it in my pocket. I take in big gulps of fresh air, trying to calm myself down and work up the nerve to go back in. Right around the time I think I've gotten myself under control, I get a text from my sister:

*Dad says to get your ass back in here or he's giving your trust fund to Sabine.*

Sabine is my seven-year-old half sister, my dad's love child with his second wife, the one he cheated on my mom with. I'm being held hostage. Screw him, I think. I don't need his money. And I don't need his bullshit.

Instead of texting my sister, I pull up my contacts and call Chris.

"What's up?" he says, like he already knows something is wrong. I hardly ever call. We usually text.

I should have brought my skateboard, but I didn't. I could walk home, but this is an area I'm not familiar with, where the houses are all cookie cutter and the streets look the same. I'm not sure I could find my way out if I tried. Oh, and look at that, it's starting to rain.

"Can you come get me?"

"Sure thing. I'll be there in twenty."

"I'm in Todesta." I glance around, looking for a street sign to give him an address.

"I know where you are," he says.

That's right, Find My Friends.

# NINE
## GRILLED CHEESE

Just the sight of Chris's Volvo coming up the street fills me with a full-body flood of relief. I'm hopping from foot to foot as he approaches, under the bus stop overhang where I'm waiting for him out of the rain.

"What happened?" he asks as I climb into the passenger side. I shake the water from my head like a dog and Chris shields himself from my spray with his hand.

"Dinner with my dad."

I think back to this one time my dad came and picked me up for the day. One of the rare occasions it was just me because Tabs was busy elsewhere. We watched football at a sports bar and ate chicken wings until we were both uncomfortably full. I asked a lot of questions about the game, and my dad was pretty patient in answering. All in all, it was a good time. Then, when he dropped me off, he picked a fight with my mom about how bad my table manners were, how I didn't say *please* or *thank you* and how he was embarrassed by my behavior while we were out.

It was bullshit—all of it—and he didn't seem to care that I was standing right there. Their fight escalated, and it made me question everything I thought I knew about my dad. He was using me to get back at her, that much I understood. I was so angry and felt so betrayed, I swore to never let my father use me as a weapon against my mother again.

In Chris's car, I tell him everything about the night up until the point where my dad said Chris was strange and asked if he was gay. Chris listens and commiserates with me until I start to feel better. What a relief it is to unload on him, knowing he's one hundred percent on my side, unlike Tabitha and my mom, who are always defending my dad and trying to make me see his point of view. In a way, Chris has suffered through my relationship with my father right alongside me, so the whole feelings part of it is covered without me even having to explain it. This is how it used to be between us before everything got awkward and strained.

"You should stay at my house tonight," Chris says. "We'll eat junk food and watch scary movies. Fart on each other's pillows."

I smile at that. It actually sounds like fun. Who cares if we have to be up at 6:00 a.m. the next morning to get ready for school? There's honestly no one in the world I'd rather be with right now.

We get back to his house, and Chris makes me a grilled cheese sandwich, since I never did eat my expensive froufrou dinner. Dad's probably pissed about that too. I watch Chris move around the kitchen, thinking how nice it is, how comfortable and safe I feel in his kitchen, how lucky I am to have him in my life. Even if things with my dad are kind of messed up. Even if my sister thinks I'm a selfish asshole.

Chris slides the grilled cheese onto my plate. He uses the edge of the spatula to slice it in half, diagonally. Even my mom doesn't know I prefer it that way.

I get to thinking then about when we first started hanging out. I was wearing this expander in my mouth so my upper jaw could fit my huge horse teeth. It made me talk with a lisp—*Seadore Woosen*—I couldn't even say my own name right. Sixth grade was pretty rough, especially because in addition to our dad ditching us, that was around the time Tabitha realized I was a dweeb and started ignoring me at school. Tabs was always good at knowing what movies and shows and web videos were popular. She, like, studied up on how to be cool, whereas I just liked to sit in my room with my Magic cards or else mess around with a soccer ball outside. Our mom never introduced us to any of the American pop culture that most kids are exposed to, and we were too broke for devices or video games, so I was pretty clueless when it came to finding common ground with other kids my age. I read a lot of fantasy books, which probably didn't help. When I tried to talk about my own weird obsessions, I was met with blank faces, or else teasing.

I got so uptight about where to sit at lunch, I couldn't eat. Then, a few days after the bullying incident in our neighborhood, Chris saw me at school and told me to sit with him and his friends at lunch, an honor for any sixth grader. Tabs and I started catching rides with Chris and Paloma, who drove us to school. Once people saw Chris and me palling around, they pretty much left me alone. I learned how to be cool, or at least, how to keep my dweeby thoughts to myself. And even when something weird snuck out, Chris went with it and made it acceptable.

He really saved my ass.

"Whatcha thinking about?" Chris asks.

I shake myself from the memory. "When we first started hanging out. Why you stuck it out with me. I'm kind of a dweeb, Chris. Let's be real."

He smiles. "Maybe I like dweebs."

I glance around at all the new, shiny appliances that adorn his state-of-the-art kitchen. Nice cars, nice family. Nice, nice, nice.

"You've got, like, everything, you know? Money, personality, looks. And you're so cool about it."

"What's cool about me?" Chris asks like he's baffled by it. I roll my eyes. There's no way he can't know. In all the ways Chris could be an asshole, he isn't.

"Your hair, for one. It always looks awesome. You're, like, super buff without even trying. The girls are always throwing their panties at you. You're generous and smart and funny and you always know the right thing to say."

"Not always," he says. His brow wrinkles in the middle. "And who's throwing their panties at me?"

"Kelli Keyhoe, Isabelle Demonte, that girl in California offering you a blowjob. I have to, like, wade through a pile of used panties just to talk to you."

He laughs.

"Your laugh." I turn back to my grilled cheese, sad as hell because I'm in love with my best friend and I'll never be able to have him the way I want him. I should just be grateful I have him at all, instead of being such a wiener about it.

"What about you?" he asks, leaning on the counter so he's close enough I can see his individual eyelashes.

"What about me?"

"Tall, dark, and handsome. Mysterious. Smart as hell. Those eyes. That smile." He sighs like a lovesick maiden, and I shake my head. He's messing with me. "And you don't give a shit whether people like you or not. That's punk rock, man."

"Yeah, that's my problem."

He nudges my shoulder with his knuckles. "That's not the problem. Your dad's a dick. We've always known this. Your mom knows it too. That's why she left him. So why are you making this about you?"

He's right. Sort of. But it's my fault too. If I tried harder, like Tabitha, I could at least have some kind of relationship with my father, instead of constantly fighting with him about stupid shit.

"See, you always know what to say." I take a bite of the grilled cheese. The warm, salty goo melts in my mouth. The bread is buttery and crisp. A perfect pairing.

"I don't always know what to say." Chris turns away to put up the dishes and wipe down the counter—he even tidies up after himself. I get the urge, then, to talk about what happened in Sebastian. To ask him if it was just some weird mood, or if it meant something to him, but I don't want to ruin this moment we're having, and I really can't afford to lose any more allies right now.

"If it was legal, I'd totally marry this grilled cheese sandwich," I tell Chris in appreciation of his culinary abilities.

"How would you consummate the marriage?" he asks with a leer. I grin and poke a hole through the sandwich with my finger. Chris shakes his head and throws a dishtowel at me, so I wiggle my finger a little more until he cracks up. God, I love his laugh.

"I've seen worse matches," he says, and I grin, excited by it because we're talking about sex, even if it is with a grilled cheese sandwich. My mother would be so horrified.

I finish eating, and we head upstairs. Chris keeps this trunk of snacks at the end of his bed—I call it his treasure chest. It's filled with every kind of snack cake, candy bar, and potato chip imaginable. I'm surprised he doesn't have ants in his room. We gorge ourselves on snacks. Then I convince Chris he's going to get fat from all the junk food he eats, so he tells me we should go swimming to work it off. It's stopped raining, so I borrow one of his pairs of board shorts, and we go out back. We goof off in the water, acting like total idiots, horsing around like we haven't since before he left for summer.

Afterward we lie back on lawn chairs and stare up at the hazy, light-polluted sky. The scent of chlorine is in the air and the faint sweetness of cut grass. Smells like summertime.

"I missed this," Chris says.

"Yeah, me too."

"You've changed since last year," he says and rolls over to face me. The shark's tooth dangles from his neck and the light from the pool plays on his face, making his eyes dance. He's gorgeous in all lighting.

"How's that?" I ask.

"You've, like, grown up. Started shaving. Got a J-O-B. Mr. Man."

"Trying to please you, Boss," I joke, only not really. When I think about the male role models in my life, Chris is who comes to mind. I'd be truly lost without him as my guide. Maybe I can't tell him how I really feel, but there are other emotions I have for him that have nothing to do with my sexuality and everything to do with the kind of person he is.

"I really admire you, Chris. The way you've always stood up for me, and other dweebs like me. The way you keep peace in the jungle at school. And you're always doing nice things for other people. You've been a really good friend."

"Are we breaking up?"

I chuckle. "No, man, I'm trying to express myself. Isn't that what you're always telling me I need to do?"

"Yeah." He rolls onto his back and clasps his hands over his perfect, ripped abs. I give myself to the count of three—three seconds to stare, and then I look away.

"Anyway, you've always been there for me, since that first time. I hope I'm there for you too, when you need me."

"You are, Theo." He sighs. "You are."

WE DON'T END UP WATCHING ANY HORROR MOVIES. I'M EXHAUSTED from all the emoting of the day. I roll out the futon cushion I normally sleep on when I spend the night, and Chris pulls out my favorite old comforter, well-worn and smelling of him. Even stale-smelling Chris is pretty nice.

We each get comfortable in our beds, and Chris shuts off the lights. After a few minutes, he leans over the side of his bed.

"You awake?" he asks.

"No," I tease.

"Come up here."

I don't question it. His bed is a king-sized. I used to share with him before it got weird. I even have my own side. I climb up and lie on my side, facing him in the dark.

"Remember the time we watched *It* and you made me barricade the bedroom door to keep Pennywise out?" he asks.

"And developed a phobia of clowns?" He grins and I continue the thread. "And when we watched *Dr. Giggles* and you asked me where my dad kept the dead bodies."

Chris starts cracking up. "And you were taking a shower...." He can't stop laughing long enough to finish, so I do it for him.

"And you shut off the lights and screamed like your head was being chopped off." He's laughing so hard there are tears coming out of his eyes. "And I busted my ass in the shower and almost got a concussion. Your mom was so pissed."

"You were buck naked," he says, wheezing. "Tore down the shower curtain and everything."

Some of the plaster came out of the wall as well. I felt really bad about it. Not to mention the embarrassment when we had to explain it to his parents.

"So not cool," I say.

"You were so pissed," he says between gasps.

"Yeah, and I seriously went looking for the dead bodies the next time I was at my dad's office. The receptionist was all, like, what are you looking for? And I had to be, like, um, an extra toothbrush?"

"I didn't mean to traumatize you," he says, looking sad as a pound puppy, but I know he's not sorry at all.

"So messed up, man. You really get off on scaring me."

He smiles. "You're not that easy to scare, though. That time you ate shit at Tropical Smoothie and got knocked out. That shit was scary."

I bombed on a trick and fell wrong, knocked my head against a curb, and went unconscious for a spell. "And you forced me to wear a helmet for, like, weeks after, even though it made me look like a total dweeb."

"You were concussed, Theo. I didn't want you to have any more brain damage than you already did."

"So lame," I say.

"Yeah, well, someone has to keep an eye on your clumsy ass." He's quiet, and my mind wanders to some of our shenanigans over the years. All the stunts we were able to pull off because we had each other, like the time we got the neighborhood kids to meet us at this big concrete drain at the edge of our subdivision. It has a slope of, like, forty-five degrees. We "borrowed" a couple of shopping carts from Publix and tried skating them down the drain, judging one another based on distance, speed, and style. One of our many dumb ways to die.

"That day in Sebastian, though," Chris says, "I thought you had drowned, T."

"Getting soft, old man."

"You were under for so long."

"You were hoping to give me mouth-to-mouth, huh?" I say, and the words are out there, hanging between us, and I can't take them back.

A beat later he laughs, but it sounds more like he's choking. "I would have done it, you know, if it needed to be done."

I shake my head. "Lucky for you it didn't."

"Lucky me." He smiles and glances away, then pulls the sheet up over our heads like we used to when we'd be watching something we shouldn't on his laptop, aka porn, and sharing a set of earbuds between us.

"Wouldn't it be great if we could stay in here forever?" he asks.

"Yeah." I sigh, afraid to say anything more and ruin the moment.

We stare at each other until the oxygen runs out. Warmth radiates from my chest thinking about all the shared memories between us, and the contentment in knowing that at least one person in this world gets me, really gets me.

I don't know why, but I kind of start to sniffle. Chris pulls back the sheet to see me better. "Theo?" he says and shoves me a little, like I might be faking. When he realizes I'm not, he mutters roughly, "Come here," and grabs me with his two powerful arms, manhandles me so my back is against his chest. He wraps his arms around me, like a brother might or maybe even a lover. At the moment I don't really care, I just want to be held by him.

Chris rests his chin on my shoulder and breathes into my neck. I wish I could capture his noises in a bottle and keep them forever. Lift the lid a little when I'm lonely and let his sighs and moans roll over me like the waves on the sand.

TEN

# UNCLE THEO

W e wake up late the next morning because Chris forgot to set an alarm. It's kind of hectic getting ready for school. I end up throwing on some of his clothes and dash next door to get my backpack and deck, then meet him out front where he's waiting with the engine already running. We arrive at school during the end of first period and hang out in the parking lot until the bell rings so we don't have to go to the ISS room.

Chris heads straight to physics since he already has his stuff, and I head to our lockers. Dave's there when I arrive. I say what's up to him and the rest of the crew and start unloading my stuff. Dave waits until it's mostly cleared out, then says to me, "I went by your house last night."

That's a first. I guess he did text me a few times. I was too preoccupied to respond. "I was out to dinner with my dad," I tell him.

"Your sister said you were staying the night at Chris's."

I shrug. Why is Dave all up in my business?

"She said you were an asshole at dinner and you had Chris come pick you up."

Jesus, my sister has a mouth. "Did she invite you in for tea and biscuits too?"

He scowls at me. "Don't be a smartass. You could have called me, you know?"

I run my fingers down the spine of one of my textbooks. It never even occurred to me to call Dave. For some reason, our relationship doesn't seem to exist for me outside his apartment.

"Why didn't you?" he asks.

"I don't know."

"Did you think of it?"

"No," I say honestly.

He crosses his arms. I can tell he's hurt by it, but I don't want to lie. One of the reasons we work is because we're both pretty up-front about things.

"You coming over this afternoon?" he asks.

I know he wants to mess around, but I'm more confused about Chris than ever. I'm not exactly sure how Dave fits in with all this, and I don't want to be selfish or lead him on. I definitely don't want him as a boyfriend, and it seems the only way to avoid that is to cool things off for a bit.

"My sister wants me to help make food for this party she's having this weekend," I tell Dave, which is the truth.

"Yeah, I heard about that."

I realize I didn't invite him, and yet I don't want him there either, because Chris will be there, and I know it will be awkward.

"It's at Chris's house. I'm only going because I have to."

"Yeah, whatever."

"You can come if you want," I tell him, which is a shitty invitation if ever there was one.

"Forget it. I don't want to get between you and Daddy."

Daddy? What the hell is that supposed to mean? I'm in defense mode all of a sudden. I thought we covered this already. I don't like Dave insinuating things he knows nothing about. "I told you before, we're just friends."

"Keep telling yourself that."

"Well, it's not like you're exactly a tender lover. I'm lucky if I get offered a drink before I'm sucking you off."

He pushes my shoulder so I'm turned around to face him, pinned between his chest and my locker. To anyone else, it might look like he's going to fight me. "You're the one who pulls away whenever I try to touch you," he hisses through clenched teeth.

His voice is low, but a few people glance over at us. It looks suspicious. I shove him off me, turn away, and concentrate on my locker so as not to attract any more attention.

"Come over this afternoon," he says again, resting his hand close to mine on our lockers without actually touching me.

"I can't. I'm busy. I'm not making it up."

Dave's hand curls into a fist. "Fine. Have it your way." He bangs the locker with his knuckles and walks away.

ON THE RIDE HOME FROM SCHOOL, I DRIFT INTO A DAYDREAM ABOUT LAST night in Chris's bedroom when he held me, whether it was strictly for my comfort or if there was some homoerotic passion behind it as well. I steal a few glances at Chris as he drives, but he's wearing sunglasses and humming along to the music like he has not a care in the world and is definitely not obsessing on our embrace or what it might have signified.

At one point he turns to me and smiles. "What?" he asks, like I told a joke and he's waiting for the punch line.

"Nothing," I mutter and choke down my feelings. He shrugs and turns his attention back to the road and I think *I have got to get off this ride.*

Later we're in Chris's kitchen with Paloma, rolling up cold cuts for a tray, when Chris pokes his finger through one of the slices of cheese and cracks up laughing. Paloma shakes her head at us like we're immature imbeciles. She's right.

I grin along with him while wondering if he has some sort of brain damage that allows him the selective memory, where our bodies pressed together under his covers for what felt like an eternity doesn't even register. I have to admit, it's pretty damn frustrating.

The doorbell rings, and Chris washes his hands to go get the door. I hear the *clack clack* of my sister's sandals and her voice carrying through the entryway, which suddenly dies when she enters the kitchen and sees me there.

"What are *you* doing here?" she asks with a pissy look on her face, hands planted on her hips. I haven't seen her since dinner last night with our dad.

"You told me you wanted me to help. Something about my lazy ass had better be here or I was doing cleanup on my own."

"Dad's pissed at you," she says, like I don't already know it. Her eyes narrow and her mouth puckers like she's warming up for a verbal spar. If she's looking for a fight, I know already I'm going to lose. Tabitha fights dirty.

Paloma announces that she needs to go check on the laundry and disappears. Chris retreats to the egg-peeling station and turns his back on us, excusing himself from the conversation. I really don't want to have it out with my sister in his kitchen, but knowing Tabs, there's no way around it.

"I got that impression," I tell her. "The whole trust fund threat."

"You were a total asshole last night."

I shouldn't be surprised. She usually takes Dad's side.

"Was I the asshole?" I couldn't have been the only one.

"You could have at least tried. He just wants to know what's going on with you. Riling you up is the only way to get you to talk. Mom didn't even know you weren't playing soccer this year. Or me. Chris is the only person you talk to." At this she shoots an accusing look at Chris's back, and I want nothing more than for her to leave him the hell out of it.

I take a deep breath and let it out through my nose. De-escalation is the name of the game with my sister, but she doesn't let up to give me the floor.

"And then you totally ditched us without saying anything. Dad was so pissed, Theo, and *I* had to deal with it. It makes me look bad, too, when you do stuff like that. He spent the rest of the night talking about how ungrateful and spoiled you are and how it's Mom's fault you don't have any manners."

"That's bullshit, Tabs."

"And what about the car?" she goes on as if I didn't say anything. "We could have had the Range Rover, but no, you've got to prove some stupid point about how you don't need anyone or anything. And screw things up for me too."

"He'll give it to you when you get your license."

"No, he won't, Theo. He won't give it to me because I'm not you. He never asks me to do stuff unless you're there. He never came to one of my dance competitions, but he went to a ton of your soccer games. You're not the one on Facebook, liking all of Susan's stupid pictures of Ellie or babysitting or picking out baby clothes. It's me. And you're still the one he wants. It's not fair."

She stomps her foot like a child and pivots away from me. I feel bad because what she says is partly true... maybe. And even if it isn't, it's sad as hell that's how she sees it, unloved by our dad even more because she's a girl.

"I'm sorry for ditching you, Tabs. If it makes you feel better, I'm a total disappointment as a son."

She sniffs and rubs at her eyes. "Yeah, well, you're a total disappointment as a brother too."

"Tabitha," Chris warns.

The insults that hurt the worst are the ones that ring true. I don't see how we can recover from this for the time being, and I'm not going to cower in the corner like a kicked dog because of some bullshit my dad pulled. I yank off my apron and toss it on the counter, rub my hands on my shorts.

"Theo, don't," Chris says, letting his demand float there between us.

"Tell Paloma I'll do cleanup." I head for the door while thinking that's one more thing my dad and I have in common: we both bail when things get tough.

I GRAB MY SKATEBOARD AND CONSIDER GOING OVER TO DAVE'S, BUT I don't want to use him as a stand-in, which makes Dave just another one of the people I've disappointed lately. I zone out to the steady rhythm of my skateboard on the concrete while thinking on the people closest to me and how I can't seem to give them what they want. And my dad. How I wish I could believe what my sister says, that he wants a relationship with me, even if it's not the kind of relationship I want. Maybe he is trying. What is it about me that I have to have things on my own terms? All or nothing. Like Chris. I should be happy with this awesome best friendship we share, but I'm not. Maybe Tabs is right; maybe I am selfish.

When I finally come out of my stupor, I find myself on the corner of Palmetto and Lake Avenue, the block where Saint Ann's is located, which is where my Uncle Theo lives. Impulsively, I decide to follow up on my earlier commitment to myself and pay him a visit.

I roll up to the double glass doors on my skateboard and tuck it under my arm. The lady at the reception desk asks me, like, five times who I am and who I'm here to see. It's obvious she doesn't believe me or thinks I have some nefarious motive, which is sad that anyone would come to an old folks' home with bad intentions, so I show her my permit to prove I am indeed Theodore Wooten III, related to TW II. She apologizes and remarks that Uncle Theo doesn't have too many visitors, which prompts me to ask her when the last time someone's stopped by to see him, and she answers that she can't remember, which means it was probably the last time I saw him, Easter.

Apparently Tabs and I aren't the only ones my father is neglecting.

I make up my mind that if I can stand the salty old bastard for the next hour or so, I'll make it a point to visit him more often. The receptionist tells me he's likely upstairs in the rec room playing solitaire, and it kind of depresses me to find out when I get up there that she's right.

The rec room smells like old people and polyester with a hint of urine, but the place is pretty clean overall and bright, thanks to the row of windows overlooking the water. A room with a view. I suppose when you're this close to the other side, that's all any of us can hope for. Uncle Theo was in the Navy for, like, thirty years and worked as an engineer on cruise ships after that, so he had a pretty good retirement package after his life at sea, plus the Wooten Family Trust fund, that mythical creature my dad and grandmother both reference when I show the slightest indication of not having my shit together.

Still, it must be costing him or my grandmother a pretty penny to keep him in a place as nice as this. I suppose that almost makes up for the fact that he has no one visiting him.

There are a couple of nurses and a few elderly folks milling around, some of them with walkers and others propped up in wheelchairs, half-comatose. Uncle Theo sits by himself at a round card table. He's got good posture for an old man, maybe because he was once military and the mannerisms stuck. His white hair is neatly combed and he's wearing a button-up shirt and slacks, which sets him apart from the other residents, some of whom wear housedresses, the men included. I wonder if he has any friends in here, people he can talk to who are at least as lucid as he is. I hope so.

I watch as he methodically sets up another round of solitaire, carefully placing the cards so that the edges line up with a uniformity that reminds me of myself. I also like things to be tidy. His face is a scowl, or maybe it's just the weight of eighty-plus years wrinkling up his mouth. Regardless, he doesn't look happy to see me when he lifts his blue eyes, which are the Wooten trademark and the reason my mother, presumably, fell in love with a gringo.

"Who are you?" he barks like a naval captain, which he was and, I suppose, still is. I take up the chair across from where he sits and lay my skateboard across my lap.

"I'm Theodore Wooten the third," I tell him, hoping that will spark some recognition.

"Huh," he grumbles, then flips a card and says, "pretty dark for a Wooten."

I smile at that. Maybe I should be offended, but I find it kind of hilarious. "Yeah, my mom's Puerto Rican. Your nephew had a thing for island girls, I guess."

Uncle Theo nods like that makes perfect sense. "If you're looking for money, I don't got it."

I shake my head at that. Maybe that's what the receptionist was worried about, like I'd come up here and shake down my elderly, senile uncle. I wonder if that's a thing. Sad.

"I didn't come for money," I tell him. "I've got a job."

"Good for you. So what do you want?"

I shrug and glance down at his cards. I didn't think much about what we would talk about. We got along well at the Easter party, but there were a lot of distractions. This is just him and me in a room that smells like death. "Thought you might be up for a game of gin rummy."

He scoffs at that. "You look like a shifty sonuvabitch to me."

I laugh out loud. I can't believe his mouth. "You don't look all that honest yourself."

Uncle Theo grins or grimaces, it's hard to tell. "You don't win at cards by being a schmuck."

I nod. "That's true." A nurse comes over then, a woman in her mid-forties, and asks my uncle who his visitor is. (Me.) My uncle shrugs and won't answer her, so I introduce myself. Her name is Gloria, and she has an accent. I ask her where she's from, and she says Trinidad. She asks me if I'd like some water, and I tell her I would, thank you, that I skateboarded here and I'm a little thirsty. She smiles like I'm an upstanding citizen and a good nephew for visiting my uncle in the old folks' home. As soon as she walks away, my uncle leans in and says, "Now there's a dark one."

I wonder if there's some reason for his racism or if it's just residual, something he acquired at an early age, like my distaste for asparagus. Uncle Theo lived in a condo in Palm Beach during his later years, golfing and boozing it up at the country club with the other old, white dudes. He also never married, though I vaguely remember a couple of live-in girlfriends, all white women.

"Do the white nurses take better care of you?" I ask.

"No," he admits. "They're all cocksuckers here."

I'm glad he at least has the good sense to keep his voice down.

Gloria comes back with paper cups of water for both of us, even though my uncle didn't want any. I thank her and my uncle only frowns and says, "Where's Manuel?"

Gloria smiles knowingly and checks her wristwatch. "He'll be here in about twenty minutes. Is there anything I can get you before then?"

"No, but make sure he's here," he says gruffly.

Gloria nods and smiles at me like I'm in on some inside joke. She rests her hand on his shoulder in a gesture that seems genuinely affectionate. "I will do that, Captain Wooten."

Captain Wooten. My uncle is with it enough to demand they use his proper title. And who is this Manuel? A fellow patient, a veteran like my uncle? Perhaps they have a standing card game in the rec room. My uncle didn't seem like he was looking forward to it, exactly, but it clearly matters to him that this Manuel character shows up.

"Who's Manuel?" I ask him when Gloria walks away.

"None of your damn business. You got any food on you?"

I wonder if he remembers how we bonded over Paula's Pit Barbecue potato salad. "No, but I'll bring you something next time."

"The chow here is terrible."

I don't doubt it. It's probably all tasteless and soft, like salty baby food. "Have you seen my dad lately?"

"Who's your dad?"

"Your nephew, William."

"William?" Uncle Theo's eyes squint a little like he's trying to place him. "No. Haven't seen him. He still do teeth?"

I smile at the way he says it. "Yeah, he still does teeth. I haven't seen much of him lately either. His wife, Susan, is pregnant. It's a boy. They're naming him William. That'd make him William the fourth, I guess."

"William was my father's name."

William Wooten II. He died before I was born. Neither my uncle nor my grandmother talk about him much. He owned and managed a small chain of five-and-dime stores in the Northeast called Wooten's that were started by his father and later sold by my grandfather George, who my grandmother married a billion years ago and who died when I was little. From what I understand, William II worked a lot and was also a high-functioning alcoholic.

"Did you get along with your dad?" I ask Uncle Theo.

He shrugs, "Eh." Then shakes his head. "No."

"Was he an asshole?" If Uncle Theo can say cocksucker, then I can say asshole.

"He didn't have much use for me. He liked my brother George."

That's news to me. "My dad and I don't get along so well either," I tell him, revealing more than I ever intended in coming here.

"Is he an asshole?"

"Yeah, a little bit."

Uncle Theo shrugs. "Must run in the family."

I laugh. I don't know if he realizes what he's saying or if he's just being agreeable, but it does make me feel a little better that I'm not the only one having a hard time of it.

A male nurse comes up to us then, short and chubby, and in his midthirties if I had to guess. He rubs his hands together as he greets my uncle with a little bow and a deferential "Good afternoon, Captain Wooten." Then he turns to me. "My name's Manuel." He offers his hand to me in a very gentlemanly gesture. My limited-range gaydar goes off immediately as I shake the guy's hand and eye him up and down. He's cute in a cuddly sort of way. His demeanor seems very gentle, and he has sweet brown eyes with long lashes, kind of like a Jersey cow.

Manuel turns back to my uncle. "Gloria said you were asking for me."

"I'm ready to go back to my room," Uncle Theo says. He drops his cards and braces his hands on the table to stand. I don't bother reminding him we were supposed to play a game of gin rummy. I don't think anything could distract him from Manuel at the moment.

"What about your visitor?" Manuel says, looking apologetically at me.

Uncle Theo glances down and glares at me, irritated that I might ruin whatever rendezvous he has planned.

"I was just leaving." I stand, curious to know where this thing is headed.

My uncle nods sharply, as though saluting. He lifts one hand, and Manuel supplies his arm for my uncle to take. Manuel glances back at me, "Nice to meet you," he says with a smile and then softer, to my uncle, "Should we take the long way?"

"Yes, of course," my uncle says gruffly.

They shuffle slowly out of the room. Manuel walks much slower to match my uncle's pace, perhaps letting him think he's leading. They cross the hallway to the elevator, and Manuel waves at me from inside it. My uncle stares straight ahead, at attention.

I wander back to the window, stunned, while Gloria collects the playing cards and places them back into the cardboard case. "I'll bring these back to him later," she says. "He hates it when the other residents lose his cards."

I open my mouth to ask Gloria about my uncle's relationship with Manuel, which seems to me almost like... a crush? But then think better of it—this is something for me to investigate further on my own, and I wouldn't want Uncle Theo to find out I've been meddling. As I'm about to turn away from the window, I see Manuel leading my uncle down the sidewalk toward the concrete seawall that overlooks the water. Manuel talks animatedly and my uncle, I'm shocked to see, is smiling.

# ELEVEN

# WTF, PART 1

I'm still contemplating my visit with Uncle Theo when I return home to find Chris out front in his driveway shooting hoops, shirtless, of course, and glistening with sweat. Positively mouthwatering. Ugh.

"Up for a game?" he asks, faking to my left, then dribbling around me for a basket. I could watch him shoot hoops all day, in slow motion, on repeat.

"Yeah, sure." I roll my skateboard into the grass where we won't trip on it and toss my shirt on top of it because I'm already sweating. "To fifteen. Make it, take it," I tell him. If I don't settle the terms ahead of time, Chris will use it to his advantage. Like if we're tied up for the win and I get the point, we're suddenly playing to twenty-one, not fifteen. Chris hates losing, and when he thinks he might be, he's a bit of a cheat.

"I get the ball first, since you've got two inches on me now," he says.

"You've got twenty pounds on me," I protest, sure he's angling for an advantage.

"Are you calling me fat again?" Chris asks with a grin, lobbing the ball at my chest for a check.

"Pleasantly plump." I beam it back at him. He's far from fat, and he knows it.

To prove his superior level of fitness, he dribbles by me and spins around my back, then does a flashy layup, using my shoulder to get more air. I let him by me because I can't take my eyes off his basketball shorts and how they hang just below his hips, exposing the waistband of his briefs, how easy it would be to yank them both down around his ankles and....

"Foul," I mutter, knowing it's useless.

"Got to get comfortable with a little contact, Wooten," Chris says, strutting back to the line while dribbling. I roll my eyes and can't help smiling at his cockiness.

This time I'm ready for his round-about move and when he turns, I'm there to use my height to my advantage and strip the ball from him, then double back and take the shot. But my aim is off, maybe because I haven't played since my growth spurt. The ball hits the rim and bounces off into the bushes. I practically have to climb into Chris's hedge to retrieve it, and when I back out of the greenery, Chris is there waiting.

"Where'd you go this afternoon?" he asks, like we're not in the middle of a game.

I press the ball into his chest, thinking how if it weren't for this ball, it'd just be him and me, chest to chest, skin on skin. Wouldn't that feel good? Amazing.

"I went to see Uncle Theo." I clear my throat and back away. Distance helps.

Chris looks surprised, like that wasn't the answer he was expecting. "How is he?" he asks, passing me the ball.

"Good." My mind drifts back to my uncle's flirtation with the handsome nurse, and Chris takes advantage of my distraction to score on me.

"You letting me win, Wooten?"

"No," I protest and steal the ball back and score on the next round.

"I hate it when you and Tabs fight," Chris says. He must be

thinking about earlier that afternoon. Maybe because he doesn't have any siblings, Chris is super sensitive to any conflict between us. Usually our fights are pretty superficial, bickering more so than fighting, but that one in Chris's kitchen kind of cut to the bone.

"Yeah, me too," I tell him.

"She felt bad after, if that makes it any better."

"A little bit." I wonder if I should say something to her or just let it ride.

"She didn't mean it," Chris says.

"Yeah, she did, but that's all right. I'm sure Tabs would like for me to be more like you."

"How's that?" Chris asks, perplexed.

"You know, friendly, outgoing, popular. Whatever it is you do to get you in the cool club."

"I'm in the cool club?" Chris asks.

I roll my eyes at his presumed ignorance. "Obviously."

"Then you must be in it too."

I shake my head. "I'm on the fringe. They only put up with me for your sake."

Chris squints at me. "You really believe that?"

"Um, yeah."

I take advantage of his thoughtful expression to steal the ball and score on him. We play like that for a while. I become increasingly aware of Chris's body when he happens to brush up against me while trying to get the ball or make a run. The slick swish of skin against skin and the heat that radiates off him like a furnace, prickling the hairs on the back of my neck and sending a shiver down my spine. The smell of his sweat and the way it beads up on all that exposed honey brown skin like water droplets on a waxed car.

I'm about to go for a three-pointer when Chris bats the ball out of my hands. We both go running for it and end up getting tripped up on each other's ankles. I land on the concrete and Chris lands in the grass. My shoulder burns like I just ate it in skateboarding.

"Shit, T, sorry about that." Chris lends me his hand and pulls me up. He turns me around to check out my raspberry and brush off whatever dirt and bits of gravel are stuck in it. Meanwhile, a car rolls up to the curb. The passenger window goes down, and I see Dave in the driver's seat. I'm mildly irritated that he keeps coming by here unannounced. He slows to a stop in front of Chris's driveway. I jog toward his car and lean into the passenger side, hoping I can get him to move along before shit gets weird.

"Hey, Theo," Dave says with a smile that seems way forced.

"Sup, Dave?"

Dave makes a point of looking over my shoulder to leer at Chris. "You need a third to make this a roast beef sandwich?"

I glance back at Chris, who's gripping the basketball with Herculean strength, the tendons in his wrists standing out, biceps bulging, face stormy and scowling.

"Probably not a good idea."

Dave shakes his head. "How can I even compete with that?"

I sigh, feeling guilty and confused and sorry for Dave in that he wants more than I can give him, and I, of all people, should know how shitty that feels.

"Listen, Dave." I run my hand through my hair, remembering when he cut it for me and taught me to shave, and then, how to give a proper blowjob. That was nice of him, and I hope after all this we can still be friends, because I do like hanging out with him. "You were right. My heart's just not in it. I don't want to play games or lead you on."

"Are you saying you're done with me?" Dave asks. The smile is still there, but it looks frozen, covering up something else. He's hurt, probably a little pissed too. Dave moistens his lips, and for a moment I think maybe I'm making a mistake. Dave was good at making me forget about Chris, if only for a short amount of time.

But I'm not going to be like my dad and take what I want because I want it and not think about how it might affect the other person.

"Yeah, I guess I am."

"That's too bad." He sighs. "I liked you, Theo. Despite your bull-shit, I really did." Dave shakes his head like he's disappointed in me, turns away, and focuses on the road. "Ah well. Adiós, Papi."

I back away from his car just as he peels off down the road, which is kind of juvenile but not that surprising. My first breakup, I reflect. I take a deep breath, trying to shake off the weight of what I've just done, hoping Dave gets over it in a day or two and we can go back to being friends. When I come back up the driveway, Chris is bouncing the ball with a little too much force for it to be casual. He also won't look at me.

"What was that about?" he asks tightly.

"You don't want to know," I tell him, which is the truth.

Chris palms the ball in one hand, presses it gently against my chest, gazes up at me with his warm brown eyes. He looks a little sad, or maybe it's just the way I'm feeling. "Yeah, you're probably right."

We finish the game, and I end up winning because Chris is distracted and grumpy. I want to ask him what's wrong, but I'm afraid of what I might uncover. I fantasize about just pinning him against the wall with my bare chest against his and kissing him, not a sweet kiss either, but really jamming my tongue in his mouth and bucking my hips against him to make it real for him and find out once and for all if it's just my imagination or if he's feeling it too. There's a moment where we're standing in the shade of his house, drinking down our Gatorades, when I have the opportunity, but when I glance over at Chris, he's lost in thought, which makes me think about all there is to lose, and like a punk, I chicken out.

# TWELVE

# WTF, PART 2

My mom greets my sister and me on the morning of our birthday with a Puerto Rican birthday cake, which is like a pound cake drenched in rum with a meringue topping, garnished with strawberries. She started making it for us after my dad and her divorced. I suppose living with an alcoholic, she took every precaution.

I tell my sister happy birthday, and she does the same for me. Neither of us apologize or even bring up yesterday's fight, but I can tell she feels bad about it, and I do too. I tug on her ponytail on her way out the door, and she elbows me in the gut—hard—before running off to catch a ride with her friend Lizbeth.

"You want me to take you down to the DMV after school?" Mom asks. "I can take off early today."

"I was thinking I'd just have Chris take me." I haven't asked him, but I know he probably would.

"He's a good friend," she says with a soft smile. "I'm glad you have each other."

"Me too." I didn't have too many friends before Chris. Other than my sister, I didn't want to play with anyone else. My mom worried about me always being by myself. Like she was raising a future serial killer. Turns out I *was* different, maybe because I'm gay? I don't know. More likely I'm just awkward as hell. I should tell my mom I'm gay—she'd be cool about it—but I'm pretty content to keep it to myself for a little while longer.

"You're getting so big," she says softly and brushes the hair out of my eyes. I haven't done much with it lately, and I'm afraid it's gone feral again.

"Only on the outside," I assure her, and she laughs.

"On the inside too." She nods, looking pleased with herself. I'm flattered that she thinks she did an all right job raising me. All my good qualities I attribute to her.

"Have a happy birthday, baby."

"Thanks, Mom." I lean down and kiss her cheek, then plop a piece of cake on a paper plate for Chris on my way out. He's already waiting for me at the top of his driveway. I'm balancing all my stuff, including his slice of cake, so it isn't until I hand it over that I notice the skateboard resting under his foot. He pops it up so I can see the underside of it.

"Happy birthday, Killer." His voice is a little husky, like it gets whenever he's feeling sentimental.

"Is that a Bruce Lee Fury deck?" I ask, astonished and pleased and unworthy all at once. He nods. "For me?" I ask, just to make sure because, wow.

"Yep."

I drop my stuff and kneel down to inspect it closer. I didn't think they made this deck anymore. One of my favorite skateboarders, Paul Rodriguez, used to ride one just like it. I'd always thought it looked sick, but I haven't talked about it in ages. Chris must have remembered.

"Where'd you find it?" I ask him.

"The UK."

"Must have cost a lot to ship it over." Not to mention the Tensor trucks and Bones 100 wheels, which are my preferred brands for skateboard hardware.

"I'm sponsoring you."

"For what?"

"The Plan Z tour. I want to see you compete."

Ryanne mentioned it when we were surfing in Sebastian. I'd loosely considered entering, but then thought better of it. A lot of the entrants will be pro or semipro. Total badasses. I'll look like a total goof compared to them.

"I don't know, Boss. That's some stiff competition."

"You're the competition, T. I want to watch you land a sick trick and then tell everyone you're my biffle."

"Biffle?

"Best Friend For Life. Tabs taught me that."

I smile. "And if I land on my ass?"

He shrugs. "Then you're just some kid who needed a ride."

I smile, knowing he'd never do me like that. "I'll think about it. I'm going to need to practice, though. You going to drain the pool for me?"

"I was thinking park might be your best bet." Park is a mix between street, pool, and vert, short for vertical, or in other words, half-pipe—the big kahuna. Park is basically a little of everything, where style and originality count for more than being able to execute a standard book of tricks.

"Yeah, you're probably right."

Chris drops the board and rolls it over so it nudges my ankle. I kick it up, like I'm He-Man picking up his Power Sword. I pull Chris into a one-handed bro-hug. "Thanks, Chris," I utter into his still-damp-from-the-shower hair.

"You're welcome, buddy."

When we pull into the school parking lot twenty minutes later, I'm riding high. Maybe it's because I basically ate sugar for breakfast, or maybe it's because of my new kick-ass skateboard, or the fact that Chris said he'd drive me to the DMV after school. Life is looking up for Theodore Wooten III when we arrive at our lockers. But once there, I notice something's off right away. The vibe is strange. Our friends are all weirdly quiet, with their eyes glued to their phones. And I have this sensation that everyone's looking at me, only when

I'm not looking at them. My paranoia must be reaching an all-time high.

"Something's up," I say to Chris and immediately search the halls for Dave. I'm not sure why, instinct maybe, but he's nowhere to be found.

Chris says what's up to Corbin, who barely acknowledges him, so Chris goes up to him. "What's going on, man?"

Corbin's shaggy, reddish-brown hair is mostly covering his face when he glances over at Chris, then me. He opens his mouth to say something, then shakes his head. "No way, man. It's not gonna be me." He shuts his locker and hurries away in the opposite direction.

The hairs on the back of my neck stand on end as I notice people passing by us, giving me way too much attention, some smiling and laughing. A football player actually points in my direction and bumps his buddy. Then they both start laughing their asses off. I glance down at my shirt, wondering if there's a sign stuck there, then run a hand through my hair. I'm still self-accessing when my sister comes storming up to us.

"How could you do this to me, Theo? *On my birthday?*" she roars, her face an ugly shade of pissed.

"Do what?" I ask, while at the same time thinking I don't want to know.

Tabs purses her lips and glances between Chris and me. Whatever it is, it's bad, if even my sister is hesitating. She takes a deep breath and pulls up her phone, enters her password, and turns it toward me, her posture ramrod straight, her arm stiff enough to clothesline someone.

I can't see what she's talking about—there's an overhead light bouncing off her phone and creating a glare—so I take it out of her hand to examine it closer. Chris comes up and peers over my shoulder.

And then I see it.

Holy shit, it's bad.

It's fucking terrible.

When I first started going online to look at skating and surf videos, my mother warned me to be careful what I searched for because there are some things I won't be able to unsee. The picture on my sister's phone is one of those images I'll never be able to scrub from my mind. I know immediately Dave must have taken it. No one else has had me at this angle—on my knees, head back, eyes closed, with a mouthful of cock.

*Cocksucker.*

Uncle Theo's words come back to haunt me, only this time I'm not laughing.

"Who sent you this?" Chris asks my sister. He's snatched the phone from my hand and squeezes it as though the force from his fist alone could cause it to disintegrate.

"Who didn't?" she says, and then only to Chris, maybe so I won't hear, "It's too late. It's *everywhere*."

"Who took this picture?" Chris glances at me, then each of our friends, trying to find the guilty party.

My vision blurs and my breath comes up short. I lean back against the lockers. The metal cuts into my shoulder blades as I struggle to keep from collapsing. It's overwhelming, what this means. I'm out, like, naked in the middle of the hallway—no, worse, because it's Dave's cock filling my mouth, and the picture is so candid, you can tell I'm enjoying it. Damn, that shit is personal. Something's been taken—no, stolen—from me, my most personal, private thing. And that thing has been smeared all over the walls to be judged and ridiculed by everyone who sees it.

"Fuck," I mutter. The oxygen has been sucked out of my lungs, and I can't get it back. Our friends are silent, eyes darting from me to Chris, perhaps seeing how we're going to react. My sister demands her phone back, and Chris absently hands it to her.

My sister says something else shitty to me—what it is, I can hardly hear or process—then storms away. The only person who comes into focus is Chris, still demanding to know who sent this, and I can only figure he means whose cock is in my mouth. And I realize even the way I look at Chris is incriminating me and probably him too. I have to get out of here. Right now. I abandon my backpack completely and drop my deck at my feet—not the new one Chris gave me, which is safely stored in his car, but my old trusty that I don't care if it gets abused. I hop on my magic carpet and skate blindly down the hallway. A teacher calls out to me, but I kickflip a curb onto the walkway, sprint through the lawn, and drop my board on the sidewalk off school grounds. I pump my legs until I'm flying, hardly bothering with stop signs or traffic. My anger and adrenaline fuel me until I don't even realize how far I've gone.

I've been violated, outed in the worst possible way. Only Dave could have done this, but why? Spite? Anger? Jealousy? What an awful, hateful thing to do, which makes me question everything I thought I knew about Dave and what we did together. I feel cheap and dirty and used and stupid. So fucking stupid. Betrayed. The list goes on and on.

It's not that I'm ashamed of being gay, or even sucking off Asshole Dave—yeah, the name is back. It's the complete and utter violation of my privacy and having that on display for everyone at Sabal Palm High to judge and hate on. It's the same reason I never show off my skateboarding tricks until I've practiced them to perfection.

I hate looking stupid.

I need to focus on something constructive. I check my phone for the address of the nearest DMV. It's too far to skate, so I pull up the city bus routes and make my way to the nearest bus stop. There's a young mother there with three kids under the age of five. The baby's crying and the middle one keeps trying to totter out into traffic, and the oldest one looks like he's tired of the bullshit. I wonder how she got to this place of having three kids and waiting on the bus, which, let's be real, in South Florida kind of sucks. And then I figure that somewhere along the way, a man must have betrayed her, kind of like my own dad betrayed my mom, kind of like how Asshole Dave betrayed me, and even though I don't know her, I can relate to her struggle, so I offer to keep her one kid out of the street while letting the other one mess around with my skateboard and she tries, in vain, to get the baby to stop crying. But the baby keeps on screaming because life is hard, and even this kid, at six months old, knows it.

## THIRTEEN

## CRACK REALLY PUTS THINGS IN PERSPECTIVE

It takes forever to get to the DMV, and then there's a line. A looong line, and the people who work here are slow as hell and don't seem to mind stretching out the process. I guess they get paid either way. First there's paperwork. Then the written test. More paperwork. Then it's another hour of waiting for the driving test, and I'm jacked up on soda and candy from the vending machine, my only source of nutrition, when the woman behind the counter finally calls my name.

"You can pull your car around back," she says.

"My what?"

"Your car. You need to have a car in order to take your driving test."

"I thought you guys provided the car."

She sighs like I'm the world's biggest idiot. "No, sweetheart, we don't provide the car. You have to bring your own." She glances down at her clipboard and then, perhaps noticing I'm on the verge of tears, shows a sliver of humanity. "I'll file your paperwork. Come back next week with your own car and we'll finish it then."

"Are you open tomorrow?" I whine. It's nearing closing time, so even if I managed to get my mom's car, by the time I got back, it'll be too late.

"Monday through Friday, 9:00 a.m. to 5:00 p.m. Make an appointment next time and it will go faster."

I moan, still trying to keep it together, then exit the DMV in a huff. I'm sticky from the ride and grimy from sitting on my ass in the DMV all day. My emotions are running amok when I imagine all the people who must have by now seen my mug performing fellatio on Asshole Dave and the last thing I want to do is go home and face my raging sister making this all about her again. And Chris. I don't want to have to explain that picture to him.

Knowing Chris, he's probably got our apartment cased, waiting to ambush me. Or maybe it's the opposite and he never wants to talk to me again after today. Even though he won't admit it, some part of Chris likes being a cool kid, and this was definitely *not cool*. The thought of him abandoning me is too depressing to even contemplate.

I hop on my board and head for the beach, thinking it's the last place I can run and hide.

When I get there an hour or so later, the sun is at my back and there's a damp chill in the air. There are a few guys out surfing, but I'm not in the mood to beg for a board.

My stomach growls because all I've eaten today is cake, a candy bar, and chips. I recognize one of the beach bums, Lieutenant Sean Knox, picking through the trashcans that line the beach access. Sean's one of the guys who will reliably buy us beer if we give him a cut, and I decide to spend the last of my birthday money from my mom on getting totally shit-faced. Seems like the only way to end this awful day.

I offer up my plan to Sean with the option that he keep the difference in cash. He suggests we split the case of beer instead, and I tell him I'm game. He asks me what kind I want, and I tell him to pick since it's all the same to me. He comes back from the convenience store with a case of Miller Light under his arm. I figured we'd just split it there on the sidewalk, but he tells me to follow him down to the beach.

Once there, he ducks under the pier and climbs up to where the sand meets the pilings and creates a secluded kind of cave. Not a bad place to camp out for the night, which makes me wonder if Sean does that on the regular. He plops down and motions for me to join him, cracks open a beer, and tosses me one. I thought I'd be drinking alone, but I suppose it's just as well to drink with a friend. I pop the top and it foams up a bit. I slurp it up, thinking it tastes only a little bit better than it smells.

By this time the sun is starting to set and the surfers are all going out for their last few rides. I get to thinking about my surf trips with Chris, how I've usually punked out by this time and I'm just sitting on the beach wrapped in a towel watching him surf. If I make my eyes go wide and fuzzy, I can almost see him out there on the waves right now, and it fills me with a sense of calm and contentment that also feels dangerous, and I know I've really screwed things up this time.

While we drink, Sean tells me about his time in the army and where he spent his tours. I've heard it before, but I listen again to be polite. Then he starts telling me about this city in Afghanistan, this one particular battle, which apparently has been made into a movie and stars an ex-marine who was there.

"He was the only one of his platoon to survive. I mean, what are the chances?" Sean says with a bitter edge to his voice, and I'm not sure I understand the significance except to think that he is one lucky bastard.

"Know what I think?" Sean leans in like we're two gangsters planning our next bank robbery.

"What?" I'm light-headed and at ease. I could listen to Sean all night long. Just two buds, kicking back a few beers, telling war stories.

"I think that fucker was hiding. I think he abandoned his boys. Because the shit he was able to remember." Sean shakes his head. His upper lip curls into a snarl. "I mean, I was in some shit, man, and I can't remember anything."

"It happens so fast," I say. In the blink of an eye, everything turns upside down and you're dumped on your ass.

"Hell yeah. It was over like that." He snaps his fingers for emphasis. "And this fucker is coming up with all these details about what guns were fired—the mortars and shells, who was hit and where. Bullshit, man. He wasn't there. Maybe he was part of the cleanup crew, but he sure as shit wasn't there."

I nod in agreement, wondering how it was that Sean ended up picking through the trash on the beach, and who we are as a society if we can't even take care of our veterans.

"So, what's your story, man?" Sean turns toward me, catching me by surprise. I'm flattered he wants to know me better. A lot of the bums just want to talk about themselves, mostly to tell you a sob story so you feel bad enough to give them money to go buy beer or drugs. Not that I'm judging. We all get by however we can.

"I don't know if I have a story." I'm not necessarily looking for sympathy, but not avoiding it early. "It's my birthday today."

"Really? Shit, happy birthday." He claps me on the back and taps the rim of his can against mine. His is already empty, so he cracks open another one. "Drink up, man. These won't stay cold for long, and they taste like ass when they're warm."

I chug the rest of my beer and accept the open one he offers to me. The first beer was ice cold and went down like water with only a mildly bitter aftertaste. My stomach is full and sloshy, but I start on the second one with just as much enthusiasm.

"So, how old are you now?" Sean asks.

"Sixteen."

"Sweet sixteen, never been kissed," Sean muses.

I chirp a bitter laugh because it's true. I've still never been kissed. Saving myself, I guess.

"Where's all your boys?" Sean scans the shoreline, where the surfers are all packing up for the night, maybe wondering if I know them. I probably do, but not well enough to call them my boys.

There's something about this second beer, which is quickly going down the gullet and working its way through my bloodstream, making me giddy and light-headed with a general sense of not giving a fuck. "There's a picture of me going around school," I tell Sean. "It's pretty bad."

"Dick pic?" he asks.

If only it were that. "No. It's of me sucking off another guy."

Sean flinches like he's just woken up from a bad dream. "Shit, man, that's a lot to unpack."

I laugh at the way he says it. "You're telling me."

"That's pretty shitty, sending around that picture. You know who did it?"

I sigh because more than being pissed at Dave, I'm disappointed. I trusted him, and he screwed me over. It hurts on a superficial level— my reputation and my privacy and the fact that I don't want to show my face at Sabal Palm High ever again—but it also hurts on a much deeper level.

"Yeah, I know who did it," I tell him.

"You going to beat his ass?"

I consider it. I can't really see myself beating Dave's ass, if I even could. I'll probably never talk to him again and avoid him at all costs, but hitting people isn't really my style. "Probably not," I tell Sean. "I'm kind of a pussy."

Sean's head wobbles back and forth like he can't make the call either way. "You do that, though? Give head?" Sean glances over with what I can only describe as a hopeful look on his face.

"No." I shake my head. "I mean, not as like, a job. The guy who took the picture, I was interested in him, even though he's kind of an asshole. I guess he showed his true colors."

"That he did." Sean crushes his empty can between two fists. *Like a real man*, I think. A real man would beat Dave's ass, wouldn't he, which makes me wonder, what is a real man, anyway? All I have as a reference is my dad and all the mixed emotions tied up in who he is and what he's done or failed to do for our family.

"Anyway." I stare out at the waves, finish my beer, and toss the can in the sand. Just when I think the silence is going to be awkward, Sean starts talking about how when he came home from his last tour in Afghanistan, he was in all kinds of bad shape, how he felt like no one understood him and he couldn't adapt to everyday life. How things that shouldn't scare him did, and the things that should scare him didn't.

"Then I started smoking crack, man," Sean says. "I was working nights at Publix, stocking shelves, and there was a guy there who offered to get me high, and I was, like, yeah, sure, why not? I mean, I've survived a war, twice, what could crack do to me?"

I'm silent at that, sensing it's a rhetorical question.

"You ever tried crack?" Sean asks.

I shake my head. Until this moment, I've never gotten drunk either. Crack seems like the Mount Everest of drugs, even though I could probably score some there at the beach before the night was over if I really wanted to.

"Man, it's good. So goddamned good. Made me feel like I was *all right*. Actually, made me not give a shit about anything else but getting high, which was a relief in a weird way." Sean glances around at who might be listening, but there are only a few shifty characters gathered over in the parking lot and a couple making out on a blanket farther down the beach. The dusk settles in around us like a fat, fluffy cat.

"Wish I had some right now," Sean says longingly, like he's pining for a lost lover.

"Probably best to stay away from it," I tell him, thinking what a hypocrite I am because here I am getting drunk when my father's an alcoholic.

"Yeah, you're probably right," Sean admits.

I finish my third beer and then my fourth. I don't notice much of anything outside the steady rhythm of Sean's voice and the wave of indifference I'm currently riding. The perfect wave. Makes me a little nauseous, but I can't seem to get off. Somewhere in between Sean talking about stealing his mother's silver only to discover it wasn't real silver and nearly setting his sister's place on fire, I tell him about my infatuation with my best friend, who is straight and how he's the person I want to be with all the time. I really stress that phrase, *all the time.* Because when we're not together, I miss him, and lately it's the same way even when we're in the same room. I miss the effortless friendship we used to have when I didn't have to think so hard on what to say or what not to say, or wonder at any given second what he's thinking, worried he might see my feelings on my face. I blubber all this to Sean, not sure if I'm making any sense, but Sean keeps nodding sympathetically and goes so far as to wrap his arm around me and say, "There are worse things in the world, buddy, and it's not what happens to you, but what you let it do to you. If this friend of yours is as good as you say he is, you should tell him what's up. Clear the air, you know?"

"Clear the air," I repeat sluggishly, making sure I got it right.

And somewhere along the way, I have the sense to warn Sean I'm about to pass out, and ask him politely not to gank my shit when I do. Sean swears to me that he won't, lifting three fingers in Scout's honor. That's the last thing I remember, Sean's three fingers and the earnest look on his face, as I ride that wave into a sweet and cozy oblivion.

FOURTEEN

# SWEET SIXTEEN?

"Theo."

I wake to Chris gazing down at me, figure it's a dream, and close my eyes again to hold on to it a little longer, but then he's calling my name kind of frantically and I decide this must be really happening, because his grip on my shoulders cuts into the muscle and his panic vibrates in the sound of his voice.

"Theo, man, wake up."

My head is thick and mossy, my limbs like lead weights and mostly unresponsive. My eyes are gritty and my vision a little fuzzy. I glance around and see that I'm still on the beach. My hair and back are damp with clumps of sand stuck to me. There's a wet chill in the air and a fog on the water that clues me in that it's the middle of the night. Sean's gone, and it looks like he cleaned up after us, because there are no empty cans or cardboard box to tell of our adventures.

"Where's Sean?" I ask.

"Who?" Chris asks.

"Lieutenant Sean Knox."

"Are you drunk?" Chris asks me. "Did he buy you beer?"

I rise to a sitting position, and my head pounds like the deep bass of a lowrider. I cradle it in my hands while Chris calls who I'm assuming is my mom. "Yeah, I've got him," he says. "He fell asleep at the pier. I'll bring him home." Chris glances down at me as I mime a pleading gesture that he not tell her I was drinking and may still currently be drunk. I don't want her to see how far I've fallen since this morning when I was her sweet, innocent baby boy. Chris shakes his head like he's disappointed in me, and I don't know if it's because I'm drunk or because I can't hold my alcohol.

"You mind if I take him to my house tonight?" Chris asks my mom. "He's had a pretty rough day."

I wonder how much she knows about my day. What did my sister or Chris tell her? Hopefully they didn't show her the picture. No, they wouldn't. Tabs and I might not see eye to eye on everything, but we have a mutual understanding to not involve my mom in one another's drama. I'm thankful Chris is covering for me. And speaking to me. And cares enough to come find my drunk ass and bring me home.

Chris ends the call and drops down to sit next to me, rests his forearms on his knees, and runs his fingers through his thick, golden hair like I've seen him do before when he's stressed. He doesn't say anything, and I don't offer anything up. I appreciate the few minutes wherein I try to collect my thoughts and make the ground stop tilting.

"You hungry?" he says at last.

"Yeah." Food might be a good way to sop up the alcohol.

"Harley's?"

I nod and slowly rise to follow him to the Volvo, brushing the sand off my ass before collapsing inside it. It's immediately calming because it's warm and familiar and smells like him. There's probably an indentation of my buttcheeks on the seat. Chris turns down the music so it won't aggravate my headache but leaves it on low, so it's not just this balloon of silence between us.

"What time is it?" I think to ask as we roll through the mostly deserted streets. I must have passed out around ten or eleven. I wonder how long Chris has been looking for me.

"About 2:00 a.m."

"Wow, that late?" I glance over at him, wondering if his stony expression means he's pissed at me. Probably. There are so many threads as to why, the task of unraveling it seems overwhelming. "Thanks for finding me. I'm sure my mom was worried."

"We were all worried," Chris says stiffly.

"Sorry." All I do any more is apologize. Chris seems to be cleaning up all my messes lately.

He sighs. "You should probably know, I kicked Dave's ass."

So Chris knows what's been going on between us. He's seen it now, up close and personal. I swallow, or at least attempt to. My throat is swollen and feels like it's full of sand. Chris kicked Dave's ass. I find that I don't have many thoughts about it either way, except to hope he didn't kick it too hard.

"When?" I ask him.

"After school. I went over to his house and asked him about the picture. He got smart with me. It was almost too easy."

"He was probably expecting it." What a dumbass. "You didn't break anything, did you?"

"No," Chris says like he regrets it.

"Did it make you feel better?"

"Not really, but it had to be done."

Chris says it with such certainty, as though it were somewhere ordained that an ass beating was in order. I glance down at my phone and see Dave has texted me pictures of Chris's handiwork captioned with *Your boyfriend paid me a visit*. From the looks of it, Chris went easy on him. There are a few text apologies from Dave as well to the tune of *I was drunk and didn't know what I was doing*. I don't check his voicemails, but they're probably the same flavor. I really don't give a shit about Dave's feelings. Screw that asshole.

"That should have never happened," Chris says, like he's been holding his breath the whole time.

I wonder what he means by "that"—Dave's cock in my mouth, the scene being captured on camera, or that it spread like a virus throughout the school, so I ask him. "Which part?"

"None of it."

"I'm gay, Chris." It seems obvious, but some things need to be said.

Chris shakes his head. "Not that. You should have never gotten involved with Asshole Dave. He's been a jerk to you from the beginning. Why would you choose him, of all people?"

I've been asking myself the same question, but I know the answer already. I needed someone to keep my mind off Chris.

"He was there and he was interested." It's not until I say it out loud that I realize how lame it sounds. How needy. There was more to Dave than a warm body, though, which is why this whole thing is so messed up and only adds to my overall confusion. I thought Dave and I were friends, at least. A real friend would never do that to me.

Chris glances over at me, his lips tight against his teeth like a dog baring its fangs. "I wanted to kill him, T. I've never been so mad before in my life."

I don't want Chris hating himself on account of my dumb ass or getting in trouble for it. "I'm sorry I brought that out in you."

"It's not that. I don't want you to apologize. You're the victim here." He sounds like he's trying very hard to speak gently to me. Even now, Chris cares about my feelings enough to rein in his anger at the situation.

And he's right, mostly. No one deserves to have their most vulnerable, intimate moment blasted to the entire student body—if it's not a crime, then it should be. But I was also wrong in using Dave as a stand-in. I hurt him too, not as publicly, but I did hurt him.

"I'm a big boy, Boss. It's probably time for me to start handling my own shit."

"Did you know he took that picture?"

I shake my head, hoping Chris knows me well enough to know I'd never allow it.

"What a dickhead. Why'd he send it around?"

"Maybe he was mad I broke up with him."

"You were together?"

"Eh." I shrug. *Together* seems too strong a sentiment, especially now. "We messed around."

"Why'd you break up with him?"

I consider a few excuses that all ring false. "It didn't feel right. In any case, I think it's just me and my grilled cheeses from now on."

Chris grins at that, and I'm glad I can eke out a smile from him still. We pull into Harley's, and once inside, I order a Hungryman platter, which has just about every breakfast food you could imagine. Chris watches me eat, then helps me out when I start to lose steam and offers to pay before I can ask him to cover it because I spent my last dollar on booze. We don't talk much on the ride home, but it's a comfortable silence. It seems some of the big questions are out of the way, which is a relief.

"What did the guys have to say about it?" I ask Chris, cringing at what his response might be.

"Nothing," he says. "And they won't either."

I'm guessing some threats have been made. Chris is watching my back yet again. Not much has changed since sixth grade. Kind of makes me feel like a loser to the nth degree.

It's super late when we get back to Chris's house. I don't worry about waking up his parents. They're in the Cayman Islands for a few days, where they have a vacation home. Chris stayed back for Tabs's party tomorrow. Rather, today.

Upstairs, I ask Chris if I can use his shower, but it's not until I'm out that I realize I don't have any clean clothes. I really don't want to put on my soggy, grimy boxer briefs, so I wrap the towel around my waist and go out to Chris's bedroom, where he's reclined on his bed staring up at the ceiling.

"Hey, man, can I borrow some clothes?"

Chris looks at me then, head to toe and back again, and I swear there's something hot and illicit in the way he sizes me up. A desire that is definitely more than friends. But then he snaps out of it and hustles off his bed to grab some clothes out of his drawers, pushes the stack at me, and won't make eye contact. It's a lot like that morning after Sebastian. Like this big, dirty secret he doesn't want to talk about or even acknowledge.

Something for me to tackle another day.

I dress inside the bathroom, and when I come out, Chris has

gotten me a glass of water and a Tylenol. He points to his bed and tells me he'll sleep on the futon. I thank him again for finding my drunk ass and not telling my mom.

"Just don't let it happen again," he says.

As I'm drifting off to sleep, Chris reaches up and finds my ear, flicks it, and whispers, "Happy birthday, Theo."

And despite all the bullshit of the day, I figure I'll be all right, because in spite of being outed in the most publicly humiliating way, I still have Chris in my corner, and that's really all I need.

# FIFTEEN

# EMPTY BOXES, THE DAMN BALL, AND OTHER METAPHORS FOR THE SUCKAGE OF LIFE

I wake up around noon the next day to the sounds of a party revving up outside Chris's window. Oh yeah, that. I peer through the blinds, squinting at the assault of daylight like a vampire. The headache is still with me, only a little more muted. My sister's by the pool, one arm draped around Chris's shoulder, laughing at something one of her friends is saying. I've only been awake for about ten seconds and I already feel like puking, which is only partly from the alcohol.

I scribble a note to Chris—*Thanks for letting me crash here*—then creep downstairs and sneak a muffin from the glass case in the kitchen that Paloma keeps stocked with an assortment of goodies. I jog across our driveways, keeping to the bushes like a ninja to avoid running into any of Tabs's guests, and find my mom upstairs in our kitchen, doing dishes while singing, but the singing abruptly stops when she turns around and sees me.

I get the arched eyebrow—just one. My mom's not very strict. In fact, she's the exact opposite of strict. Around the time we started high school, my mom kind of shrugged and said *That's all I can do. It's up to you now.* Maybe it's because she's from Puerto Rico, where it seems parents are a little laxer and the kids more independent. In any case, as long as we come home at night and check in every few days, she pretty much stays out of our business.

But my mom knows something's up, and the arched eyebrow says more than words.

I have this speech prepared for my mom, which begins with my first stirrings for Casanova Guerra and how my desires have manifested over the years, growing stronger and more unavoidable. Then I was going to reference a boy who is Chris-like but not actually Chris, and conclude with the relationship I recently ended as an example of me needing to be a little choosier about who I date. As she's staring at me and I'm searching for the right metaphor with which to begin this great oration of my sexual awakening, I decide to cut to the chase and simply say, "I'm gay, Mom."

She nods and sets down her scrubby and opens her arms to me. I walk over and get this great mama-bear hug from a woman half my size who has more strength in her two arms than most men I know.

"You want to talk about it?" she asks.

I shrug, still encased in her arms, thinking about when she taught me how to dance. I was ten years old, and she insisted it was essential to my growth as a man. *You need to know how to lead, mijo.* I doubt I'll ever be leading a bride, but I'll always have my mom to dance with, and that's enough for me.

"I thought I did, but you seem to get it, so maybe it's not necessary after all."

"What happened yesterday?" she asks, pulling back to look at me, and I can only assume she knows most if not everything that went down.

"This picture went around school of me...." I clear my throat, and she holds up one hand to gesture that I don't need to go on.

"Do you want me to call this boy's mother?"

My sweet, old-school mother is a lot like Chris in many ways, only instead of beating a guy's ass, she goes for the jugular—his mother.

"He doesn't have the best home life," I tell her, feeling bad for Dave all over again because he's basically a runaway who had the good fortune of having an aunt with a spare apartment and no tenant. Then I kick myself for feeling bad for that asshole at all. "Besides, Chris already beat his ass. That's probably enough."

She nods. "Well, I can see why you call him Asshole Dave."

We share a bitter chuckle at that, and even though my mom pretends to not know what's going on in my life, clearly she does. Then she reveals perhaps more than she ever has about her relationship with my father when she says, "Make sure you fall for what's on the inside and not what's on the outside, baby. Otherwise you're just buying an empty box."

I nod and feel pretty bad at the same time. My father reduced to one sad metaphor, an empty box. I kiss my mom's cheek and tell her I'm going to visit Uncle Theo at the home. She seems surprised at that. "You're not going to the party?"

"Not my scene," I tell her. Another part of me manning up is not doing shit I don't want to do because other people tell me to. Even Chris and Tabs.

"Tell your uncle I said hello," she says. "He was always very nice to me."

I pick up pulled pork sandwiches from Paula's Pit Barbecue, including a pint of baked beans and a quart of their potato salad, even though it's about a mile out of the way. I stuff it all in my backpack and arrive at Saint Ann's in the early afternoon. The receptionist is different than the one I faced off with before—weekend crew. At first she thinks I'm delivering food and tells me they have a policy of not accepting meals from outside vendors, so I have to go through the whole exercise of proving to her I'm the nephew of one of the residents, producing my ID again, having her verify it with someone else, and finally they give me the pass to work the elevator to go see Uncle Theo.

This time he's in an activities room, where someone has stretched a volleyball net at waist-high level across the middle of the room. The old folks are all sitting in chairs, batting a beach ball over the net. Some of them are really getting into it, while others just sit there with glazed expressions on their faces. When the ball reaches Uncle Theo where he sits in the back, he bats it out of annoyance in a spike that goes straight to the floor. The instructor mimes the motion of hitting it up and over the net, then puts the ball in play again with a smile on her face the whole time, and I think I want some of whatever she's taking.

I lift the plastic bag with the Paula's logo and point to it to get Uncle Theo's attention. He stands up pretty fast for an old man and gestures toward me. His presence is commanding, and a nurse immediately goes over to assist him. It's not Manuel this time, but Gloria, who escorts him out of the room and over to the larger rec room, where we all sit down together.

"You know, Theo, outside food is prohibited for the residents." Gloria says it like it's protocol for her to say it, but I sense that her heart's not in it.

"But I brought extra for you, Gloria." I unpack the food and slide a pulled pork sandwich wrapped in foil toward her. She glances back at the door and then over at Uncle Theo, who's still scowling and hasn't seemed to have picked up on our negotiation.

"Captain Wooten doesn't have any food allergies, so I suppose we can let it slide this time."

I smile my eager smile and pull out the rest of the food. Uncle Theo taps the lid to the container of potato salad impatiently and seems to not know what to do with it. I did some reading on dementia and found out there are good days and bad days. Compared to the last time I saw him, this seems to be one of my uncle's bad days.

"Let me get that for you, Captain." Gloria tucks the napkin into his shirtfront like a bib and lays out his plasticware. She goes to the trouble of portioning out the food onto a plate she made out of one of the Styrofoam containers. When he tells her he wants more on his plate, she reminds him the food is rich and he doesn't want to eat too much and get a rumble in his tummy. Then, instead of eating, he stares at it.

"What's all this?" he asks with a frown, and she points to each of the sides, telling him what they are. He nods along like it's all very obvious.

"And what's this one?" he asks again, pointing at the sandwich.

"Pulled pork," she says.

"Stringy meat from a pig with barbecue sauce," I tell Uncle Theo, because I think he heard her the first time but still didn't know what it meant.

"Oh," he says like it's something he's never had before, but he's willing to give it a try.

"You eat it with your hands like this." I show him what I mean by taking a bite of my own.

"Is it any good?" he asks.

"Mmmm." I nod, not wanting to expose a mouthful of food to them.

I watch Uncle Theo take a hesitant bite and feel kind of sad and happy at the same time. Getting old sucks, but at least he has really nice caretakers who seem to give an actual shit about him as a person.

"Where's Manuel today?" I ask him once we've all settled into our meal.

My uncle shakes his head and says briskly, "It's Saturday." He looks to Gloria for confirmation, and she nods.

"That's right, Captain. Manuel only works on weekdays." She smiles at me. "It helps him remember the days of the week by knowing Manuel's schedule. He has it taped up in his apartment."

*Interesting*, I think and then, *is that normal?*

"Has Manuel worked here long?" I ask, trying to mine her for information without making it too obvious. Gloria smiles like she knows what I'm up to.

"A few years now."

"Is Manuel here?" my uncle asks, seeming put out by the thought that Manuel might be in the vicinity without him knowing.

"Not today. It's Saturday." Gloria rests a hand on his arm, and he nods and goes back to eating. I don't mention Manuel again because I don't want to get my uncle worked up about it or have him think we're hiding something from him.

My uncle is a tidy eater, careful about wiping his mouth and not talking with his mouth full. I've seen some of the other old folks who aren't so tidy and wonder if table manners are one of the last things to go, then feel guilty for thinking that way about Uncle Theo. Just makes me sad that it's only going to get worse for him, losing more of his memories and identity and even the habits he's had his whole life. And what's waiting for him at the end of it all? Death.

Jesus, that's grim. Even for me. I've got to get back on the sunny side.

We eat in companionable silence, and when we're through, I help Gloria clean up. I ask her if she wants the leftovers, and she says she'll keep the food in the staff fridge and try to sneak more to my uncle tomorrow, so long as his stomach agrees with it. I wonder if they do poop checks or something, then realize it's probably a situation where the old folks shit their pants if the food doesn't agree with them, and then I have all the respect in the world for the staff of Saint Ann's, because wiping another person's ass is true compassion.

When it's just my uncle and me again, I suggest we play some gin rummy, but he only wants to play solitaire. He calls to Gloria for "the cards," and she retrieves them from somewhere else, perhaps his room. I watch him line up his hand meticulously and realize there must be something calming about the ritual itself.

He's not too interested in conversation, and I find myself taking the lead. I ask him a little bit more about Saint Ann's, whether he has a roommate ("hell no") and about the activities they have here. He doesn't like most of them, including what I witnessed, which he calls "the damn ball." He's kind of grumpy about all the stuff they make him do, even though it sounds pretty stimulating and a hell of a lot better than sitting here alone playing solitaire. I get the impression my uncle was a hater before hating was cool, so I ask him what his favorite activity is, thinking he'll say being by himself or chow time.

"I like walks with Manuel," he says. His face changes then, becomes softer and sweeter. A small smile forms on his wrinkled face, subtle, like a shift in the light. It's so tender on such a tough man that it melts me a little on the inside.

"He seems nice," I agree.

My uncle nods, and I decide to reveal to him something about myself. It's not like my dad is going to visit him anytime soon, and even if he does, I doubt Uncle Theo would remember.

"I'm gay, Uncle Theo."

"Gay?" he asks, tasting the word like it's an exotic food.

"I like other boys."

He shrugs like it's not the huge revelation I think it is. "That happens sometimes." He goes back to counting out cards and seems generally unimpressed.

"My dad doesn't know." Hopefully he'll get the hint that it's not something he should share without me having to say it explicitly.

"Neither did my father," Uncle Theo says.

I must have misheard him. Is he saying he's... "What do you mean?"

"Liking boys." He stares directly at me like I'm being dense. "My father never knew."

He sighs, and it seems laced with regret and longing. And here my mind is blown. Uncle Theo just came out to me, and maybe it was rumored before among the older generation of Wootens, but if it was, I didn't know about it, and it certainly wasn't made known to me. I read somewhere homosexuality has a genetic component, and I wonder how many other queers have been hanging out in the Wooten family tree, closeted, and whether Uncle Theo was ever out or if it's something he's hidden his entire life. Did he ever have a boyfriend? Male lovers? I have so many questions, but I don't want to overwhelm or confuse him.

"Is that why you joined the Navy?" I ask.

He nods again, his face still drawn and dejected. "My father never liked me much."

"That sucks," I tell him, feeling closer to Uncle Theo than I ever thought possible. I think I have it hard now, but try to imagine seventy years ago, what it must have been like for him to be gay at my age. I can't even.

We're quiet after that—the only noise is the rasp of the playing cards in my uncle's hands—and I notice he's cheating by pulling different multiples of cards when he runs out of options, but I don't mention it. I'm not even sure it's considered cheating when you're only playing yourself.

I DRAW OUT MY VISIT WITH UNCLE THEO BECAUSE I DON'T WANT TO GO home until long after the party's over. Uncle Theo punks out pretty early, says he needs to go take a nap, so I end up skating along the intercoastal, just enjoying the sea breeze and the view of the water, until I can't stall any longer.

At home I sneak up to my room and close my blinds, consider playing the Sims but decide it's just an invitation for more pain. I queue up some of my favorite skate videos on my tablet instead, thinking about what tricks I might want to showcase at Plan Z, assuming I still have the balls to compete. A while back I found this hour-long skate video that has no music or talking, just the background noises of a skate session—the rollicking percussion of wheels on concrete, the sandpapery swish of boards grinding rails, trucks clicking and popping, and all the syncopated rhythms of tricks I can identify just from the sounds they make. I must have watched this video about a hundred times, whenever I want to relax. Now I close my eyes and zone out to the gritty soundtrack, imagining myself pulling off all these gnarly tricks.

I wake up in the dusty blue of twilight. I go over to my window and peek between the blinds at the pool area. The partygoers have vacated the premises, and Tabs is nowhere to be seen. I hope she didn't leave Chris and Paloma with cleanup.

I head downstairs and jog next door as Chris is telling Paloma that he'll take care of the rest. I ask him where Tabs is at, and Chris says he sent her off with her friends to continue the celebration downtown. I silently curse my sister for bailing.

"We missed you today," Chris says as I collect empty bottles and cans and dump them in the recycling bin.

"I wasn't up for it."

"I figured."

"Did Tabs have fun?" I hope I didn't totally ruin her sixteenth birthday.

"Yeah, I think she did."

He tells me some of the highlights, including who all was there, which makes me smile. A few of the upper echelon made an appearance, likely at Chris's request, which probably made my sister's day. She likes being included in the inner circle. Chris and I continue collecting trash for a while until the pool area is mostly clean. Then we go inside to tackle the kitchen, wrapping up the leftover food and wiping down the counters.

"What are you doing tonight?" Chris asks me when we're mostly finished. "We should go out and celebrate."

I rub my head, which still hasn't completely cleared from last night. "I think I did that already."

"We don't have to drink. What do you want to do? Anything at all. Magic cards?"

I laugh, because all I ever wanted to do in middle school was play Magic cards. God, I was such a geek. Maybe I'm simple or unimaginative, but all I want to do now is go down to the BOA and skate to get my mind off everything. I tell Chris and he's down. An hour later we arrive to where there's a small crowd of skaters we all know. It's unfortunate, but Dave's also there, looking pretty torn up from his beatdown from Chris. A flare of anger courses through me, mostly because this is my skate spot, and I hate feeling like it's not my home anymore because there's an intruder.

"I'll tell him to leave," Chris says.

"Don't. I don't want a scene. He's not going to try anything anyway. He's afraid of you."

As I predicted, Dave hardly even looks at us and keeps to the center of his cluster of friends, perhaps afraid of Chris getting him alone. I ignore the rest of them and do my circuit of the BOA. Perhaps because I know there's a competition coming up, I take it a little more seriously this time, thinking about which combinations I'll do and in what sequence. I have this combination, which is a series of 180s in quick succession that makes it look like that old-school dance, the twist. I skate goofy-footed—right foot forward—but I'm pretty ambidextrous. When I add a few backside kickflips to the combo, it looks pretty slick.

I gauge the crew's reactions, trying to determine which of my repertoire are crowd pleasers. It's hard to know, though, because as soon as a trick becomes popular or makes a comeback, it's chow time for the haters and the trick is no longer deemed worthy. I used to care more, but now I don't really give a shit what's considered cool, just try to make my tricks look smooth and effortless. I know it's not anything like ballet in terms of an art form, but there is some definite artistry to the different combinations.

After my third run, I'm thirsty and I've sweated through my T-shirt. I tell Chris I'm heading next door for drinks, and he asks me if I want him to come with me. "I got this, bro," I tell him and skate over to the 7-Eleven. While in there, I say what's up to Justin, who's working the night shift. I hang out in front of the drink cooler with the door open to cool off a bit, lifting my shirt to evaporate the sweat from my stomach and chest. As I'm paying, Justin is super slow to ring up my drinks, to the point that I wonder if he's on drugs or something.

He gives me my total and I hand him a five-dollar bill. He stares at me, holding the bill in midair, and looks so frozen I finally ask him if he's all right.

"I saw that picture of you." He says it so quietly that I almost don't hear him.

I take a deep breath and think *Shit, here we go.* "And?" My wall goes up straight away, preparing for whatever ill he's about to lay on me.

"I thought it was really hot." He smiles like he can't help it.

Not what I was expecting. At all. Also, precisely what is the reach of this damn photo? It's already spread outside of Sabal Palm High. Will my mom end up seeing it, or Christ, my dad? Am I going to Google myself and find that goddamned photo? Is it going to haunt me in ten years? Shit.

And just when I'm in the middle of this mini existential crisis at the 7-Eleven counter, Justin slides a scrap of paper over toward me. I stare at it—his phone number.

"I'm, um, into that sort of thing. So if you ever get bored, or, you know, want to, um, you know, just... give me a call."

I stare at him, stunned silent, while he hands me my change. I stuff the money in my pocket along with his number and grab the drinks, backing out of there blindly, overcome by the unintended consequences. *Who does that?* I think. *Sees a picture on the internet and then makes a move.* When I get back to BOA, Chris notices something is up and asks me what's wrong.

"Nothing," I tell him, glancing around at all the guys milling about, wondering how many of them have seen the picture, who they've shown it to, and what's been said. The panic hits me, this spiral of anxiety and fear. Will I ever be able to get past this, or will I always be that kid who sucks cock? What if I'm going in for a job interview and they Google me? Or applying for a scholarship. Shit, have I just screwed up my entire future? My vision constricts into a pea-sized view of the concrete, and I realize I'm leaned over and having trouble catching my breath. Chris is shouting, kind of panicked, asking if he should call 911 and I tell him *I'm fine*, only I don't feel the words come out of my mouth, only hear them bouncing around my head like a distant echo, and for some reason I think of the expression *bats in the belfry* and then *batshit crazy* while wondering what the hell did bats ever do to be associated with insanity?

And then I'm in the back seat of someone's car with my head between my knees. Chris is rubbing my back and barking directions on how to get us home. "I'm fine," I keep hearing me say, but I'm having my doubts.

Chris leads me up his stairs, and I sit down on the edge of the bed, still dizzy and nauseous, sweating, and short of breath. He sits across from me on the carpet, knees up, back against his dresser, and waits patiently while I pull it together. I focus on the texture of his comforter under my fingers, a loose thread I twine around my finger, the color of his walls—blue—and then his face. His face is just as it has always been. Kind eyes, square jaw, stubborn chin. Eventually everything stops shrinking and expanding, my ears stop ringing, my heart returns to normal volume and slinks down from my throat back into my chest, and it's just Chris and me alone in his room.

"I think I just had a panic attack," I tell him.

He nods without saying anything, rattled as well.

"Shit." I run my hands through my hair and pat myself down. There was a moment there where I didn't feel real—like, I had no physical presence. I was floating just above myself, like I was perched on my shoulder viewing what was going on without being an actual participant.

"What happened?" Chris asks.

"I freaked the fuck out."

"What happened to cause it? You came back from the gas station all pale and shit."

"Oh." I think back, having trouble remembering. "This guy gave me his number." Only that wasn't exactly it. It was everything else, the sensation that this would never end and I had no control over it. That my life was not my own.

"Who was it?" he asks.

"Justin."

"Justin who?" Chris looks like he's gearing up to kick some more ass.

"Justin from the gas station. He said he'd seen the picture, and he gave me his number. Told me to call him." I reach into my pocket and produce the strip of paper, uncrumple it, and stare at it—okay, at least I'm not imagining things. Chris springs to his feet and paces the room.

"He doesn't even go to our school, Chris. How many people do you think saw the picture?" My heart flutters, and the swell of panic balloons all over again.

"I don't know."

"I'm scared," I admit. "There's this whole other level to my social anxiety now, wondering who's seen it. What they're thinking, whether they'll turn around and talk shit behind my back."

"People will forget about it in a few days," Chris says.

"Will they?"

He frowns and doesn't offer any more encouragement.

"What if it follows me forever?"

"It won't."

"Shit," I curl up on his bed, squeezing a pillow to my chest. Chris sits down at my back and lays a hand on my shoulder.

"I'm with you, Theo. I'll be there every step of the way. You're not alone."

"Okay," I say shakily and then a little stronger, "Okay."

# SIXTEEN

# WHAT'S IN WOOTEN'S MOUTH?

I wake up early Sunday morning for work. I took off Saturday because of the party, but it's good to be back in the real world, surrounded by guys who have no idea I'm making the circuit on social media. Yeah, I checked my accounts that morning, and it's not pretty. There's this whole thread with the headline, "What's in Wooten's mouth?" There are all these filters people have put on top of the photo—a banana, a pickle, a dog's butt.... The dog's expression is one of surprise and dismay. Pretty creative. If it wasn't me they were mocking, I might even find it mildly humorous.

The comments range from wisecracks to propositions and then, farther down, a forum of debate between gay rights advocates and bigots. I sign out so I won't be tempted to dig further, excusing myself entirely from the conversation.

I decide then I'm not going to let Dave run me out of my own school or dwell on the fact that everyone now knows I have a taste for cock. It's time for me to man up, and by that I mean, own my shit and be real about who I am. Screw the haters. I never had much use for them anyway.

At work I enjoy the solidness of the tools in my hand, the vibrations of the mowers and edgers, the sun on my skin, and the utter exhaustion of eight hours of manual labor. At the end of the day, I text my boss and tell him I'm ready to take on more hours. I need something to occupy my time and keep me out of my own head.

After work I consider going straight to Chris's house and hiding out for a few more hours until his parents get back but figure I can't delay the inevitable much longer. I climb the stairs to our kitchen. My sister's nowhere in sight, so I tiptoe past her room so that she won't know I'm home. But when I open my door, she's sitting there on my bed, legs crossed, waiting for me.

I eye her warily and try to determine the nature of this intrusion. She crosses her arms and raises her eyebrows. She looks like a younger, sassier version of our mom.

"So, are you gay or what?" She purses her lips and looks at me expectantly.

I lean against the doorway and try to predict which way this thing will go. "Yeah, I am."

She huffs, audibly. "You could have told me, you know?"

"I didn't tell anyone."

"Not even Chris?"

"Nope." Especially not Chris.

She sighs, uncrosses her arms, and pats my bed for me to join her.

"You inviting me in to my own room?"

She tilts her head and scowls. "Come sit, baby brother."

Tabs is about two minutes older than me, and she loves reminding me of it whenever she has the opportunity. She probably elbowed me out of the way to be first. I slouch over and sit with my back against the headboard, swat at her with one of the pillows, then hug it to my chest. I need something to hold on to.

"Here's the thing," she begins. "I always thought you were being weird on purpose—"

"Why would anyone be weird on purpose?" I interrupt.

"I don't know. You're so good at everything, Theo. I figured being weird was one more thing you were good at." She shakes her head. "But I realize you probably had a lot on your mind, and because you don't *tell* anyone anything...." Here she pauses to give me an accusing look, then rolls her eyes to further her point. "Anyway, I'm sorry I was rude to you on your birthday. Whoever did that... they suck, and if there's anything I can do—"

"It's fine, Tabs. I'm handling it. Just... don't tell Dad, okay?"

She looks stricken. Her mouth falls open a little. "I wouldn't, Theo. Trust me. And I'm sorry about that night at dinner. If I had known...." She looks thoughtful for a moment. "I didn't mean to be so insensitive."

"It's okay. I shouldn't have walked out like that. I should have just...." I drift off, not knowing what I should have done... cared less? Kept it all bottled up inside? That's the story of my life. "Anyway, I'm sorry too. I don't like it when you're mad at me."

"Then you shouldn't do things to make me so mad." She punches my shoulder playfully. Her phone dings, and she checks it.

"Can you believe this shit?" she demands, shaking her phone in the air like the device is the problem. I figure it can only mean she's found the controversy brewing online—What's in Wooten's mouth and why does it matter?

I watch as she furiously types into her phone.

"You're not commenting, are you?" I bury my head in the pillow, dreading her answer.

"Of course I am. I'm not going to let them get away with this. Carson Fuller is dead to me."

Carson is one of the guys calling me a faggot with AIDS and blaming gays for the economy. I'm surprised he even knows enough about the economy to make the leap. I really bring out the crazy in people, apparently.

"You can't take them all on," I tell her, though I'm flattered she would try.

"Yes, I can. They can't treat my brother like this." Her face is pinched and furious, and I realize that same fierce protection she exhibits for our father, she also has for me.

"I appreciate it, Tabs. I'm going to stay off the interwebs for a while, so don't feel like you have to keep me updated."

"Don't worry, Theo. I got this."

I stand to go take a shower, then shove her on impulse.

"What was that for?" she asks.

"That's me showing affection," I tell her.

She smiles and holds up both arms, asking for a hug. "Come on, it's not going to kill you."

"It might."

She turns her wrists, insisting, so I reach down and hug her.

"See, that doesn't hurt, does it?"

"A little."

I grab some clothes and head out to the hall bathroom to take a shower, thinking how lucky I am to have Chris and my sister on my side. And my mom. Apparently Uncle Theo as well. Then I think about Dave being kicked out by his parents and find myself feeling sorry for him again, wishing he hadn't gotten drunk and been so spiteful as to spread that picture of me around, because I could have been a friend to him too. Fucking asshole.

Afterward I'm alone in my bedroom when I hear something buzzing outside my window. I glance over to see a big, black bug. A bat? Shit, am I seeing things now? I go over and pull up the blinds. It's a drone. I throw up the window to find Chris is in his driveway, holding a remote control. "Come over," he calls. "My parents' flight got delayed, and I'm bored."

I tell Tabitha I'm going next door. She's moved to the living room but remains glued to her phone. Even though it'd probably be better for all of us if she didn't suffer the trolls, it's the thought that counts.

Next door, Chris seems to know I'll be hungry, because he's pulled out the leftovers from my sister's birthday party, and we pick through the platters and tubs of salads until we're both full. Then we head upstairs and play video games. Chris is telling me about this story he saw online about a cockroach that crawled up a woman's nose while she was sleeping and how she could feel it scooting around inside her head, so she went to the doctor and some surgeons had to operate on her to get it out.

"She said when it moved around it made her eyes burn," Chris says, squinting. There's a hint of a smile on his face, like he's waiting for my reaction—he knows how I feel about roaches. Creepy, crawly little fuckers. Just when you think you've killed them, they're all, *psyche*, then they reanimate and scurry away.

"That's such bullshit," I tell him. Chris has been known to exaggerate or even make shit up in order to freak me out. He's good at it too.

"I'm not lying, T. There's a YouTube video of the surgery and everything."

"Did you watch it?"

"Hell no. I don't like roaches either."

"Pull it up." I pause the game and set down the controller.

"You don't believe me?" he says like I've insulted him, still with that mischievous grin on his face.

"Pull it up and we'll watch it together." He pulls out his phone and finds the video, shows me the story to prove he's not lying. We dare each other to watch it, going back and forth like morons until I finally just hit the Play button. It's only about two minutes long, but the shit is straight-up nasty and totally makes me want to barf, yet neither of us can look away. There are tubes all in the woman's nose and mouth and some god-awful long instrument like a tiny snake the surgeons are manipulating. And here's the grossest part: the cockroach is still alive when they pull it out. You can see its legs twitching and everything. Chris keeps saying *holy shit* over and over again.

"That's fucking gross," I tell him, pushing his phone away. "I'm never falling asleep again." Cockroaches are everywhere in Florida, even with pest service. They love that swampy heat, just like the snowbirds.

"I'd kill that motherfucker twice," Chris says, slapping his hands together and grinning.

Chris goes on about what it would be like to have a cockroach squirming around in your head, trying to gross me out even more, making his fingers like insect legs and crawling up my arm to freak me out until we're both cracking up. We go back to playing our video game, and it's so normal and right between us that I'm overcome by Chris's devotion to me, even in my lowest of lows. He's an even better friend when I'm down, and how many people are there out there like that? Heart of gold, man. He's not going to abandon me, no matter what it seems. Seriously, I don't think his loyalty could be tested any more than it has been.

It hits me in a moment of clarity that I don't want to lie to him anymore. And I'm no longer afraid he's going to ditch me if I tell him about my infatuation with him. Sure, it might be awkward for a while, but maybe if Chris tells me he's not interested, I'll be able to douse the flame and move on.

I pause the game for the second time and toss the controller on the carpet, turn to him with my legs crossed in front of me like we're in kindergarten during share time.

"We need to talk," I say and coach myself to be honest. Just lay it on the table. Now's the time, no more stalling. Real men share their feelings, right? At least, this one does.

"I'm sorry I made you watch that video," Chris says, perhaps thinking that's what this is about.

"It's not that." I study my hands for a minute, willing them to stop shaking. "I lied to you about a few things."

"Oh yeah?" I glance up to see his eyes shift away. He looks guilty, like this one time he cheated in Risk by gaming the dice and I caught him. That look.

But I know deep down that Chris is true blue and whatever I tell him, our friendship can handle it, and if I don't tell him now, I might never do it. Even while I don't expect him to act on it except to be mildly horrified, I know I can't continue on like this, constantly thinking about what I should say to him and worrying he's going to find out I like him because I'm smiling too eagerly or staring at him for too long or whatever crazy nonsense my head has convinced me not to do.

I clear my throat and submerge my fingertips into his plush carpet to have something real to hold on to. "That night in Sebastian. It meant something to me." I exhale and study him. He still looks caught, but he's nodding slowly, eyes locked on mine.

"It meant something to me too," he says softly.

*Umm, okay, but what?*

"It didn't seem that way." I wish I didn't sound so whiny about it.

He stretches his arms in front of him, then tucks his hair behind his ears and stares at the carpet. "I panicked, Theo. I didn't know if it was something you wanted, or if you just did it because I told you to." He looks up and searches my face. "I still don't know."

"I wanted it," I say before I can back out or blow it off. I try to keep my voice even and not falter because I don't want to sound weak and needy. "I have for a while. I didn't want to tell you because I wasn't sure if you were into guys or me and even if you were, I didn't want it to ruin our friendship."

He takes a breath that seems to last forever. I watch his chest expand and then deflate. Chris isn't one to rush his words. "How long have you felt this way?" he asks.

"I don't know. A year? Maybe longer. I started noticing... things... last fall."

"Things?" His eyebrows lift, the hint of a grin on his lips.

"You're going to make me say it?" Chris nods, his smile growing wider. He's going to make me say it. "Boners, Chris. Huge friggin' hard-ons. Don't act like you haven't noticed."

Chris laughs for, like, a while, to the point where we're no longer laughing together, if we ever were. "I thought you might have a medical condition," he rasps between guffaws.

"Har dee har har."

When he finally stops, he reaches out and squeezes my shoulder. "I've felt this way longer."

Poof. Mind blown.

"Why the hell didn't you say anything?" I say in a rush of passion. I'm not going to lie, I'm a little pissed. I've been wrestling with this for a while. Completely paranoid. Completely out of my mind.

"It freaked me out, Theo. I mean, it still does."

"For how long?"

"I don't know, eighth grade?"

I do a little mental math. "Eighth grade? That was, like, *years* ago." I can't even believe this. We'd only been friends for a year or so, and he already had feelings? How did I not pick up on this? Oh, that's right, all the making out with chicks. "What about all those girls... freaking Kelli Keyhoe?"

He shrugs. His nonchalance is making me crazy. "I didn't think you'd be into it," he says, "and I didn't want to screw up our friendship either. Kelli was easy compared to you."

I have no idea what he's talking about. Easy? Like, she's a slut and I'm not? "What does that even mean?"

He shakes his head and smiles at me with brotherly affection, like he does whenever I say something completely dweeby or weird.

"You're a little clueless sometimes, T."

"*I'm* clueless?" I point to myself, completely baffled and indignant. He's the clueless one as far as I'm concerned.

"Yeah, I've been making moves on you for years."

"You *have*?" I ask incredulously. There's absolutely no proof of that. I mean, I would know. "When?"

"My whole eighth-grade year. All we ever did was wrestle here on my bedroom floor."

I glance down at the carpet. Chris did go through a phase where he wanted to show me all these wrestling moves. I had an awful lot of rug burns that year. I thought he'd go out for the high school team, but he never did.

"I thought you were just trying to prove how much stronger than me you were."

Chris gives me a hard look. "By pinning you against the ground over and over?"

It did take an awful long time for him to count to three. How could I not have noticed that? But straight guys do that sort of thing all the time. There's no way I could have known there was anything behind it.

"Shit." I look at him. "So, are you gay?"

He shrugs and goes wide-eyed. "I don't know. All I know is I think about you all the time. Dirty thoughts, T. Really filthy. Like, pornographic. That night in Sebastian...." He sucks in a deep breath and lets it out slowly. "All I've wanted since then is to get you alone in my tent. I have these schemes to kidnap you and...." He shakes his head, a small smile curving his pink lips. His face looks a little flushed. "You don't want to know."

I probably do, in fact. I can't believe he's had feelings for me all this time and hasn't said anything. He tells me *everything*. "You should have said something," I reiterate.

"I tried. I mean, I thought you'd pick up on it. Then after that night in Sebastian, you said it was a mistake. I saw you giving your number to Ryanne on the beach and thought there might be something there. Then you started hooking up with Dave." He shakes his head and facepalms. "What a mess."

I cannot believe we were both struggling with the same exact thing, in silence, for so long. In fact, I'm a little bitter. The whole Dave fiasco could have been avoided if we'd just manned up.

"So, what do we do now?" I ask him.

"I don't know. I still don't want to screw this up." He lifts his eyes to stare at me, and my gaze drifts to his mouth, thinking about how long I've wanted to kiss those lips, how many girls have straddled his lap, draped over him like a flesh Snuggie, how badly I've wanted that permission to touch him myself.

"Maybe the reality won't match up to the fantasy," I tell him. "Then we could just, you know, move on."

"You think we should test it?" Chris asks in a deep, gruff voice.

I scoot toward him so I'm kneeling in front of him with my knees spread wide. I reach down and cup his face in my hands while leaning in. Our mouths knock together somewhat awkwardly. His top teeth scrape against my bottom lip. I don't think he was expecting my advance. Instead of pulling away, Chris grips the back of my head so it's solidly in his grasp. Our mouths meet again, softly this time. I part my lips a little and his tongue slides across my own, like licking an ice cream cone, then curls inside my mouth. *Chris's tongue is inside my mouth.* My brain shoots off a string of fireworks, and I force myself to relax and let him show me what to do. My hands migrate to the back of his neck, where my fingers get tangled in the soft curls of his hair. I forget for a minute that it's Chris and think *Wow, he's a good kisser,* then wonder if I'm moving my tongue at the right speed or opening my mouth wide enough, if I'm being too slobbery or eager.

*Just shut up and enjoy it.*

"Come here." Chris shifts so he's on his knees with our chests pressed together. His body radiates heat and his chest so fits nicely against my own. My mouth opens wider as our tongues find their groove, making sweet, sucking noises as we kiss. It could be only seconds or several minutes—I lose track of time and my thoughts drift away. There's only room for the soft press of Chris's lips against mine, the slow give and take of our tongues as they become better acquainted, and the flame of desire he ignites in my belly.

The rest of me gets all gooey and bendy except for my lone soldier, at full attention and nudging Chris's thigh somewhat obscenely.

Chris pushes me back roughly, and I think it might be to make me stop, but then my back is flat on the carpet and he's on top of me, grinding against me. His hands grip my wrists so they're pinned above my head, his mouth mashed with mine while he makes his little humming noises. He positions himself so his hips are between my thighs, and I spread my legs wider to make room for him.

"Unghh." I mutter something unintelligible and arch my back as my cock strains painfully against him like an arrow seeking release. Chris's mouth latches on to my neck while he props himself on either side of me on his elbows like he's doing push-ups, still thrusting against me.

"Take it off," he orders and backs off for a moment. I can only assume he means my clothes. I rip off my shirt like Superman, and Chris does the same. His physique is decidedly more in the vein of an actual superhero. I almost come right then at the sight of him, his broad tanned chest and pink, rubbery nipples, his smell flooding my senses like a tantalizing mist. "Everything," he commands, "take everything off."

I have no reservations with Chris. Unlike Dave, I trust Chris implicitly. Anything he wants, I'll give it to him. It's just that simple.

"You feel so good," Chris growls as he climbs, naked, on top of me again, riding his dick alongside my own. The heat rises like a fever and radiates out of my every pore as I reach down and grab both our cocks in my hand, jacking us off at the same time in a fervor. Chris's mouth covers mine and then trails off across my cheek like he's forgotten we're kissing. He buries his face in my neck, sucking hard, teeth scraping my skin as he rides me like a dog. I love how wild and unrestrained he is, how perfectly Chris. He doesn't care about how he looks or the sounds he's making, which makes me not care either so I'm really able to let loose. Our bodies grind against each other, rough and dirty, trying to get each other off as fast as we can. There's a sticky wetness on my stomach, and I think I must have come, but no, not quite. Still hard and aching and tender to the touch. Chris climbs off to access the damages, then bows down to finish me off. He's barely latched on before I explode inside his mouth.

Sad to say, neither of us lasted very long.

"Whoa," he says and spurts a mouthful of jizz onto my stomach. Like I said before, I'm not very tidy.

He wipes his arm across his mouth and stretches out across my chest, panting in my ear like an animal, hot and breathy. I love the weight of him, love that he's crushing me into the carpet, his limbs spread over me in conquest. P.S. I surrender.

"Shit," he says after a minute. The haze of carnal lust clears, and he glances around like he can't believe what just happened. He sits up on his knees, his muscular thighs still straddling my hips, fine blond hair against tanned skin. I rub my hands along his muscular quads, and he stares at me with a wide-eyed look on his face. "What are we going to do now?"

I recognize this face from the morning after in Sebastian. He's freaked out. I thought it was because he regretted it, but I realize now he's truly scared shitless. Thinking you might be gay is one thing. Acting on it is another. I'm so used to Chris taking the lead, so effortlessly, that I didn't realize he might need me to take the lead on this one.

"I need a shower," I tell him, pointing politely to the pile of jizz pooling on my stomach, some of which is his and some of which is my own, "and you might want to rinse your mouth out."

"Screw you, man," he says and punches my shoulder.

I laugh and grip my arm like it hurt, but it's only for his benefit.

"I think I gave you a hickey," he says and turns my chin to inspect it closer.

"Yeah, for a minute there I thought you were a vampire."

"I can't believe I did that." He touches my neck as though needing proof. "It's, like, bruised and shit."

"It's cool. I like it a little rough."

"You do?" Chris says, stupefied, because somewhere in the last five minutes, he misplaced his sense of humor.

"Maybe. I don't know. I was just kidding." I snap my hips to remind him of the plan, and he climbs off me in a daze.

Chris is kind of zoned out while I shower, sitting on the toilet seat, watching me wash up. He wiped himself down with a wet washrag, but I got most of the spillage. After the *Dr. Giggles* incident, his parents replaced the curtain with a glass door. I'm tempted to invite him in, but I don't think he's ready for cutesy couple shit like washing each other's backs. He looks pretty stone-cold terrified right now, coming to grips with the fact that he also has a taste for cock. Even in South Flaaarida where straight guys wear pink, there's some real homophobic haters out there. For proof, just check out What's in Wooten's mouth?

I turn off the water. Chris's eyes track me as I dry off and wrap the towel around my waist. Chris is still naked as he grabs hold of the towel and gently tugs. My dick is definitely ready for round two and makes it known rather obnoxiously, but I sense from the way Chris kisses me softly on the lips, he's looking for something gentler and sweeter.

"Come on." He leads me back to his bedroom, nods at my junk, and says, "Put that away so I can focus." He tosses my boxer briefs at me and puts on his own. He sits on the edge of his bed looking sort of dejected, like he just got told he didn't make the team.

"What's up?" I ask him while I redress.

"I thought I might be bi, but this is, like, straight-up gay." He looks like he might be on the verge of a panic attack himself.

"How's the reality match up to the fantasy?"

"It's hot," he says, and I smile, but he doesn't look too pleased about it.

Chris leans forward, cradling his head in his hands, doing his wrinkled forehead stress face. "I have to tell my parents. My dad...."

He's definitely panicking now. I kneel down at his feet and resist the urge to touch him. Even though we just did things we've never done before, I don't want to assume he wants my affection or force myself on him. "We don't have to do anything you're not ready for. Or tell anyone. We don't even have to do this again if it's too much."

"I want to, I'm just...." He glances up at me, brown eyes wide. "I'm freaking out, T."

I reach for one of his hands and squeeze his fingers to bring him back to the here and now. "I get it, Chris. It's a big deal. It's okay to freak out."

"I need some time," he says, and I sense that he needs a little space to process as well. I back away, find my phone and keys, while Chris watches me with a stoned expression on his face.

"Can you take me to the DMV tomorrow after school?" I ask him. My mom could do it for me, but I want Chris there, partly because that's how it was always supposed to be, and also because I want to show him we can be friends, just friends, if that's what he wants.

"Yeah, of course." He stands to walk me out. He's still shirtless, wearing only his briefs, his junk bulging against the thin material. I bite my lip. This isn't going to be easy, but at least I no longer have to lie to him or hide it.

"See you tomorrow," he says absently, then grabs for my shirt with one hand and pulls me in close for another kiss. My mouth melts against his like warm chocolate. When we finally break apart, Chris seems reluctant to let me go.

"Take care, Boss," I tell him.

"Don't let your mom see that hickey."

"Heard."

I gallop down the stairs and out of his house. It's late now and the streetlights are on, bathing the streets in an oily yellow glow. I grab an old skateboard from my garage and take a tour of the neighborhood, thinking about Chris and all the thoughts that must be swirling around in his head right now. I'm not going to pressure him or make any demands. I've made my feelings known, and that's all I can do. I think of Gloria tucking the napkin into my uncle's shirt and laying out his food for him in preparation for the feast.

I've set the table for Chris and served up the meal. It's up to him to take the first bite.

SEVENTEEN

# HEADROOM, SOMETHING THAT SOUNDS DIRTY BUT ISN'T

Monday morning is my first day back at school post-outing. To hide the huge gnarly hickey Chris gave me, I wear one of his old polo shirts and pop the collar, like some of the assholes at school who do it as part of their preppy look. I also bring my cans to school, even though you're not supposed to wear them in the hallways. I need to drown out the static coming my way. Mostly it's dudes asking me what's in my mouth and girls giggling when they think I'm not paying attention. A few guys call me a fag, but it's pretty halfhearted. No one tries to kick my ass or says anything as nasty as what's online. I'm not sure if that's a good thing.

Right before lunch I'm at my locker, just trying to keep my head down, when someone taps me on the shoulder. I glance over and Ryanne's holding up her phone. If it was anyone else, I'd ignore them, but I have a soft spot for Ryanne, who always goes out of her way to say hi to me when we pass by in the hallways. I slide my cans around my neck and say what's up.

"I have something I want to show you," she says with a smile on her face.

"I've already seen it." The answer to What's in Wooten's mouth, it's cock.

She shakes her head. "It's my cousin's car. He's moving to New York, and he wants to sell it quickly." She hands me her phone, and I scroll through the pictures where her cousin posted it on Craigslist. It's a gunmetal gray Honda Accord sedan, six years old. From the photos, it appears to be in pretty good shape.

"Sixty thousand miles," I muse. "Not bad."

"The first owner hardly ever drove it, and Hondas last forever. It looks small, but my cousin's a tall guy like you. Says he bought it because of the headroom."

I'm definitely interested. I tell Ryanne I'm going for my driver's test that afternoon, and I'll text her to let her know how it goes. She offers me a ride to go see it later in the week.

"Good luck," she says brightly. "I'll let my cousin know you're interested."

At lunch, Tomás has a Hacky Sack, and I stand around with him and Corbin and a few other guys and bat the ball around. No one says a word about *the incident*, and I don't think it's because Chris is there. I think they're all a little tongue-tied with me, not wanting to embarrass me any more, which I appreciate. Dave's not around, and he hasn't come to his locker either. I'm tempted to ask about him, but my sister informed me that morning the big question has evolved from What's in Wooten's mouth to Who's in Wooten's mouth, and I don't want to give the gossip mill any more grist.

At the end of school, there's a note stuffed in my locker, folded like a paper football with *Theo* written on the outside of it. I don't know Dave's handwriting, but I figure it's probably from him. I blocked him from my phone and deleted his number, and I haven't responded to any of his previous appeals. I tuck the note in my pocket. Maybe I'll light it on fire later.

The DMV still takes forever, but at least Chris is there to keep me company. We sit in a corner of the waiting room, away from everyone else, because Chris has questions of a delicate nature. It's strange, because I've always been the one going to Chris for advice. For now, it seems our roles are reversed. It's kind of refreshing.

"What'd your mom say about it?" he asks me about coming out.

"She was cool, but I figured she would be."

"And your dad?"

"I haven't told him yet."

"Are you going to?"

"Not if I don't have to." Yeah, I'm a wiener, but every time I imagine it, it ends in disaster. In fact, I'd rather imagine an actual disaster than think about coming out to my dad. Maybe I should upload my dad to the Sims and come out to him there to see how it all plays out.

"How are you going to manage that?" Chris asks.

"I went six months this summer not seeing him. Plus, he's about to have another kid, so that should keep him busy for a while."

"You think he'll be mad?"

"Yeah." I don't need to explain it to Chris. He knows our relationship is walking a tightrope as it is. I can see me being gay as the thing that makes my dad want to cut all ties. I guess I've been living in this weird limbo for so long, hoping beyond hope that my dad and I will find some sort of common ground. But me coming out seems like it might be the last straw. "I'm pretty terrified," I admit to Chris.

"It might be better to know one way or another," Chris says, "instead of worrying about it. Maybe he'll be more accepting than you think."

Chris, ever the optimist, one of the reasons I love him.

"Maybe."

"I'm not too worried about my mom and Jay, but my dad...." Chris shakes his head. "He's like a mountain man, all rugged and shit."

"You're rugged," I tell him. "Just look at all the ass you've kicked over the years." Chris is a manly man already. I figured that would make it easier—to have your manhood already proven—but maybe, in a way, it makes it harder. Like, I know my dad has wondered in the past if I was gay—that's probably why he always pushed me so hard in soccer. But Chris? That's going to be a huge bomb he drops on his parents.

"My mom will want me to tell him right away," Chris says.

"Is it up to her?"

"No, but she won't want me to keep it from him. I just hate doing it over the phone. Not being able to see his face or how he's reacting to it."

"I bet your parents would fly you out."

"Yeah. It just sucks that it even has to be done at all, you know?"

I didn't want to come out. I was quite content to keep my business to myself. If Dave hadn't outed me, I probably wouldn't have said anything to anyone, not even my mom. I'm torn about it. In one way, it's good to not have to hide it, but in another way, it's like I'm naked in front of people all the time. Like gay is my whole personality. I'm not smart or funny or an awesome skateboarder, I'm just gay, gay, gay.

"You don't have to come out to them, Chris. You might not even be gay. Maybe you're bi."

"Maybe," he says like he's having doubts. "But what about us? Do we just start making out in front of them?"

That sounds like a bad idea too. "No, I mean, let them wonder. Plus, if you tell them, there go our sleepovers."

Chris laughs at that, which is good. I don't want him to lose his sense of humor in all this.

"Seriously, though, I'll keep this a secret if that's what you want," I tell him.

"That's shitty. Why would you let me get away with that?"

*Because I love you.*

"I just would," I say.

"I don't want to keep it a secret, Theo. Especially not with all these randos giving you their number every time I turn around."

"They are not," I argue. Although I have been hit on a couple more times since Justin. It's probably the strangest thing about being out. I'd never approach a girl—or a guy—just because I saw a picture of them going around online, but maybe some guys would. "Guys are dogs," I tell Chris.

"Yeah, they are. Hey, I don't want you messing around with anyone but me, okay?" I glance over to find him staring at me intently, giving me the full-body meltdown. The look that has me saying, yes, yes, yes.

"You want to go steady with me, Boss?" I nudge him with my elbow, and he grabs for it.

"I want that shit on lockdown."

I smile. It's the cherry on my chocolate fudge sundae. "Done."

Chris smiles, then glances across the waiting room and eyes up the vending machine. He seriously can't go two waking hours without eating. "How are you so cool about all this?" he asks.

Something has changed since coming out to Chris. There were so many thoughts and emotions I was keeping from him, little things and big things, that now it's like a dam has broken and I can tell him anything on my mind, no matter how embarrassing or personal.

"As Lieutenant Knox would say, I've been in the shit."

"Fucking Sean." Chris shakes his head. He's still bitter Sean got me wasted on the beach, even though I asked for it. And Sean did make me feel a hell of a lot better about *the incident*. My problems seem pretty small compared to his.

"You know none of this has anything to do with how I feel about you, right?" Chris says.

"It kind of does. You're willing to be this whole new person for me."

"Not new. Just... out in the open."

I take a moment to reflect on the gravity of what we're doing. Straight couples don't have to go through near as much bullshit to be together. Make great proclamations about their sexuality or worry about which of their family members are going to disown them, or in my case, cut off my mythical trust fund. *West Side Story*, my ass—what bliss.

"Hey, guess who else is gay?" I say to Chris.

"Who?"

"Uncle Theo."

"Cocksucker Uncle Theo?"

"Yup."

"Wow."

"I know. He totally has a crush on one of the nurses at the home."

"Really? Is that how you found out he was gay?"

"Yeah, and he more or less told me after I came out to him. It's this whole secret society, Chris."

"Apparently."

"The cool club."

"That might be overselling it."

I chuckle. "Maybe so."

The lady behind the counter calls me up then, and Chris tosses me his keys. "Good luck, Killer."

I pull Chris's car around back, and an older guy gets in and introduces himself. We go through the three-point turn and parking between the orange cones. Then we go out to the road, and he tells me to stop, and I do so without making it too abrupt. I make a few turns with signals and handle some traffic lights. I merge and adhere to right-of-way and do everything I think I'm supposed to. When the car is safely parked back at the DMV, I ask the guy how I did.

"You did great," he says with more enthusiasm than anyone working inside has shown me. "Remember, no drinking, no drugs, and no texting."

"Yes, sir."

Driver's test: slayed.

The smile on my face is huge when they take my picture. I come back out to Chris, show him my new license with the plastic still warm from the machine, and ask him if he thinks my smile is too eager.

"What?" he says like I'm crazy.

"Does it look like I'm trying too hard?"

"To do what?"

"I don't know. Do I look stupid?"

"No, Theo, you look happy." Then, in front of everyone in the DMV, he hooks his arm around my neck and plants a big fat kiss on my cheek.

No one at the DMV is impressed. Except, of course, for me.

And I get to drive us home.

WE TAKE THE LONG WAY HOME, ALONG THE INTERCOASTAL WITH THE windows down and the wind in our hair. I'm driving legally at last. The moment I've been dreaming about for so long is finally realized and even better because Chris is here with me. *My boyfriend.* I say it in my head a few times. It sounds so strange, but I love it.

Chris is smiling and humming to himself. I ask him what he's thinking about, and he glances over like I caught him up to no good.

"Nothing." He shakes his head like he's embarrassed.

"Tell me."

"I've been thinking about all these little things between us, times when I thought maybe you were into me, but I was actually too afraid to go for it."

I smile. Sounds familiar. "Like, when?"

"When I first got back from Cali and I was showing you my board. I was totally going to kiss you in the shed, but I wussed out."

A lustful heat rises up in me at the memory of it. Boy, that would have cleared up some things.

"Sebastian, obviously," he continues, "and then, that night you slept over when we were cuddling. All I wanted was to make out with you, but it felt wrong because you were all sad and depressed about your dad. I promised myself the next day I'd make a move."

"So why didn't you?"

He shakes his head. "I was warming up to it during our basketball game when Dave pulled up."

"That's when I told him I was done."

"I figured."

"The only reason I ever started hooking up with him was to get over you."

Chris frowns. "I wish you hadn't told me that. I really hate that guy."

"He's not all bad."

"He's a fucking asshole, Theo. Look what he did to you. And I hate that he got to you first."

I shake my head. Chris is an only child who's never had to share his toys unless he wanted to. Same with his parents' affection. His jealous streak comes out in moments like these where he practically says *mine, mine, mine.*

"I hated watching Kelli Keyhoe slobber all over you my entire freshman year."

He sighs. "Yeah, my bad." He runs his hand over the dashboard and inspects his fingers. Chris's car is filthy. Maybe because his mom's kind of a neat freak, he totally lets his car go. Talk about roaches. I'm never falling asleep in here.

"So, what'd you guys do when you were together?" Chris asks, going out of his way to sound casual about it, like he's asking for the morning surf report.

"Me and Dave?" I ask, playing dumb.

"Yeah, who else?"

"I got pretty good at FIFA."

I expect him to laugh at that, smile at least, but instead his frown deepens. "Fine, don't tell me," Chris says with a pout. I give him a look.

"Don't make that face." His mouth shouldn't hold so much sway over me.

"What? I tell you *everything.*"

That's true; even when I'd rather him not tell me, he does.

"Hand jobs. Blowjobs. That's about it."

"Was it good?"

I clear my throat. This is what they call a trick question. "It wasn't... bad."

"Did you want to have sex with him?"

My face heats up. There are really no limits to what Chris will ask me.

"Butt sex?"

He chuckles a bit. Nothing gets Chris going like a little crude humor. "Yeah, Theo, *butt* sex." He really accentuates the word *butt.*

I lick my lips, unable to wipe the giddy smile off my face I get whenever the topic of sex comes up between us. Feels like I'm sucking on helium. "Not really."

"Why not?"

"I don't know. We didn't have a super strong connection. We only knew each other for like, a month."

Chris is quiet for a moment, and then, "Do you want to have butt sex with me?"

I laugh, a nervous little giggle, and steal a glance. Chris looks pretty serious about it. It's difficult to have this conversation and still pay attention to the road. "Um, yeah," I say when I've recovered.

"Really?"

"Why do you sound so surprised?"

"I don't know. A couple months ago, you'd never even kissed a girl, and now you're like this sex-crazed horn dog."

I shake my head at how quickly the tables are turned. Suddenly I'm the horny one, not him. "You're the one who brought it up, Chris. I can't help my hormones. And you're still the only person I've ever kissed."

"Yeah?" He sounds pleased with that.

"Yeah."

"Cool."

We drift off into silence. Chris stares out the window, and I concentrate on my driving. But the cat's out of the bag, only in this case, it's butt sex. He never told me how he feels about it. Chris got me to show my cards without revealing his own hand. It's on the tip of my tongue to ask him, but I'm afraid he'll say no. Or he'll feel like he has to say yes and I won't be able to tell the difference. Does he think I'm a slut because I want to have sex with him? Maybe he'd rather wait, but now there's this pressure to act. We can wait if that's what he wants. I just want him to be my first, whenever the time comes. I know him better than anyone else, and most importantly, I trust him.

When we get back to our houses, Chris tells me to come up because his parents won't be home for a couple of hours and he wants to make out with me. He says it so directly that I stutter and blush and get really tongue-tied. I would never in a million years say something like that, even to him. I guess that's why we work.

"Is Paloma home?" I ask him as we're walking up his driveway.

Her hours are pretty irregular. On the weekends when they travel, she house-sits and doesn't work at all during the week. I've never had a housekeeper before, so I don't know what's normal, but ever since Chris became old enough that he didn't need someone to watch him or drive him places, Paloma pretty much sets her own schedule and does whatever she thinks will help out the most. I think Chris's parents feel bad about being gone so much, and they like having Paloma around to keep Chris company.

In response to my question, Chris shrugs. "If she is, I'll shut my door."

I follow him inside. We say hi to Paloma and tell her the food she's cooking smells delicious. Chris asks her what's for dinner, and she gives him the rundown of the roast chicken and sides in somewhat excessive detail. It's this whole exchange between them. I can practically see Chris salivating over it. Paloma loves the way he eats, as does my own mother. Chris asks if she's going to make "the flaky biscuits," and they have this whole back-and-forth about which specific biscuit he means. I can tell they're both loving it, Chris because he gets to go into further detail about food, and Paloma because she loves the way he appreciates her cooking. She has all kinds of pet names for him—Cristian (the Spanish version of his name), Rubito (blondie), and my favorite, Gordito (little fatty). Finally they reach a consensus on which biscuits will be prepared for tonight's feast, and by now I'm about to beg for a seat at the table because my mouth's watering as well.

On our way upstairs, I tease Chris about his food fetish.

"I could listen to Paloma talk about food all day long," he says.

"You have no idea how spoiled you are, Gordito."

He grins. "I have some idea."

In his room, he shuts the door and turns on some music—this weird electronica I've dubbed "Club Mario Kart." Maybe he wants it to sound like we're playing video games. I don't have time to be nervous because he heads straight for me like a shark, bumps me with his chest until I'm backed up to the edge of his bed. Once there, he peels back the collar of my shirt to inspect his handiwork.

"I still can't believe I did that," he says, but he seems a little excited by it. I've looked at the mark several times since he gave it to me, even poked at it to feel the bruise. Evidence of his mouth on my skin.

With his finger, he traces up my neck, along my jaw, stopping to turn my chin toward him. He stares at me with a look I've come to recognize—dewy eyes, parted lips, heavy breathing. I like the way lust looks on Chris, especially knowing it's for me.

"The first time I saw you," he says as he nuzzles his nose against mine.

"Yeah?" I curl my fingers in the hair at the nape of his neck and lean down to kiss just below his ear, breathing in his beach-salt skin, tangy with sweat. I take deep breaths, letting his scent wash over me, thrilled and amazed that this is happening and I'm allowed to do this. I'm making out with my boyfriend. The rest of the world could be crumbling outside our window, but in this room at this moment, life is fucking fantastic.

"I thought you were super cute," he says. His voice is thick and husky, both of us speaking in half sentences, drowsy with the desire. "I liked your pretty eyes. And your smile. And the funny way you talked. All the weird things you said."

"Like Doom Blade is the answer to a Tarmogoyf?"

Chris chuckles. "You were so sweet and geeky with your Magic cards. You taught me a whole new language."

"Yeah, it's called Dweeb."

"I like dweebs. You follow your own beat and do your own thing. That's sexy."

I smile, and he kisses the corner of my mouth, grips my hips, and draws them forward until our groins bump together. "You're sexy," I tell him. I want him all the time.

"What did you think of me when we first met?" he asks, glancing up at me, his eyes hooded with desire.

"I thought you were scary." I hook my thumbs in the waistband of his shorts, my hands cupping his muscular ass. When Chris is fired up, he blazes brighter than the sun. I wouldn't want to be on the receiving end of his anger, that's for sure. "And then I wanted to be just like you. You were good at everything—surfing, basketball, making friends, cracking jokes." This is weird to think, but I probably developed my sense of humor based on what Chris thought was funny. There is no greater pleasure for me than in making him laugh.

"Even back then, before it was anything, I wanted to be around you all the time," he says dreamily as I kiss his neck.

"Me too."

"I missed you this summer. Did you miss me?"

"Yes," I whisper. *Yes and yes and yes....*

"Then why didn't you call me?" He sounds hurt by it.

"I was trying to get over you."

"But you couldn't."

I shake my head. *Lord, how I tried.* He grips the nape of my neck with one hand and draws my mouth to his, kissing me softly at first, deepening as our tongues find each other, a slow and sensual dance. I let him lead. Wherever Chris goes, I'll follow.

My hands crawl up under his shirt, and he pulls it over his shoulders in one deft move. He tugs at mine, and I lift my arms for him to disrobe me.

"This isn't fair," I tell him as my fingers travel over the grooves in his abs, making their way down to his hipbones, all those hard lines on smooth skin. I sit down on the edge of his bed, eye level with his dips, kissing one exquisitely sculpted groove and then the other.

"All yours," he says, thrusting his pelvis forward and turning me on even more. I go to reach for the button on his pants, and he pushes my shoulders until I'm flat on my back on his bed, climbs on top of me, and splays both hands across my chest to hold me down. As if I would go anywhere. "Is it weird I want to lick all of this?" he asks.

"I'm not edible," I remind him, using my arms to shield my chest from the intensity of his gaze.

He pulls my hands away and anchors them to the bed. "Don't be shy," he whispers into my ear. "Not with me." He kisses my throat, drags his lips across my chest to suck on one nipple and then the other, flicking the tip of it with his tongue. I squirm and he holds my wrists more firmly. He draws his nose down the center of my chest to my happy trail, stopping just at the waistband of my briefs, tugging a little at the elastic with his teeth. I shiver because it tickles and gets me all twisted up inside, wanting more and more and more.

"You like that?" he asks.

"I like *everything*."

Chris sits up so he's straddling my thighs, gyrates a little, revving me up. He turns me on with the slightest touch. I love his body—its texture, shape, and smell, the way he moves with confidence in who he is and what he wants.

He grips my upper arms with both hands, tells me to flex, then squeezes my biceps.

"Are we going to arm wrestle?" I tease.

"I'm doing all the things I could never do before," he says so matter-of-factly. "Now, sit up." I oblige, taking the opportunity to scale my hands down his smooth back, squeezing the tight bands of muscle at its base, kissing his neck and shoulders, every little freckle that's tormented me over the years.

"Your skin's so nice," I murmur, warm like honey and tastes like spice. "You taste so good."

Chris juts his hips forward so his hard-on strains against my own. I'd like to go down on him, but he seems to want to keep our touching above the belt, so we make out like that for a while, him on top of me, me on top of him, scissored side by side. Chris likes to get a little rough, grappling me into submission. He still has the ability to pin me every time, but here's the secret: I let him. Chris's door doesn't have a lock, so even though it's closed, there's a slight danger of getting caught, which makes it that much sexier and forbidden.

After what seems like hours, my nerves are raw, my lips are swollen and tender, and my stomach has another hickey because it seems Chris really does want to devour me. I'm a little afraid to turn him loose on the boys.

"So... you really want to do it?" he asks, picking up from our earlier conversation. I wonder if he's been thinking about it this whole time. He's leaned on one elbow, staring at my chest while tracing one of my nipples in slow circles. It tickles a little, but I don't stop him. His golden hair is a mess of waves, his lips are plump, his skin ruddy and glowing. His confidence is dimmed only a little as he waits for me to respond.

"Only if you do." Having this conversation with anyone else would be completely mortifying, which makes me wonder how other couples get through their first time, perhaps by not talking about it.

"How?" Chris asks, placing a light kiss on the center of my chest.

"I think it involves our...." I nod to the downstairs department.

He pinches my nipple so hard that I cry out. "I know that, T. I mean, who does what?"

"I don't know. I figured I'd let you decide."

Chris is quiet at that. Strangely quiet. He looks like he's been called on in class and is trying to come up with the right answer. He licks his lips, and I watch the slow, careful path of his tongue, wishing to lean up and intercept it with my own, but he's deep in thought and it doesn't seem right to disturb him.

"What is it?" I ask, worried I've freaked him out again.

"Nothing. I'm just really turned on at the thought of it." He presses his boner against my thigh to let me know how aroused he is. My heart races at the prospect.

"You think we're too young?" he asks.

"For butt sex?" Chris nods. "I don't know. Maybe if we were talking about hooking up with strangers, but we've known each other forever."

"I think about it all the time." He rests his chin on my shoulder with his mouth turned toward my ear like it's a secret. He draws one finger along the inside of my arm, and I shiver down to my toes. I want to know all his secrets.

"Me too," I confess.

"I want to touch you," he says in a husky voice.

"You can."

He reaches for the button on my pants and unfastens it, plunges his hand inside, and grabs hold of my cock. I can sustain an erection for a pretty long time, one of my many marvels. In any case, this is some sort of record. My breath goes ragged as he strokes me up and down. I love the way he touches me. Possessively. Passionately. Like I belong to him. I moan and curl inward, gripping his back with one hand and the fabric of his comforter with the other. The wave builds toward its apex and my body is full of it, a thimble in a fire hydrant. I didn't think it possible, but this make-out session just got better. "Chris—"

"Cristian." Paloma cuts me off, her singsong voice coming from down the hallway.

"Shit," Chris mutters, and we both jump off the bed like our pants are on fire and grab our shirts off the ground. I button up my pants faster than you can say *hand-eye-coordination*. We're in the process of pulling on our shirts when Paloma opens the door, glances from me to him to me to him, down to Chris's raging boner straining against his shorts, and then over at mine.

"Biscuits are ready," she says and quietly backs away, shutting the door behind her.

"Shit," Chris whispers and starts to panic, pacing his room.

I grab his shoulders and give them a little shake. "Relax, Chris. Paloma's cool. She won't care."

"What?"

"Go downstairs, tell her we're together, and bring us back some food." I settle down in front of his television and adjust myself so my junk knows good times are over for now.

"Should I?" he asks, his mind likely working over all the possible outcomes.

"Yeah."

"Come with me." He nudges me with his foot. I remember the *Dr. Giggles* incident, when he made me come down with him to tell his parents what happened with the shower. He knew they wouldn't get too mad if I was there with him.

"Okay." I hop up while Chris rakes a comb through his hair like he's getting ready for a date, then freshens his pits with body spray.

"You look fine." And smell even better.

"I don't want to look sloppy."

"Like you just got done making out with your boyfriend." He gives me a look. "You don't." Except he totally does—all wild-eyed and flush-faced. I bet if I pressed my palm to his chest, I'd feel his heart still racing. *I did that to him*, I think with satisfaction.

It takes another five minutes for him to work up the nerve to go downstairs. When we do, Paloma is in the kitchen putting away dishes from the dishwasher. Chris and I sit down at the counter, and she retrieves the biscuits and sets them down in front of us without a word. Before Chris can grab for his, I push away the plate and give him a pointed look. He glares at me. He hates being separated from food.

"Paloma," he calls, because she's trying to pretend nothing's out of the ordinary.

"Yes?" she asks without turning.

"Theo's my boyfriend."

She sets the dish gently on the counter and crosses the kitchen to perch delicately on the stool across from us. "Theo's your... boyfriend?" She tilts her head, like maybe she didn't understand him and is giving him the chance to correct her English.

"Sí, mi novio. I'm gay, but Mom and Jay don't know yet."

"Oh." Her mouth makes a little O shape, and she says it again in a different key. "Oh."

"It's cool, though. I'm going to tell them."

"Yes," she says with a nod. "Yes, you should, Cristian. Soon."

"Very soon," he says.

"Okay, then I won't say anything about...." She glances between us, then smiles at Chris affectionately, the same smile he got earlier when he asked for his flaky biscuits.

He nods. "Gracias, Paloma."

"And you?" She looks at me. "Are you the gay too?"

I nod, suppressing a smile at the translation.

"Well." She points at the biscuits. "¿Tienes hambre?"

"Sí, muy, muy," Chris says, a grin breaking over his face. His Spanish, while not always grammatically correct, is adorable.

She slides them over, and we each eat our biscuits—already

buttered—while Paloma finishes putting away the dishes. As we're standing to go back upstairs, Paloma taps me on the shoulder. "Be good to him," she says to me in Spanish.

"Prometo."

"And change your shirt. That one's Cristian's. I know because I washed it yesterday."

I glance down to discover she's right.

# EIGHTEEN

# THE PART WHERE I PUNK OUT, YET AGAIN

After school the next day, I catch a ride with Ryanne to her cousin's house. On the way there, we talk about school—classes and workload, when we'll be taking the SAT's, and where we'll apply. Ryanne is in a similar situation to mine in that she has a couple of siblings, and her parents can't afford to help much. The conversation is pretty tame, and I figure I might as well get the elephant out of the room. Even though I'm guessing Ryanne doesn't give a shit about my sexuality, I need to state it just to, as Lt. Knox says, clear the air.

"Hey, you know about that picture, right? What's in Wooten's mouth?"

She glances over at me. "I heard something about it."

"So, I'm gay."

She nods. "Yeah, I kind of figured that already."

"Before the picture?"

She nods again.

"Is it because of my smile?"

She gives me a funny look. "No, I figured Chris was too."

I don't confirm it, because I'm not going to out him, even to

Ryanne. "Why would you think that?" I ask like it's the craziest thing ever.

"Something about that day in Sebastian. The way he was when you went under. And after. Like he didn't want to leave your side, and you were just sleeping on the beach. I know he's your best friend, but it was something deeper."

I marvel at that. "Isn't it funny how you can be so close to something, you don't even see it?"

She smiles. "Yeah."

Then I get to thinking about Chris and how, if he's my boyfriend, then I really don't have any friends left. My sister's cool but not always that easy to talk to. There's something about Ryanne I really click with. Kismet.

"I don't have a lot of friends," I tell her.

"I'm your friend."

I smile at that. It's kind of exactly what I wanted to hear. "Cool."

She glances at me over the tops of her sunglasses. "I don't know if you remember, but you asked me to go with you to Plan Z."

It's kind of awesome she remembers that and still wants to go with me as a friend. "Yeah, I want you to. I think I'm going to enter."

"As a contestant?"

"Yeah. I try not to think about it too much. If I do, I might punk out."

"You nervous?"

"Yeah."

"About the tricks or something else?"

"I don't know, but since coming out, I feel like I have this responsibility or something. Like I'm less a person and more a figurehead. This is what a gay kid looks like eating his lunch or walking down the hallway, smiling at his teachers. Or this is how a gay kid pulls off a kickflip. It's kind of weird. Maybe I'm a narcissist and no one really gives a shit. Just, the thought of being in front of all those people is already pretty terrifying, and if I screw up, then what if the bros are like, 'yeah, he sucks because he's gay'? Seems like the stakes are higher or something."

She tilts her head thoughtfully, and I worry I've overshared. That was a lot to unload all at once, more than I even realized I was holding on to.

"I can see why you'd be freaked out," she says. "But what if you're this really talented skater, who happens to be gay and has the courage to compete against some real ballers? I mean, those punks judging you either don't have the balls or the skills to do that."

I nod. "That's a good way of looking at it."

"Haters gonna hate, Theo. If people have a problem with you being gay, fuck them. That's their problem, not yours."

"Punk rock," I tell her and give her fist a bump where it rests on the steering wheel. She smiles. Ryanne has a good attitude, and she's so laid back about everything. I should ask her advice more often. "Hey, how's your sister?"

"She's a mess...." Ryanne tells me how they've checked her into rehab—I'd heard as much—and she's not handling it well. She doesn't want to see them, and when she does, she's hateful and bitter. "It's like she doesn't want to get better. And my parents are spending all this money. It's really frustrating."

"That sucks."

"Yeah, and meanwhile I'm working my ass off to save up for school and get good grades. I know it's selfish, but I'm sick of her getting all their attention and resources."

"Squeaky wheels, man."

"And she hates me, Theo. I mean, *hates* me. She thinks I'm this goody-goody suck-up. Trust me, I'm not, but that's how she sees it."

I think about my own sister and how we don't always see eye to eye, but I know she has my back. I hope it stays that way. I wouldn't want to be on her bad side.

"It probably has more to do with how she feels about herself," I tell Ryanne. "It's hard being the screwup of the family. Hopefully she'll get better and get over it."

Ryanne vents a little more about it, and I try to offer help where I can, wishing I could do more to help her out, but maybe listening is enough for now. She pulls into a subdivision that used to house military families during World War II. It's modest by West Palm comparison, but it's tidy and well-kept. It looks like the kind of neighborhood where the men spend their weekends mowing the lawn because taking care of your yard is a source of pride and not an inconvenience.

Ryanne pulls up to a small, boxy house the color of a Creamsicle. She goes up to knock on the door while I check out the Accord parked in the driveway. Looks even better in person, all sleek and shiny. The rims are customized too, which is a nice bonus.

Ryanne introduces me to her cousin, Rob. I ask him some questions—How does it run? How long have you had it? Anything wrong? Rob says it belonged to an elderly neighbor who hardly ever drove it, and he bought it off her when she got too old to drive. Mechanically it's solid, he says, and I can see for myself how it looks. He shows me the stereo system and a couple of subwoofers in the trunk, which is a nice little add-on. I ask him if I can take it for a test drive, and he agrees. I climb in, and the seat's already kicked back to fit my long legs. Ryanne was right about the headroom. It's pretty spacious. I adjust the mirrors, even though they're mostly good, then get a little nervous because this is the first time I've ever driven alone and what if I, like, hit a mailbox or something? I pull out, taking it extra slow. Rob asks Ryanne if I have my license, and I pretend I didn't hear him.

In the actual driving of it, I do fine. I like how it handles, not a boat like Chris's Volvo, where I'm always worried I'm taking the turns too fast and going to clip someone or hit a curb. This car turns on a dime. I reach an empty straightaway where the subdivision butts up against a canal. I floor it and appreciate its get-up-and-go. Not bad for a compact car.

Back in the driveway, I ask Rob his price. He gives me the same amount listed on Craigslist. Ryanne lowers her glasses to look at him, clears her throat a little. Rob shakes his head at her.

"Since you're a friend of Ryanne's, I'll knock off $500."

Luckily his price is just about what I have. My dad would probably want me to play hardball, but that's not really my style. I looked the car up already, and it's a good deal no matter which way you slice it. I pull out my bankroll and count off the cash in hundred-dollar bills and hand it over to him.

"Sweet," he says and goes back inside to get the title to transfer over to me, along with the paperwork. The keys are already in my pocket.

I didn't even realize my hands were trembling when Ryanne grabs hold and does an excited little dance. "Congratulations!"

"Yeah, thanks for hooking us up and for the friend-of-a-friend discount." I'm elated and nervous at the same time. I can't believe I just dropped my life savings on a car, but damn, it does feel good. *My car.*

She smiles. "Don't forget about our date to Plan Z."

"I won't. But can I drive?"

"Sure."

"And bring Chris? I kind of told him I'd go with him too."

Ryanne smiles and shakes her head in mock displeasure. "Two-timing me already, Wooten?"

I don't even need to answer her because I'm sure my smile gives me away.

I DRIVE THE CAR HOME THAT SAME DAY, PULL INTO OUR DRIVEWAY, AND decide the first thing I need to do after showing it off to my mom and sister is wash, wax, and detail it. I'm out front vacuuming the inside when Chris gets back from surfing.

"Nice wheels," he comments.

"Thanks, Boss." I climb out of the back seat and take him in. He's wearing one of those distressed shirts, so worn through it's practically see-through, board shorts, and flip-flops, carrying the surfboard he named Baby Blue.

"Are your parents home?" I ask, kind of hoping they're not.

"Yeah, they worked from home today."

"Bummer, dude."

"I told them. After school."

"Yeah? How'd they take it?"

"Pretty good. There were some lectures about safe sex. My mom wants me to write a five-paragraph essay on the importance of using condoms, including blowjobs. Think that prompt will be on the SAT?"

"Blowjobs too, huh?" Dave and I were pretty careful, but it never hurts to be 100 percent sure. The risk is low, but it's still a risk. "I should get tested, just to be safe."

Chris nods. "I didn't tell them about us. I will. I was just hoping to give them some time to adjust."

"It's cool." I haven't told my mom or sister about Chris either, but I'm pretty sure my mom has figured it out. She gets a little smile on her face whenever I mention hanging out with him.

"They're flying me out to Cali this weekend," Chris says.

"That's good."

"Yeah, but I wanted to spend the weekend with you, practicing for Plan Z."

"I'll stick to the regimen."

Chris did some research online and listed combos he thinks the judges will like. He's laid out all the tricks I need to master and where the best spots to practice them are, including the skate park where the competition will be held, which is fine, but it almost feels like cheating. I appreciate the thought behind the design, but I find skate parks a little condescending. The curbs are all smooth and rounded, and the concrete is softer with these tire-tread textures in between stations, like we're toddlers on the playground. Part of the thrill of skateboarding is the fear of getting hurt and pulling off stunts on structures that were never meant to be shredded. Also trespassing.

"I expect you to slay," Chris reminds me. He thinks I'm not taking it seriously. I definitely am, even more so than he knows. In a way, it's my coming out as a skater who shreds—hopefully—and is also gay.

Chris offers to help me out with the car, and I take him up on it. He shines up the interior while I take a toothbrush to all the cracks and grooves to get out the dirt and dust. Chris makes fun of my OCD and asks if we can do his car next.

"Your car needs a power washer."

Once the inside is gleaming, we get to work on the outside. I "accidentally" spray him with water, hoping he'll take off his shirt. Predictably, he does, taking his time to stretch his arms and really preen for me. I ask him with a wink if he has wax in his shed, and he catches my drift. We end up making out in there like the horny teenagers we are—all sloppy and frenzied, grabbing at whatever we can with our hands and mouths without completely dropping our drawers, worried one of our moms is going to see the car out there only half-washed and get curious about where we've gotten off too. Sure enough, I hear my mom calling my name from my bedroom window, and when Chris and I emerge, him holding the towels and me holding the car wax, she gives me the all-knowing eyebrow and points to the street, where my dad's Tahoe is parked on the curb.

"Your dad's here," she calls. "He wants to see you."

"Shit," I say to Chris, getting all weak-kneed and jellified thinking he's here because he finally saw that damn picture and has come to confront me about it.

Chris lays a hand on my shoulder and squeezes. "You want backup?"

I straighten up and steel my resolve. "No, I got this."

"I'll finish washing the car for you."

"Rain check on the wax?" I ask.

Chris just shakes his head and smiles. "You betcha."

I put my shirt back on and climb the stairs to our apartment super slow, consider bailing a few times or faking an illness, then chide myself for being such a wiener. When I enter the kitchen, my sister's handing my dad a Coke and my mom's making herself busy at the kitchen sink. My dad sits at the kitchen table where we normally eat, looking large and imposing in the small space, kind of like an intruder. I glare at my sister, thinking she's the one who tipped him off, but she lifts her hand and makes a pointing motion behind it, directed at our mom.

*Et tu, Brute?*

"Your mom says you have something to tell me," Dad says,

confirming the traitor. He looks tired and worn-out, like he hasn't been sleeping well, or maybe he was out drinking the night before and this is how he looks the day after—he still goes on benders from time to time. His skin is paler than normal and hangs off his face kind of haggard-like. He looks straight-up old. I feel a little bad for him.

"We have some errands to run," Mom says and grabs Tabs by the arm. Mom won't look me in the eye, sealing her guilt.

"Maybe we should—" Tabs starts to say, and my mom cuts her off with a look. Mom plucks up her purse from the counter and blows me a kiss. They whirl out of the kitchen in five seconds flat, leaving me alone with my father, who looks a little put out by this impromptu visit, like he should be charging by the hour.

"So?" Dad leans back in the chair, legs spread wide, an expectant look on his face. Something about his posture and his almost bored expression makes me think my mom didn't clue him in all the way, just arranged this visit in the hopes I'd tell him myself.

I search for the words to share the news with him in a way that's not such a shock to the system, the perfect sentiment that will convey it has nothing to do with him and everything to do with me, that I'm not just doing this to upset him or rebel. It's just the way it is.

I open my mouth. What comes out is, "I bought a car." I plaster a huge, fake smile on my face.

Dad's eyebrows raise, and he frowns a little, like that news alone probably didn't warrant a trip all the way out here. "Yeah? Well... let's see it."

He stands, and I wonder *Could it really be this easy?* I lead him outside, where there's more room for the both of us to breathe. Chris is toweling off the car, still shirtless, looking mouthwatering and delicious. *My boyfriend is soooo hot.* My lower half starts acting up, so I avert my eyes and focus on my dad instead.

"You remember Chris," I say.

Chris comes over and shakes my dad's hand, looks to me for a sign. I shake my head slightly. My dad nods at Chris like nothing's amiss.

"You need me?" Chris asks, code for, do I want him to stay?

"Nah, I'll finish up here."

"Cool." He tosses the towel into a pile with the rest, throws his wet shirt over one shoulder, and grabs his board where he set it down in the grass. "Catch you later, Mr. Wooten," Chris says with an air of cockiness I could never pull off in talking to a friend's parent.

My dad circles the car, inspecting the body like he's looking for a cavity. "How much you pay for it?" he asks. I tell him, and he nods. "Not a bad price. You going to take me for a ride?"

I grin at that and unlock the doors with my key fob. Dad climbs into the passenger seat and comments on the headroom. "Bigger on the inside than I expected."

I back out of the driveway and take him on a tour of the neighborhood. Dad asks more questions about the car—how many miles, who I bought it from, whether it's had an oil change lately. At one point he turns to me and goes, "Your mother teach you how to drive?"

I shake my head. "Chris."

"Is that legal?"

I shrug. "Not really."

Dad shakes his head and harrumphs. "I could have taught you, Theo."

"It's cool, Dad. I know you're busy." Too little, too late, I guess.

"Well, all you had to do was ask," he says with irritation. If I begged and pleaded like my sister, he might have taken me out once or twice, but that's not my style. It's better to not need him than risk getting rejected. Maybe that's my own shortcoming. Pride or whatever.

"Quite frankly, I'm a little surprised to see you after that stunt you pulled the last time."

Of course he'd bring it up when we're both trapped in the car.

"Yeah, I wasn't feeling too great," I tell him, technically not a lie. "Did you get my text?"

"I don't consider texts a legitimate apology. And you could have at least come back to the table to let us know you were leaving."

I take a deep breath and let it out through my nose. "Sorry, Dad." I consider telling him about my anxiety and occasional panic attacks, but then he might ask more questions as to why, and I definitely don't want our conversation to veer into that territory while I'm driving.

"I figured you'd get the hint I was still angry when I didn't send any birthday money," he says.

I actually hadn't noticed—the drama of What's in Wooten's mouth kind of overshadowed everything else. "I figured it was because I got a job," I say, making up an excuse on the fly.

"Mowing lawns makes you financially independent, huh?"

I clench my jaw so I won't be tempted to argue with him. I want this to go as smoothly as possible.

"You know, I hear from your sister pretty regularly," he says. "I'm assuming your cell phone still works."

I nod. "I've been busy with work, I guess. And school."

"How's that going?"

I give him a rundown of my schedule. Dad seems impressed by all the AP classes I'm taking. I also have an above A average thanks to the weighted grades. It kind of goes along with my OCD and perfectionist tendencies.

"Sounds like you'll be starting college as a sophomore."

"Yeah, probably."

"Keep up those grades and you might have a shot at med school. Or dental?" he says hopefully.

I like working with my hands, but not in a life-or-death way or an in-your-mouth kind of way. "That's pretty far off, Dad. I don't really know what I'm into yet. One semester at a time, you know?"

"And soccer? You change your mind about that. Plenty of colleges recruit, you know."

We both know I'm not good enough to get recruited at the collegiate level. "Like I said, I'm more into skateboarding now. There's a competition coming up that I'm entering."

"Oh yeah?" he asks like he's interested.

I tell him about it, listing some of the pro skaters who will likely be there, even though he probably wouldn't know them by name. I explain the different events and what I'll be competing in. He asks more questions, so I give him a rundown of some of the tricks, using the most basic of terms.

"And there are people who do this professionally?" he asks.

"Yeah, they help sell stuff—skateboards, sodas, clothes.... The point, I guess, is to look like a badass while wearing a certain shoe or skating a certain board, drinking whatever energy drink they're trying to push. Kind of like sports endorsements."

"You think you're good enough to do that?"

"I don't know. Chris thinks so, but he's kind of like my dad sometimes." I freeze, hoping he doesn't take it the wrong way. There's really no right way to take it, though. "Just in the way he's always telling me to try harder, reach my potential and all."

"I see," Dad says, not missing the implication. "Pro skateboarding is reaching your potential, huh?"

I chuckle like he made a joke, even though that's not quite the tone of his voice. "Anyway, the competition is in a couple weeks. You should come check it out, see what I've been up to the past couple years."

"Yeah, I'll do that." He rubs his hand over the dashboard of the car. "I remember my first car—an '84 Camaro, cherry red with pinstriping. Looked amazing, but it was only a four-cylinder. Didn't have much get-up-and-go. I didn't know much about cars then."

I glance over to see him smiling sheepishly. I appreciate his honesty. My dad hardly ever admits when he was wrong, about anything. "Oops," I tell him.

"Yeah, oops." He chuckles at that, and it's nice to see a more laid-back version of my dad. I bet he used to be a lot more fun before adulting got him so down.

When we arrive back at my house, I realize we've gone a whole twenty minutes without arguing, and it almost makes me feel hopeful that there might be a space we can both occupy amicably.

"I don't know what to do with the Range Rover now," Dad says when we're both standing in the driveway. "I guess I'll have to sell it."

"Tabs still wants it. She'll be getting her license soon, and I'd rather not have to share my car with her." I don't say this to him, but Tabs isn't the best at sharing.

"You think she can handle it?"

I don't know what he means by it, but I nod enthusiastically. "She's got a few more months to practice, but she'll be fine when the time comes."

"Well, if you think so." Dad stares at me, and I know I should just tell him—man up and get it over with. But do I really want to ruin this moment by coming out to him right now in my driveway? Maybe we should have a few more visits like this one, and then I can come out.

While I'm stalling, Dad's phone rings. He pulls it out of his pocket, tells me it's Susan and that he has to take it. He drifts over toward his Tahoe while their conversation veers into argument territory. My dad pinches the bridge of his nose and talks through his teeth. *Been there, done that*, I think. Makes me feel a little better that I'm not the only one who can provoke that reaction from him. Meanwhile I inspect the rims on my car, making sure Chris didn't miss any grease spots.

Dad calls me over, his hand over the phone. "Was there anything else you needed, Theo?" The irritation is back in his voice, like he has a million patients in the waiting room and I'm taking up more than my allotted time.

"No, Dad, I'm good."

"All right, then, see you soon."

He walks over to the driver's side while fussing into the phone. I watch his Tahoe pull away and round the corner, out of sight. I pull out my phone and think about texting him "I'm gay." Just keep it as simple as that, but knowing how my dad feels about text apologies, that would probably be the worst way to come out to him.

Instead I text him the details of the Plan Z competition and tell him I hope he can make it.

Looks like I chickened out again.

# NINETEEN
## EXIT ASSHOLE DAVE

When my mom and sister get home that evening. I tell them, politely, to butt out.

"He's waited sixteen years to hear about it," I say. "He can wait a little longer."

I also tell Chris about punking out with my dad. His response: "It's cool. You'll do it when you're ready."

Like, never.

Over the next few days, Chris and I prowl around town for prime skating terrain, spending a few hours at the skate park to appease him, but significantly more time in places like Tropical Smoothie and BOA and random drainage ditches, where I feel a little freer and more spontaneous, where I can try out crazy combinations without worrying I'll look stupid in front of my colleagues. Chris films me with his phone and says he's going to cut up the videos and upload them to YouTube in preparation for my big debut. I'm a little worried What's in Wooten's mouth will follow me to a YouTube channel, but there's only so much I can stress about. My top priority for now is not looking like a total amateur at Plan Z.

"Homework assignment, Wooten," Chris says to me Thursday night before we part. He's heading out to Cali in the morning to visit his dad for a long weekend, leaving me to my own devices for a few days. "That two-story rail outside of BOA—I want you to be able to slide it any which way—front, back, nose, tail, and board."

"Grinds are so basic." I much prefer the aerial tricks, preferably over long flights of stairs. I like the "wow" factor.

"Grinds show off your technical ability, and judges love them. Plus, the skate park has a hell of a lot more rails than it does stairs. Curbs too. You should work on your mounts and dismounts. Transitions matter," he says with emphasis, because I'm starting to nod and smile like I do whenever he goes into boss mode. "For the three-step flight of stairs, I'd practice your nollie laser flip. That's a crowd pleaser. Save the nightmare flip for the finale."

"Yes, Boss."

"I want your no-comply's so smooth it looks like you're moon-walking."

"Are you done?" I'd rather our goodbye kiss not be interrupted by Chris's verbal diarrhea.

He smiles and cups my face in both hands, plants a big sloppy kiss on my mouth for fun, then comes in again for something softer and more meaningful. "Wish me luck," he says.

"Good luck." I pinch his ass for a little extra, and he yelps and swats at me.

The next morning between classes, I watch on my phone as Chris makes his transcontinental flight, arriving safely in California by midafternoon. He sends me text updates about his great coming-out weekend. Apparently his mom hinted to his dad at what was going on, so his dad was prepared with some celebratory festivities, including a fancy dinner at Chris's favorite restaurant and night out at a gay nightclub owned by a client of his dad.

I'd be lying if I said I wasn't jealous, but even more than that I'm glad Chris and his dad have the kind of relationship where coming out only brings them closer. That's pretty damn special. Even though I've envied Chris's blessed life over the years, I want only the best for him. He deserves it.

On Sunday night it's gotten pretty late at the BOA. Most of the skate rats have all gone home for the night, and it's just me and a couple of other guys. Word has spread that I'm entering Plan Z, and like Chris, everyone has an opinion on which tricks are my best and which ones need work. Dave is there, too, but he hasn't tried talking to me since *the incident*. There was another scandal at Sabal Palm High, a tryst between an assistant coach and a senior. What's in Wooten's mouth has faded a bit.

I'm taking a break between sets when Dave approaches me. I briefly consider getting on my skateboard and jetting home or else going in for another round, but I decide instead to stand my ground and face him once and for all, even better since Chris isn't here. Dave's been giving me puppy-dog looks in the hallway and joining in the chorus of supporters when I'm skating. I know he wants to make up.

"I heard you're going to compete in Plan Z," Dave says, keeping a couple feet of distance between us. Like a shamed dog, he also won't make eye contact.

"Yup."

"You're going to murder it."

I shrug. The silence is deafening.

"I've been trying to call you," he says.

"Yeah, I know."

"You read my note?"

"No." I ended up burning it, which is way better than sticking pins in it. In any case, I found it to be therapeutic.

"I fucked up, Theo."

I nod, unable to find it in me to accept his apology. There's a wall about ten feet high between us, with razor wire, and I can't scale it.

"Can you kick my ass to make me feel better?" Dave asks.

I'm not built that way. All the anger and frustration I felt toward Dave has morphed into this tough little nut of bitterness, candy-coated with regret. When I think about what he did, I feel sick and weak and betrayed, so I try not to think about it at all. "What you did was so uncool, Dave. I don't even have the words for it. And I know a lot of words."

"You didn't deserve that."

"No one deserves that."

"I'm sorry, Theo. I was getting some things off my chest to one of the guys, and your name slipped out. He didn't believe we were hooking up, so I sent him that picture. I was stupid. And an asshole. Everything you ever said about me is true."

I don't like how he's making me out to be the asshole, like all he could do was live up to my expectations. Besides, that was before I even knew him.

"You played me twice," I tell him. "First in taking that picture without me knowing, and then in sending it around."

"If I could take it back, I would. I swear."

For a moment there's nothing between us but the sticky sounds of wheels on pavement. I wish I could forgive him—I really do—but he totally screwed me over, and just like some things can't be unseen, some deeds can't be undone. Whenever I look back on how I came out, I'll think of that goddamned picture and how Dave stole it from me, like that scene in Indiana Jones where the guy gets his heart ripped out and the ripper presents it to the crowd like it's some kind of prize. I was a trophy for Dave. Whether or not it was his intention, that's how it feels.

"I thought we could be friends," I say to Dave. "I wanted to, but now when you're around, I just feel...." I search for the word. "Unsafe."

Dave nods, and I glance over at him, feeling that familiar tug inside me. In a way it'd be so much easier to forgive him. I really did like hanging out with him.... But he's not trustworthy, and I'll never risk getting played by him again.

"I just wanted to tell you to your face I'm sorry," he says.

I'm afraid to say anything that will give the impression he's allowed back into my life, so I just stand there in a fortress of silence.

Dave sighs. "Good luck at Plan Z. I'll be cheering for you."

I watch him walk away, feeling massive amounts of emptiness and regret—for the friendship we lost and the one we could have had.

Goddamned Asshole Dave.

CHRIS MAKES ME TRAIN THAT WHOLE WEEK AT THE SKATE PARK. HE even wears a whistle, tube socks, and a headband to keep the sweat off his forehead. He means for it to be funny, and it works. He looks so ridiculous that I can't even get mad at him when he pushes me to work harder or land a trick with more finesse, or when I bust my ass, to get back up.

There are a lot of shorties at the skate park who want to learn my tricks, so we take some time each afternoon giving them pointers. Needless to say, we have a sort of following by the end of the week. Chris talks me up, telling the kids to come out on Saturday for the competition and cheer for me. I can't believe it, though, when we show up on Saturday morning and there's a crowd of middle schoolers all chanting my name. Ryanne is with us, and she gushes over how adorable it all is, and Chris ruffles my hair. We already registered online by sending in Chris's video of me skating, so all I have to do is show my ID and get a number. There are a few members of Plan Z's pro team already testing the concrete—T-Bo Hendrix, Austin Schriller, and Javi Martinez. Seeing them shred gets my gut doing a spin cycle, and I remember to breathe deeply and concentrate on the steady sound of my wheels on pavement as I warm up.

I scan the crowds to see if my dad is here. Nope. I check my phone, and there are no messages or calls from him either. I see my mom and sister in the stands and wave. My mom calls my name and blows kisses. It's embarrassing but also sweet. Chris notices me scoping out the bleachers and asks me who I'm expecting. I tell him, and he shakes his head. Then we drop it. I can't let it distract me. I've got to focus.

The competition is spread out over the entire park, with sections cordoned off with metal blockades. Bleachers have been set up for viewing, but most of the people we know are clustered around the blockades up front. Plan Z was here the day before setting up proper half- and quarter-pipes for vert skating, so most of the skate park structures are reserved for park. The competition is set up in heats, where the top twenty in points continue on to the second round, and then the top five go into the finals, which are televised live on Plan Z's web channel. By noon I've made it into the top twenty, along with the pro and semipro skaters and a few guys who must not be from around here because I've never seen them before. After a lunch of chili dogs—Chris's suggestion—we do our second heat, and I bust my ass on the laser flip but kill it on the nightmare flip. I make up for the biff in grinds, which Chris was right, the judges seem to score higher than the less technical tricks.

When the news comes through that I've made it through the second heat, I can't stop smiling. Ryanne hugs me and Chris smacks my ass. Our gaggle of middle schoolers all cheer when the announcer calls my name, and I jog down the line where they're hanging on the metal guard rails like the little street urchins they are. I slap all their hands, and they go totally nuts. Some of our skater friends are here and they give me props as well, but there's something about the littler kids' blind admiration that strikes a chord. It's like their dreams haven't been sapped out of them just yet, and they're looking at me like if I can do it, then they can too. I guess that's what it's like to be a role model.

"You came with your own fan club?" a man asks me. I saw him before at the registration table. I noticed him because he seemed overdressed for the occasion—slacks and fancy dress shoes, a long-sleeved collared shirt open at the top, and hair that was once carefully styled but has since melted in the heat.

"Local kids," I tell him.

"Are you local?"

"Yeah."

He seems to perk up at that. "You must know the area pretty well, then?"

"I do."

"Then I'm in luck." He offers his hand for me to shake. "I'm Vincent Longorio with Plan Z. I do marketing and arrange the skate sessions. I have a few guys getting ready to do a Dirty South tour...." He pauses. "You know what Dirty South means?"

I laugh because this guy is, like, ten years older than me. I'm not sure if Dirty South is a new term to him, or if he thinks it will be for me. "Like rap music from the south?"

"Exactly," he says with a smile. "We're taking a road trip through the South during winter break. We were thinking of going straight to Miami from Daytona, but if you'd be willing to be our tour guide, I'd love to stop in here for a day or two."

"Totally," I say, then think to ask, "What does a tour guide do?"

"Shows the crew where the best skate places are. You eighteen?"

"No, sixteen."

Vincent nods. "We'd need your legal guardian to sign off on it. You'll probably be in some of the footage. We'd pay you for your time. And who knows, if you do well, Plan Z is always looking for talented and photogenic youth."

I smile, feeling a little bashful. "Yeah, cool," I tell him. He asks me for my number, and I give it to him. Then he hands me his business card, and I tuck it into my wallet. Chris comes up while we're exchanging information, and I introduce him to Vincent as my boyfriend.

"Boyfriend?" Vincent asks, his eyebrows hitching up a little like it's a scandal.

"Is that a problem?" I ask, keeping my tone neutral.

"Not at all." His smile widens. "We're a very inclusive group."

"The finals are starting soon, T," Chris says, commanding my attention. He gives Vincent a hard look, and I chalk it up to Chris's territorial nature. Whether it's surfing at the beach or skating, he's always a little suspicious of outsiders, especially those who end up selling photographs or footage of a session without permission—it happens pretty often.

I grab my board and wait in line behind the other contestants. I'm slated to go last, which is good because I want to see what tricks the others pull off before my run. Now it's just the pros and me—all of them execute their runs more or less flawlessly, with a lot of style and charisma. T-Bo sends his skateboard under the rail while jumping over the top of it and landing on the other side. It's so simple, yet flashy at the same time, that I kick myself for not thinking of it first.

And then it's my turn to go. I decide to abandon my routine, which feels stale by now, and just go with whatever feels right. I don't know if it's the crowd's energy or knowing that I have nothing to lose, but everything comes so easily—every grind, kickflip, and ollie feels effortless, like my board is an extension of my body. I nail all my best tricks, some of them twice, so that by the time the buzzer goes off, I'm sweating and breathless and totally amped because even if I didn't score the highest in points, I really did kill it.

"Dude," Chris keeps saying over and over as he embraces me in a big, sweaty bro-hug. Ryanne bounces and claps and doesn't know our skater lingo, so she just keeps saying, "Wow, Theo, that was amazing." My mom and sister sandwich me in a hug, and Tabs asks me if I'm famous now.

I end up coming in second, just shy of first in points behind Austin Schriller because of his wicked 720 flip I've never seen anyone land in real life. Kudos to him. He comes up to me afterward and asks if I'm with anyone, and it takes me a minute to realize he means if I've signed with someone. "No," I tell him.

"You should talk to Vincent," he says. "We could use someone like you on our team."

As if being summoned, Vincent materializes a moment later. "I'm going to call you in a couple weeks about being our guide, Theo." He says it almost like it's a warning. "You do well in that, we might have room for one more on our team."

"Yeah, sure, that'd be great." I'm still reeling from the fact that I got through the competition while keeping my rep intact. The chance at a sponsorship is a total bonus and not anything I was expecting.

The second-place prize is $1000, which couldn't come at a better time, because I owe my mom for putting me on her car insurance. As we pack up to leave, I scan the crowds one more time, thinking it would have been cool if my dad had showed up.

Well, there you have it.

# TWENTY

# SEBASTIAN

We go out for pizza afterward—it's my go-to cuisine after grilled cheese. Then we say goodbye to Tabs and my mom and drop Ryanne off at her house. When it's just Chris and me back in my car again, he says with a little grumble in his voice, "Guys are always giving you their number."

"Who's that?"

"That Plan Z guy. He was totally hitting on you."

Vincent? I just saw it as him being friendly—maybe even a little charming—in order to get what he wanted. "You think he's gay?"

"He was totally checking you out, and not in the sponsorship-potential way. I liked it better when I only had to worry about girls liking you. Guys are dogs."

I agree with him on that, but Vincent seemed pretty business-oriented. "He was pretty old, Chris. Pushing thirty."

"Gay life doesn't have the same age-difference rules."

"Gay life? Is that like Salt Life?" I tease. All of a sudden Chris is the expert on being queer? I swear it's the same as when I taught him how to ollie back in seventh grade, and then suddenly he was the authority on skating. "I'm pretty sure the law doesn't give a shit if you're gay or not. And besides, he should know my boyfriend is the jealous type who will kick his ass if he tries anything."

Chris is quiet for a moment then goes, "Am I *that* guy?"

I glance over to see him experiencing a rare moment of self-doubt. "I don't know. Are you?"

Chris shakes his head as though ridding himself of the persona. "Sorry about that, T. I've just waited so long for this. I'm a little worried someone's going to swoop in and steal you away."

It's funny to me that Chris would stress about that. If only he'd been in my head the past year or so, he'd know he has nothing to fear. "Consider my ass bolted to the floor like the furniture in Juvie."

He smiles. "Cool."

Chris opens his legs so his knees are spread wide and adjusts his balls. I wonder if it's for my benefit. I have the urge to swerve off the road and park in the nearest secluded spot and demonstrate the skills I learned from Dave, but I've heard too many stories about kids getting caught by the police with their pants down and being brought into the station for their parents to come claim them. I'm not getting charged with indecent exposure at the tender age of sixteen or worse, having to make that call to my mother.

"You have to work tomorrow?" Chris asks.

"No, I took off. Why?"

"I want to go to Sebastian."

"When? Tonight?"

"Yeah," he says in a deep, throaty voice.

"To surf?"

Chris hums, giving himself away.

"You bringing your tent?"

He chuckles, deep and sexy. "Yeah. So... you want to come?"

"Yes, again and again."

Chris laughs. "Don't psyche me out, T."

I smile, loving that slow burn in the bottom of my groin, knowing whatever happens in Sebastian, it's sure to be memorable.

"Go easy on me, Boss."

He leans his head back against the seat rest and glances over at me with that cocky grin I adore. "No promises."

WE NEVER MAKE IT TO THE BEACH. THE SUN SET LONG AGO BY THE TIME we arrive at the campground in Sebastian. Chris builds the fire. I set up the tent. It's like it's always been, except I'm too keyed up. I can't calm my thoughts long enough to concentrate on any one thing, which makes setting up camp kind of scattered, with me forgetting basic things like making sure to anchor in the stakes. Then I have to force myself to be still and sit down next to Chris, so my anxiety doesn't spread like a brushfire to him.

Chris reviews the day, somewhat methodically, going over all the good rides the skaters had and all the biffs, each of their strengths and weaknesses. My strength, according to him, is making my tricks look easy. My weakness is not taking more risks because I haven't practiced a trick enough times. I actually have a target ratio of attempts vs. completions for any given trick before I'll go public with it. While Chris doesn't know the exact details, I think he suspects it.

Chris seems pretty serious about me getting a sponsorship, and despite his personal feelings toward Vincent, he agrees that hosting the Dirty South tour is my ticket to more exposure. Chris prattles on, and I get the sense he's nervous too, like he doesn't know how to begin this part—the big build-up. We're probably both overthinking it.

At a lull in the conversation, I reach over and nest my fingers in the back of his hair, scooting closer at the same time, so that when he turns, my mouth is there to receive him. Chris grabs my shirt and pulls me to him, starting out slow and letting it build. We're the only ones camping out here tonight, so there's no need to rush. No parents or housekeepers within a hundred-mile radius.

We make out by the fire on one of Chris's old comforters, taking breaks to add more wood, then coming together again. I can tell by the way he nips and paws at me that he's growing impatient. "Let's go inside," he says in a lustful, throaty voice. He goes over to the tent, fumbles with the zipper, holds the flap open, and shutters it behind us.

Inside the tent it's a little darker, lit only by the faint glow of the fire. We shed our clothes and roll around on the sleeping bags like puppies, groping each other with more urgency, wrestling like we used to, only with a different goal in mind. The air is sticky sweet with the smell of our sweat and desire. My erection is uncomfortably hard, leaky, and tender. Every time he brushes up against it, a thrill races through me that makes me shudder. When he leaves one area of my body for another, that part of me gets jealous and wants him back. Chris pins me on my back and grabs my cock firmly in one hand. I like the way it looks in his fist: fat, flush, and at the ready.

"Bend your knees," he says, and when I do, he touches my hole with his finger, tapping lightly, then pressing harder with his knuckle. "How's this?"

"Feels good."

He edges one finger inside me, and I squirm a little because it's a sensation unlike any other. I take a deep breath and marvel, *Chris is inside me.*

And then he isn't. I open my eyes to find him sitting back on his heels. He watches me with a hungry look in his eyes, but he makes zero moves toward me.

"I know that face," I tell him, sitting up. "Talk to me."

"Maybe we should wait." He licks his lips, and I lean in and place a gentle kiss on his mouth.

"For what?"

He rubs my shoulder. "I don't want to hurt you."

His concern is touching but unnecessary. "I'm a big boy, Chris. I can handle it."

"Maybe you should do me. I think I could take it better."

For some reason this rubs me the wrong way. "Really? Between the two of us, you think you can handle pain better?"

"This isn't a competition, T." He draws his hands through his hair, upset about it.

Everything is a competition with Chris, even when it isn't. "Well, I might inflict more pain, based on diameter and depth."

His mouth drops open. "Are you telling me in a really geeky way that my dick is small?"

I chuckle. "No, I'm telling you in a really geeky way your asshole is small." His brow furrows and he looks past me, so I try again. "Listen, I want to experience this with you. If you want to wait, that's fine. But I don't want the reason to be because you don't want to hurt me. I can take it. I want to take it."

I expect Chris to laugh at that, but he doesn't. Just sits there, stiff and unmoving, with a blank look on his face. I scoot around so I can kneel behind him and rub his shoulders, thinking how lucky I am to be touching him, to have the freedom to explore. My palms glide over his smooth skin, warm to the touch. The pads of my thumbs knead into his tense muscles while my mouth trails along his shoulder and up the slope of his delicious neck. His hair brushes along the ridge of my nose and tickles my nostrils.

"This is enough for me," I tell him, sorry for pressuring him at all.

I lean my cheek against his back, then reach around to comb through his chest hair, fondling his perky nipples with the tips of my fingers, then scaling down his muscular abs. I kiss the space between his shoulder blades and rub my nose against his skin, inhaling his scent. I try to angle my junk so I won't poke him in the back, but I really can't help it. He has that effect on me.

Chris grabs hold of my wrist and fills my palm with his thick cock. I stroke him lovingly. I want to make him feel better than he's ever felt before, to be the one to give him this feeling, with all my love and devotion.

"Whatever you want," I whisper into his ear. He moans and rocks back into me, then rises up to his knees. I drape myself on top of him, kissing the ridges of his spine until I reach his tailbone. He leans back into my lap, so I spread his asscheeks and let my cock flop against his crack, gliding slowly up and down, getting heated and antsy from the friction.

"Try me, Theo," he whispers. My stomach drops and my senses sharpen. I pause for a moment to make sure I heard him correctly.

"You sure?" I ask.

"Yeah, you go first."

I'm no longer in the mood to argue. My body only wants to keep on going. I finger his hole, poking gently with my fingertip, teasing, and testing to see how much pressure his muscle will allow before yielding. I just barely breach his hole and his muscle throbs against my fingertip.

"That's good," Chris says and stretches his arms forward to rest back on his heels. I love seeing him bow before me. Smooth skin and hard muscle curled in submission, giving me control.

"Do you like it?" I feel really unprepared for this part. I should have practiced on myself beforehand.

Chris hums in response, and I warm some lube on my fingertips and try again, going a little deeper this time. My other hand is splayed across his lower back, holding him steady while my finger penetrates him. I experiment, moving it slowly in and out, twisting a little, curling it. Chris rises to his knees and mutters "More, Theo," in a raspy voice. I add another finger, leaning on his back for leverage. We move like that for a while, sweating and growing increasingly agitated, but knowing we have to go slowly. My cock weeps and throbs for him, but I have to focus on Chris's needs.

"Let's do this," he says in a deep, ragged voice.

"Now?"

"Yeah, go for it."

I remove my fingers and prep myself with shaking hands, position myself at his entrance. *Shit, shit, shit* rattles through my brain like a runaway train as I nudge him with the barest amount of pressure, and he opens up like a morning glory. Chris rocks back into me, forcefully, perhaps thinking that will make it easier, then freezes. His whole body tenses as he tightens up around me. I freeze, afraid to move or even breathe and risk making it worse.

"Do you want me to take it out?" I ask him.

"No, just give me a minute."

He takes a few deep breaths, and I can tell he's uncomfortable, maybe even in pain. I know it's supposed to hurt, but I hope it's not too bad. I draw my hands down his rippling muscles and rub my thumbs over his tailbone to help him relax. He repositions himself, then drops back down with a grunt.

"Tell me what to do," I say to him.

"You're good. Just... stand by."

I brace myself against the ground with my knees while Chris rocks slowly back and forth, determining the depth and pressure. My body hums like a live wire, but my worry for him is more present in my mind. My gaze is drawn to the point where we're joined, still amazed that this is even happening. Awestruck.

"Take over," Chris says. I add more lube and grab hold of his hips. He grunts as I ease in deeper. I've never felt this close to a person before in my entire life, connected so deeply on so many levels. All I want is for him to feel good, cherished, and special.

"I love you," I whisper. He nods, back heaving with every breath. "Does it hurt?" I'm afraid of his answer.

"Yeah, but it's okay. I can handle it."

I'm nearly to the base now, and Chris groans so deeply, I feel the vibration in my balls.

"That's the spot, Theo. Keep doing that."

I angle in so that I'm hitting whatever feels so good to him. To me it's *all good*—every nerve ending being massaged in all the right ways. Pleasure cascading through me with every thrust. We hit the right beat—breathing, rocking, and grunting as one, unraveling together. Chris grabs hold of himself, jerking his fist along his shaft while I drive into him. My eyes roll back into my head, pleasure ballooning inside me like hot, spitting lava. I'm relieved when I hear Chris cry out that he's coming, because I can't hold out much longer.

Stars explode behind my eyes, and I flood the condom with my release while the last delicious tremor dances through me. I lean over and pant on his slick, strong back.

"Don't move," I tell him and gingerly pull out.

We collapse in a heap on our sleeping bags, bunched up and in disarray, sweating and breathless. Chris holds on to me like he doesn't want to let go, and the words fall from my lips between kisses.

"Thank you... for everything. I just...." My eyes get a little misty and my breath hitches, overwhelmed by it all. "I couldn't have done it... like that... with anyone else... I can't believe you let me."

He grips the back of my head and draws me to his chest so I can hear his rollicking heartbeat. "I love you too, Theo. I think I always have. Since that first day. The only way I could be happy was if you were happy too."

"Does it hurt?"

"Let's just say, you're getting the wet spot tonight."

I know why he did this, because he's always tried to protect me, even when I didn't think I needed it. It's what Chris does. He rolls over and scoots his ass against me so we're spooning. My mouth finds his shoulder and I rest it there, on his archipelago of freckles, soaking up his smell, the feel of him, the way his body fits against mine so comfortably. The sense of being whole in a way I only can with him.

We drift off for a while, curled in each other's arms. I'm breathing in his exhales, and then Chris is kissing me back from the brink of slumber, his mouth traveling down my chest while he massages my inner thighs with both hands, stirring me awake in more ways than one. He massages my balls and strokes my cock with amazing dexterity, making me twitch and moan and grip the fabric of the sleeping bags with both hands. I'm wide-awake now, strung out on sensation and eager for what comes next.

"Can I do you?" he asks.

"Yes." *And yes and yes....*

He pushes back on my knees and gives me the same preparation I gave him, only more tenderly, it would seem. The sensations escalate until I'm restless and bucking, worked into such a frenzy I'm begging him to get inside me.

"Say it again," Chris commands in a deep, throaty voice, towering above me like a god.

"Please."

He plunges into me. The stretch burns worse than any raspberry from skateboarding, like being split wide open, but it feels good too, and maybe it feels better because of the pain. A kind of sacrifice.

"More," I tell him, the same as he told me. More and more of him until there's no clear divide between us, like the moment after sunset when the horizon blurs and you can't tell where the ocean ends and the sky begins, when everything is blue.

Chris straightens his broad shoulders and yanks down on my thighs, tugging me to him, filling me up completely so there's no room in my body or mind for anything but him. I moan his name, and he seems to know how much I need him because he thrusts deeper than before, deeper than I thought possible, tearing me apart and pouring himself into me. In his expression is tenderness, everything we've shared, all those little jokes, arguments, and competitions, all our memories... I'd go through worse pain to share this with him because he is my person.

He leans down and kisses my forehead, tells me he loves me. I close my eyes and Chris takes hold of my cock, piloting us both to new heights.

To understand and be understood and trust someone so completely that there's nothing I wouldn't do for him. I come with the slightest provocation, easily and eager to please. Chris smiles smugly, taking all the credit, then turns his attention to his own needs. He quickens his pace, pumping me like a surfboard, snapping his hips. His thighs slap against my ass as he works my body to get himself off. His face is flushed, tongue poking out the corner of his mouth, the shark's tooth like a talisman around his arched neck. His lips part, making a sweet little O face. His eyebrows knit together as he calls out my name. I want to see that expression again and again, be the one who rattles his bones and makes him cry out.

He strains against me and I feel him finish inside me, his breathless moaning at the final thrust, his hesitation as he withdraws. I feel everything, including the loss when he's no longer inside me. Chris disposes of the condom and collapses on top of me like I'm a human mattress. For a few moments, the only sound is our ragged breath and the crickets buzzing outside our tent. My ass is raw and my bones ache and the pool of jelly that is my body slowly reforms in a new way.

"That was awesome," Chris says with unbridled exuberance.

"Yeahhh...." I slur the word like I'm drunk. I'm still suspended in the cloud of sensation, waiting for my mind to rejoin my body.

"Which did you like better?" He noses my shoulder, and it takes me a second to realize he means which position.

"Don't make me choose, Boss."

He chuckles, his voice thick and scratchy. "I love it when you call me that."

"I know you do."

I listen to his breathing, the steady rise and fall of his chest against mine, the heat and weight of him on top of me. I grip him to me with both arms, thinking how lucky we are. How amazing this is.

Then I think about Uncle Theo and what he must have endured in keeping his secret all those years. What Chris and I have is special, and I don't want to hide it. My relationship with my dad is important to me, but it has to be based on something real. The only way for him to know me is if I show him. Not who he'd like me to be, but who I honestly am.

"What are you thinking about?" Chris asks, laying his cheek on my chest like it's a pillow.

"I have to tell my dad."

"Whenever you're ready, I'm there."

"It might get ugly," I warn him.

"Ride or die, baby." He squeezes my thigh.

I sigh, swept up in all the emotions of the night, worried about what I'll say to my dad and how he'll react to it all. I talk a big game right now, but when faced with him, I might not have the guts to go through with it.

"Don't stress, T. Put that energy to good use and rub my back till I fall asleep."

I draw my hands down Chris's strong back, wondering how I'll ever manage to fall asleep with this big beefy blanket on top of me.

I wouldn't want it any other way.

# TWENTY-ONE

# OLD PEOPLE ARE THE WORST

"So, what now?" Chris asks. We surfed all morning and headed back to West Palm early. Now it's nearing lunchtime, and Chris is hungry.

"There's someone I want you to introduce you to."

"Awesome. Where we headed?"

"Paula's Pit Barbecue."

"They have the best potato salad," he says happily. I make a mental note to remember. The feeding and care of Christian Mitcham is my sacred duty.

I realize when we pull into Saint Ann's, both of us loaded down with contraband barbecue, that I might want to be a little subtler when breaking the nursing home rules. This time the woman at the front desk recognizes me, and only Chris has to produce his ID in order to get a visitor's badge. We hide the bags of food behind the counter, even though the whole lobby smells like a barbecue joint. As soon as they hand us the passes, we head for the elevator before they can call us back.

Upstairs, I find Uncle Theo in his room, sitting in a recliner watching what appears to be a Netflix original, and I wonder who set him up with the account and password, since I'm not sure he could navigate that sort of thing on his own.

"Uncle Theo," I call from the hallway where the door is slightly open. "Can we come in?"

"Who's that?" he asks, neck straining, and points at Chris.

"It's my boyfriend Chris." I step aside so Chris can pass in front of me.

"Who?" Uncle Theo stands as if to get a better look.

"Hi, Captain Wooten." Chris walks up to him and holds out his hand while I set the food on a small dining table. "I'm Chris. Nice to meet you."

"I know you," my uncle says stubbornly while grabbing on to Chris's outstretched hand. "Adam?"

Chris glances over at me with a questioning look, and I shrug my shoulders like, go with it.

"We brought food," I tell him. "Barbecue like the last time. You hungry?"

Uncle Theo makes his way over to the table using an aluminum cane for support. I've never seen it before now, so maybe he just uses it when he's alone in his room. He glances sideways at Chris like Chris might steal something while his back is turned. He's probably not used to having strangers in his apartment.

I check out his digs. Uncle Theo's suite is larger and homier than what I expected. The walls are painted a buttercup yellow with pictures hanging on the walls. There's an adjoining bathroom that looks a little more hospital-like with all the old people add-ons. There's also a bedroom where his Navy memorabilia and old family photographs are on display. After a quick survey, I start unpacking the food. Chris sits across the table from Uncle Theo, and the staring contest continues. Chris keeps glancing over at me for a sign, while Uncle Theo studies Chris like he's trying to memorize his face.

I present the food to my uncle, but he doesn't even acknowledge it.

"I like your place," Chris says, perhaps trying to put him at ease.

"What are you doing here?" Uncle Theo asks earnestly. He seems confused and a little upset. His mouth pulls down into a frown.

"Do you want me to leave?" Chris glances between the food and the door. Leaving barbecue on the table would be a near impossible feat for Chris.

"No," my uncle barks. "You stay right there, *Adam*."

Chris nods, and because he can't control himself around food, starts digging into our lunch. I eye the two of them, trying to read the situation. Uncle Theo's still not eating, just staring at Chris with a mixture of disbelief and suspicion.

"Uncle Theo, what's up?" Maybe this is something he needs to get off his chest.

"It's Adam," he says plaintively and points at Chris.

"Are you sure? He's pretty young. Looks more like Chris, my next-door neighbor. Maybe he reminds you of someone else?"

Uncle Theo's mouth moves but nothing comes out. I notice he's trembling. His eyes squeeze shut, and he shakes his head. Then he starts making the most terrible moaning noises.

I scoot my chair over to him and lay a hand on his shoulder. "Uncle Theo, what's wrong?"

"Adam, Adam...." He moans the name over and over again, more pitiful each time. It hurts my heart to hear him so distraught. Chris sets down his sandwich. His eyebrows pull together, and he too looks upset by it.

"Wait here with him," I tell Chris and jump up to find Gloria. I ask the floor receptionist for her, and she makes a call. A minute later I see Gloria come out of another resident's room, and I meet her halfway down the hallway.

"I think we upset him," I tell her. "I brought my friend with me, and he called him Adam and started crying."

Gloria nods. Her mouth turns downward. "He does that sometimes."

"Really?"

"We think Adam is a friend who died or lost touch. Your uncle's memories don't always go in order. The pain is very fresh."

Imagine reliving your greatest heartache over and over again like it just happened yesterday. "Jesus, that's awful," I tell her. She nods. "I tried telling him it wasn't him."

Gloria rests her hand on my arm. "I don't think arguing with him helps. It only confuses him more."

"Okay. What do we do then?"

"Just hold his hand and wait for it to pass."

When we get back to my uncle's room, I'm shocked to see Uncle Theo cradled in Chris's arms. He's still sobbing, and Chris just holds him there gently. Uncle Theo's cheek rests against Chris's shoulder. Chris's expression conveys the same warmth and compassion that made me trust him from day one. My heart blooms again for him now. Gloria smiles. Then her eyes alight on the contraband food, and she makes little clucking noises.

"This is far too much for you, Captain." She swoops in on his plate and portions some of the food back into their containers. "You have to think about your figure."

My uncle pulls himself away from Chris and blinks away his tears. He glances at the two of us, scowls at Gloria, and resumes his seat at the table. He pulls out the chair next to him a little and glances up at Chris, who takes the hint and sits down next to him. Gloria fusses over my uncle, making sure his utensils are lined up and the napkin is tucked into his collar. My uncle smoothes it down over his shirtfront, straightens up, and proceeds to eat his lunch as if nothing happened. Except, every now and again, he'll glance over at Chris and smile warmly or reach over to pat his arm.

We invite Gloria to eat with us, and she comments on how good the food is, and how she didn't know about Paula's before I introduced her to it. She says she's developed quite a taste for it, though her hips could probably do without. We chat easily about the goings on of Saint Ann's—there's a talent show coming up, and we tease Uncle Theo about his talent. He glowers at us. Not Chris, though. For Chris, he's all smiles. I tell Gloria about yesterday's skate competition. At one point she mentions Manuel in passing, and Uncle Theo points to the calendar on the wall, which has the seven days of a week with big red X's over the boxes under Saturday and Sunday.

After a while, Uncle Theo announces that he's tired and wants to take a nap. We condense the leftovers into one container for Gloria to hide in the staff fridge and throw the trash away. When we go to leave, Chris pulls Uncle Theo in for another hug.

"I missed you," my uncle says to him.

"I missed you too, buddy," Chris says and rubs his back. "I'll be back soon, okay?"

Uncle Theo nods and turns away. I have to fight to keep my composure as we leave. The only conclusion I can draw is that Chris reminds him of someone from his past he was close with and maybe even loved. On the elevator down to the first floor, I turn to Chris, "Are you okay?"

"Yeah, that was... crazy. Your uncle was so sad. Kind of broke my heart."

"Yeah, mine too. Old people are the worst." He chuckles, because he knows I'm just kidding. He grabs my hand, and I squeeze him back. "I have one more favor to ask you, Chris."

"Anything."

"I want to tell my dad. Today, if possible. And I want you to come with me."

He pulls me in for a sweet, barbecue-flavored kiss. "Let's do it."

# TWENTY-TWO

# I'D RATHER BE SELLING INVESTMENT PORTFOLIOS

"That was wild," Chris says when we're back in his car. We're still processing our visit with Uncle Theo. Chris can't get over the fact that Uncle Theo is gay. "So, no one in your family knows?"

"If they know, they're not saying anything."

"That's incredible." He shakes his head.

"And kind of sad that he had to hide it his whole life. Or he felt like he did. I mean, what if he had a chance to be happy with someone?"

"Maybe he's happy now."

"Yeah, maybe." I wonder how happy a person can be in Uncle Theo's situation. I see a lot of myself in my uncle—stubborn, prone to solitude, cranky on the outside but sensitive on the inside. I'd be so miserable if Chris got sick of me and we stopped being friends. The thought of not having him in my life kind of terrifies me.

"Are you sure you want me there?" Chris asks, bringing me back to my most immediate concern. Our plan is to drive straight to Todesta, call my dad when we're close, and totally blow his Sunday all to hell.

"If it goes really well, I want you there," I tell him, "and if it goes really bad... I still want you there."

Chris nods and gives a little half smile. If this whole thing goes to shit, I'm going to need someone to lean on. Chris thinks I'm overreacting, but I think it's just because his relationships with his parents are so solid. Even though he was worried about telling his dad, I don't think he ever considered abandonment as a real possibility.

"I don't want to stress you out even more," Chris says, "but I think we should have a plan."

A plan right now seems like a great idea, whatever will reduce the chance of screwing this up royally. "I'm listening."

"Okay, check this. Whenever my dad goes into a meeting with a client, he has a set agenda of what he hopes to get out of it. Goals, you know? That way, even if the meeting goes off the rails, he has in the back of his mind what he wants to accomplish, and he can work toward it. Make sense?"

I'm not sure how coming out to my dad is like sealing the deal, but I'm interested to know more. "Go on," I tell him.

"For instance, other than telling him you're gay, is there anything you want to accomplish?"

"That's a pretty big deal." Let's hope, given my track record, I can even do that.

"I know it is, but is there anything else you want him to know?"

That's a good question, and one I haven't really thought about. "I guess I'd want him to know that our relationship is important to me."

"That's good. Then you should probably say it."

"Maybe I should see how it's going before I unload my feelings on him."

"See, here I disagree," Chris says. "I mean, you're basically making a pitch—not an investment—but yourself. You want to come out of this meeting with your relationship intact. Why not put it all out there—how you feel, what you want from him, how you'd like your relationship to grow."

That seems like a lot for one conversation. "Lay it all on the table?"

"Exactly."

It actually makes a lot of sense, even if the idea of making myself so vulnerable to my dad is terrifying. I'll show him everything—total honesty—and let him decide how he's going to take it.

"I don't want to get angry or emotional or blame him for not being part of my life," I tell Chris. "I'd like to avoid getting into all that drama, you know? In a way, I'd almost be able to forgive the years of noncommunication if he could just be cool about this one thing."

Chris nods. "That seems pretty generous of you, but here's the thing. You can't really control how your dad will react. You can only do your best in any given situation. That's why my dad says he doesn't get mad when he doesn't close a deal. He only gets mad if he feels he didn't make the best possible case for the client. So, regardless of outcome, if you make a good pitch, you can be happy with the result."

"I guess so, but this isn't some faceless client we're talking about; it's my dad."

"But it's still all about relationships. Do you have some things worked out you want to say to him? Maybe you could try it out on me."

It seems like this conversation is all I've thought about lately, but I've mostly been imagining what my dad will say in reaction to the news and not the way in which I might present it.

"Well, Dad, I'm gay. This hot piece of man right here is my boyfriend. I know it might come as a surprise, but I'm hoping you're okay with it, because our relationship means a lot to me, and I'd like for us to be closer than we have been in recent years."

"That's great," Chris says with a smile. "But you might just want to call me Chris. *Hot piece of man*, while true, might be too much for him. I think you should lead with that and then let him have a chance to express himself. Give him, like, five minutes to say everything he wants before interrupting. You want him to feel like he's been heard."

"You study psychology this summer?"

"I checked out a lot of coming-out websites in the past couple weeks. Now, do you want me to say anything or just stand there quietly?"

Chris has a tendency to jump in and defend me, which wouldn't go over well with my dad. I also don't want my dad blaming Chris or thinking he's the reason I'm gay.

"Just stand there. If he takes it badly, you saying something will probably only make it worse."

"Okay, then I think we have a plan."

Chris's smile is so positive and hopeful that it almost makes me think everything's going to be all right. I wish I had a tenth of his confidence. Chris tells me more about what we dubbed his "gaycation" with his dad, and even though he's not trying, it does make me long for something like that with my own dad. "He wants you to come out with me this summer," Chris says.

"Really?" I wouldn't want to intrude on their father-son time.

"Yeah, my dad's got a ton of miles from work, so you don't have to worry about the flight. We can just hang out and surf, skate, go to Disneyland, whatever you want."

I smile at that. In middle school I went with Chris and his family to Orlando to do the circuit of theme parks. It was a blast, and something my mom could have never afforded on her own. Chris made me go on all the roller coasters even though I was scared shitless. Like now, his courage is infectious.

"I'm there," I tell him.

Chris keeps up the conversation while my stomach gurgles and my head spins. When we reach the outskirts of Todesta, I think he realizes I'm not really paying attention, so he puts on music for the rest of the ride. I call my dad.

"Theo?" he asks, sounding huffy in his typically impatient way.

"Hi, Dad."

"What is it? I'm on the golf course."

That smarts a little, that he skipped out on my skateboarding competition yesterday, but managed to fit in eighteen holes of golf today.

"When do you think you'll be done?" I ask.

"I'm finishing up now. Twenty minutes or so."

I plaster a smile on my face so I'll sound more positive than I feel.

"Great. I have some big news I want to share, so if it's all right with you, I'll see you back at your house when you're finished."

"Fine. Susan should be home if you get there before I do."

"All right. See you soon."

Chris gives me another pep talk in their driveway, telling me again it probably won't be as bad as I think and citing his own irrational worries as evidence that everything will work out fine.

I knock on the door, and after what seems like a long time, Susan answers. "Theo," she says, trying to sound cheery, but she looks tired, in addition to being as big as a house, and I can hear my sister Ellie wailing in the background. "You caught us at nap time," she says, like she's apologizing.

"Sorry for showing up like this," I tell her. "I was just hoping to talk to Dad for a few minutes. He said he'd be here soon."

"Of course, come on in."

"This is my friend, Chris," I tell her. By this time, Ellie has caught on that her mother's distracted and waddles her way out into the foyer. She's wearing a pink tank top with some old food crusted on the front of it and a diaper. Her eyes are still wet with tears, but she's no longer crying.

"What's up, Ellie?" I lean down to mess up her hair, and she glances from me to Chris, then smiles at Chris. Chris gets all the smiles from my family.

"Who dat?" she asks and points at Chris.

"This is my friend, Chris. Chris, this is Ellie."

"Put her there, lil mama," Chris says and presents his fist for a bump. Ellie slaps his hand. Chris's fist explodes and rains down in front of her, poking her once in the belly. Ellie giggles at that.

"Sorry we're such a mess," Susan says, scooping up Ellie and dabbing at her shirt.

"It's cool. Pants are optional on Sundays."

Susan motions to the living room. "Why don't you have a seat, and I'll get you boys a drink."

"Don't worry about us, Susan. We'll just chill until Dad gets here. We'll be quiet if you need to put Ellie down or whatever."

"Okay." She smiles. "Say night-night to Theo and Chris," Susan says to Ellie.

"No." Ellie crosses her arms. She looks a lot like Tabs when she does that. I hope she gives my dad hell.

"Night-night, Ellie," I say to her, and Chris tugs at her big toe, which brings about another little giggle from her.

Susan and Ellie go upstairs, and Chris and I hang out in the living room. There are toys everywhere and the air feels a little stale and sour, like old milk. I wonder if my dad helps out with cleaning and childcare. I hope so.

"You cool?" Chris asks.

I nod as the front door opens and shuts. Chris and I stand to greet my dad. He sets his clubs by the front door and enters into the living room.

"I didn't realize you were bringing a friend," Dad says. "Chris, right?"

"Yes, sir." Chris and my dad shake hands. Then it's my turn. Chris and I sit back down on the couch, and my dad collapses into his recliner, just short of putting his feet up and turning on the TV.

"You kids want something to drink?" Dad asks and glances toward the kitchen as though about to call for Susan.

"No, Dad, we're fine." I lean forward and rest my elbows on my knees. "Like I said on the phone, there's something I want to tell you. Something I probably should have told you before now."

"That good, huh?" Dad says gruffly. He sits up straighter. His eyes widen as if hurrying me to get to the point.

"Well, this may or may not come as a surprise but...." I swallow and the words get lodged in my throat like a chicken bone.

*Just say it.*

"I'm...grrray. And Chris—"

"You're *what*?" His words are sharp and loud, edged with disbelief. He leans forward and braces himself against the arms of his chair.

"I'm... gay." The word shouldn't be that hard to get out. It's one syllable, for chrissakes. I go still—fugue state—and wait for his reaction. He huffs a little, blowing his breath out through his nose.

"Is this his influence?" Dad points to my shoulder where Chris sits rigidly, his hands folded in his lap, fingers slowly closing into fists.

"No." I shake my head. I'm not sure which is the better answer, so I go with honesty. "This is all me."

"Really?" he says skeptically, like he could argue me out of my own sexuality. "This is all you? Were you gay the last time I saw you?"

I take a deep breath and let it out slowly so that I won't say something snotty or sarcastic. "Yeah."

"And the time before that?"

I nod. "Yep, then too."

"And just when did you decide you were gay?" My dad narrows his eyes. It feels like he's trying to catch me in a lie. His question is loaded. To answer would be to agree that my being gay was a choice.

Instead of giving him some arbitrary age, I tell him, "Being gay wasn't a decision, but coming out to you was."

"And what does your mother have to say about it?" His mouth twitches like Tabs's does before she's about to launch a barb.

"She's okay with it." Even as I say it, I know it's the wrong answer. My dad has always tried to pit us against my mom, to make it seem like she was the one who left him, even while he was the one shacking up with another woman.

"Of course she is." He shakes his head, disgusted. He stands and crosses the room to the entertainment system. "I bet she *loves* it, one more thing to blame on me." Dad opens a cabinet and reaches behind some old VHS tapes, selects one of the cases, cracks it open, and pulls out a metal flask. It's *Winnie the Pooh*, one of my old favorites. I'm pretty sure Piglet was gay for Pooh, but that's neither here nor there. Dad twists the cap of the flask and takes a drink. Looks like I'm driving him to drink.

"No one blames you for anything." I try to keep the emotion out of my voice, because why would you *blame* anyone for this? I remind myself of my goals in telling my dad. Goal #1 has been met. Maybe we should just get up and leave.

*No*, I tell myself, *I'm going to see this thing through, and then leave knowing I couldn't do any more.*

"Is this because I didn't spend enough time with you when you were a kid?" Dad asks, still theorizing. "That turns kids queer, you know."

Next to me, Chris repositions himself, and I lay my hand on his knee because I know how hard it is for him to stay silent.

"I don't think that's it," I tell him. I'm tempted to ask him if he heard that on Fox News, but I don't.

"You think if your mother and I were together, you'd still be a queer?"

That's an interesting *what if* statement and one I'd never consider in a million years, because it's somewhat irrelevant.

"Probably, Dad. I don't know the exact statistics, but I'm pretty sure queers come from two-parent households too."

He shakes his head and runs his tongue over his teeth. "I knew she coddled you too much growing up. I told her over and over you needed a strong male influence in your life."

And here I almost laugh at the irony of it all, because he should have been that strong male influence. I'd still be gay, but at least there wouldn't be this chasm between us, this distrust born of not really knowing each other because we've hardly ever hung out one-on-one. Chris knocks his knee against mine, a reassuring gesture. His presence gives me the strength to continue.

"Dad, maybe we shouldn't focus right now on what might have been. The reason I'm telling you this is because I want to be honest with you. And my sexuality aside, I'd like for us to have a relationship."

Dad runs one hand through his thinning hair and smiles like the actor in *American Psycho*. I never know what the hell that smile means. "I don't know what I'm going to say to your grandmother, Theo. She's not going to like this one bit. I wouldn't be surprised if she revokes your trust fund money."

I stare blankly at the gaping flat-screen TV. I should have known we'd get into trust fund territory sooner or later. For my dad, it seems his world revolves around money, and the trust fund has always been his bargaining chip. That carrot he's always dangling just in front of my nose. And maybe because it's always been a threat to take it away, I've never thought of it as mine, so in this moment, I honestly don't give a shit about the Wooten Family Trust fund.

"I don't really care about the trust fund, Dad."

He looks offended by that. "Oh no? You think you'll be able to afford college without it?"

I feel myself growing more and more despondent, retreating entirely from this conversation like I'm overhearing it from across the room, thinking *that poor kid is screwed.*

"I don't know, Dad. I hope so."

"You hope so," he scoffs. "You think being queer is worth throwing your life away?"

"He's not throwing anything away," Chris says with a rumble in his voice. Only I know how much it's killing him to stay calm. "He's smart enough and works hard enough that he doesn't need your money. You should be proud of him for that. I know I am."

Chris puts a hand on my shoulder and I grab for it, smiling almost by accident. It reminds me of Uncle Theo's face when he spoke of Manuel, that sweet, private happiness, contrasted with the despondency when he mentioned his own relationship with his father. Chris was right. There's nothing I can say that will bring my dad around to my side. He has to want this too. Even knowing that, I try again.

"I came to you, Dad, because I wanted to tell you to your face that I'm gay before you hear it from someone else. It's not going to go away, and you're not going to be able to talk me out of it. Chris is my boyfriend. I love him. He's also my best friend. I'd like for you to get to know him better and me as well, because I want us to have a relationship, and I hope after you've had some time to think about it, you'll want that too."

My dad stares at his flask, grumbling for, like, a minute. His phone rings, but he doesn't answer it. All three of us listen to it ring while I count the seconds in my head, the most excruciating of awkward silences. Instead of feeling angry, I start to feel bad for him, this man who's pushing fifty and sneaking drinks on a Sunday afternoon while his pregnant wife is upstairs, frustrated and unhappy. His phone quiets and nobody moves. I want him to say something.

"Maybe we should go," Chris says, not trying to hide his disgust.

Even though my dad is weirdly silent, I want to give him the chance to respond. This is an opportunity to show me I mean something to him. His big chance. He takes a long swig from his flask and sighs heavily.

"You know, Theo?" He draws his finger along the edge of the entertainment system. "I'm not really sure what's going on in your head. Tell you the truth, you always were a weird kid. I never could quite figure you out. I tried, kid, I really did, but the fact of the matter is, I just don't have time for this. I admit I made some mistakes, with your mother and you and your sister both, but you're practically an adult now. And me?" He shakes his head and plasters another one of those strange smiles on his face. "I've got another kid on the way. You realize I'm going to be in my sixties by the time that kid is eighteen? Jesus." He squints at the sliding glass doors that lead to their in-ground pool and screened-in patio.

"So you want to be a queer," he continues. "Go on and be a queer. Good luck to you. As for me...." He shrugs. "I've got enough on my plate as it is." He tilts the flask back all the way so it goes completely vertical, then caps it and places it back into the VHS case.

My father's an empty box. I wonder if he was always like this or if life has sucked the good stuff away. For me, I'm in a bit like a free fall —my father doesn't care enough to even pretend to try. Maybe he's been pretending this whole time by trying to fill a role he was never interested in the first place.

I stand so that we're eye to eye. I wish I knew the magic words that would bring him around, something I could harken back to that would bind him to me, some great father-son memory to make him want to put in the effort to accept me and maybe even get to know me better, but I don't have it, and even my desire to do so is dwindling. Maybe I've always wanted more from him than he could give and in his own way, that's what he's telling me now.

"Listen," I say, "don't punish Tabitha for this. She needs you and wants to be part of your and Susan's family. She's really excited about the new baby, and it would crush her if you cut her out of your life."

Dad clears his throat, frowns, and studies me for a moment. He nods once and holds out his hand. I take it, and he gives it one hard pump. "It's too bad it had to be this way," he says like it's completely out of his control. I'm a deal gone bad. I'm guessing it's partly an apology, but mostly it's a goodbye.

"It doesn't have to be this way," I tell him. "This is a choice you're making."

My dad's mouth forms a grim line. He lets go of my hand and walks out to the patio, shutting the glass door behind him. He must not want me to follow him. I turn blindly to find Chris's arms. I lean my head on his shoulder and he rubs my back, whispering encouragement into my ear, most of which I don't hear because I'm overwhelmed with the finality of it all.

I could say it's my dad's loss, but I know it's mine too.

# TWENTY-THREE

# BIFFLE

"You can cry if it'll make you feel better," Chris says. His arms are wrapped around me and my face is buried in his neck where we stand in the middle of my dad's driveway. I think of Uncle Theo just hours ago in this same warm and comforting embrace. What a treasure.

I take a deep breath and release it into his skin. I feel strangely empty. Maybe the tears will come later, but for now I mainly just want to get the hell out of here and go home.

As we break apart, Chris grabs my hand. "I'm really proud of you, T. That took a lot of guts."

I tear up then, a little bit, not really because of my dad, but because Chris has always been there for me—after every shitty visit with my dad, every argument, every rejection. He's been the constant in my life, my role model, and my best friend. "Thanks, Chris."

"Maybe I shouldn't have pushed it."

I sigh, trying to expel all the bad feelings I absorbed inside my father's home before climbing into Chris's car. "I'm glad I did it. Like you said, I made my best case."

"If your dad doesn't want to make time for you...."

Chris doesn't finish his sentence. We both know it's about more than making time, but in a way maybe it is just that. My dad has never made me a priority in his life, and he likely never will. That's the cold, sobering truth. At least I can accept it, knowing I tried.

"He might still come around," Chris says, ever the hopeful one.

"Maybe," I agree, though I truly doubt it.

"Any time you want to talk about it, I'm here for you."

"Your dad would have never done that," I say, not really as a comparison, but as an observation.

Chris's jaw sets in a hard line, and he shakes his head. "No."

It's hard not to take it so personal—the gravity of the realization that my dad really doesn't want me. It's going to take some time get over, if that's even possible. At least Chris was there. I can talk with him about it, and he'll understand completely. I'm less alone, because I can share the burden with him.

"I'm really glad you were there," I say to him.

"Me too." He shakes his head. "Man, I wanted to beat his ass so bad."

I smile at that. "I appreciate your restraint."

"What an asshole," he says, gripping the steering wheel a little tighter.

I wish I could get angry like Chris, instead of feeling all sad and dejected, but I'm just not wired that way. Chris projects his emotions outward, whereas I suck them up and stew on them.

"If you were my son, I'd be totally stoked," Chris says. "You're, like, the coolest person, you know?"

My spirit lifts a little. "Thanks, Chris. You always know just what to say."

We drift into silence, and I get to thinking then about Chris and me, and how, if he's my boyfriend, we can't really be best buds anymore, and that's something I'm going to miss.

"Still thinking about your dad?" Chris asks, perhaps picking up on my silence.

"No, actually, I'm stressing about something else now."

"You going to make me guess?"

"It's nothing."

He pulls into his driveway a few minutes later, and I help him unload our stuff. I pile my bags on the side of his car, then help him haul the boards back to his shed. While we're in there, he grabs my hand and draws me to him.

"Talk to me, T." He pulls me in close so our noses are touching, warming me up for a kiss. "Whatever it is, you don't have to hide stuff from me."

I hesitate because I don't want to jinx us or have Chris think I'm not into this 110 percent. "I was just thinking about how, now that we're together, we can't really be best friends anymore. And that sucks."

Chris frowns. "Yes, we can."

"I mean, sort of, but what if we break up?"

"We just got together," Chris harrumphs.

"I'm not saying I'd ever want to break up, but if it happens, then what?"

Chris's eyebrows furrow, and he stares past my shoulder for a moment. "I don't want to think about it. That would really suck."

"Yeah, I know. It would be *the worst*."

"We should make a pact," he says. "Like, no matter what happens with this, we'll always be friends."

"Can we make that promise?"

"I can," Chris says stubbornly, a challenge in his voice.

"Well, I can too."

"Bet me, then."

"Bet you what?"

"That we'll always be friends."

"To make a bet, you have to be at odds. Otherwise, what's the bet?"

He groans at my literal interpretation of things. "Just this once, let's bet on the same thing. The consequence of breaking the bet is a lifetime of suck."

I'm tempted to ask him to define "lifetime of suck," but I figure it to be more symbolic than anything else, and regardless, not having Chris as a friend *would* suck, for at least a lifetime. So I agree to his bet and we shake on it, as our deals have always been sealed in the past. It's settled. No matter what happens, we'll always be friends. I'm relieved. Chris is good at making complicated things seem easy.

"Be honest if you get sick of me," I tell him.

"It's been five years and I'm not sick of you yet. Be honest if I'm getting too possessive or jealous."

"I don't see that happening." He lifts his eyebrows like he doesn't believe me. "Fine, but honestly, I kind of like it."

He grins at me like a scoundrel. "Awesome, then if you're done, I brought you in here to make out with me."

"It's all about you, isn't it?" I tease, and he peppers my lips until I kiss him back with fervor. I'll never get tired of this—kissing, touching, talking—all our little intimacies and exchanges. I think of Uncle Theo's friend and what a loss that must have been for him to endure, how a person can spend their whole life searching for the kind of connection Chris and I found in each other. How lucky are we? Wherever I go in life and wherever I end up, I want to remember this feeling of being understood and accepted exactly as I am. And I want to love and honor Chris with the same devotion.

"You have my heart completely," I confess to him.

"You've got mine. Even though yours is probably bigger, judging from the rest of you."

I chuckle and he grips me tighter, demanding my full attention. We make out in the fading buttery light of his shed until my mom calls me home from my bedroom window, reminding me there's a whole world outside, and we can't keep it waiting forever.

I press one gentle kiss on the tip of his nose. "I gotta go, Boss."

"See you tomorrow."

We exit the shed to find my mom shaking her head at us with a small smile on her face. As soon as she turns away from the window, Chris grabs my ass, and I dive in for one more good night kiss. "Best friends for life," he reminds me with that cocky grin as he struts up his driveway. I watch him until I can't anymore.

## TWENTY-FOUR
## MUY, MUY

I thought it would be weird dating my best friend. Like, it might be awkward at first, or we might need to give each other some space so we don't wear ourselves out. But as it turns out, our romantic relationship is a lot like our best friendship, only with sexy times. Like, we'll be playing video games and one of us will get horny and then we're rolling around on the floor with our mouths mashed together or dry humping to get ourselves off before anyone catches us. Or we'll be skating somewhere, and Chris'll corner me behind a building for a quick make-out sesh. Our friends all know we're together, but we don't do a lot of PDA's. Chris probably wouldn't mind it, but I don't like having our relationship on display, especially after What's in Wooten's mouth? I'd like to keep our business between us.

Sometimes we get lucky and our parents will be out of the house, and one of us will put out the bat signal that we're in the clear for some heavy petting.

Like today, we're in Chris's bedroom because his parents aren't home from work yet, and Paloma has the day off. Chris cleverly added his parents to Find My Friends so he can track their commute from work to home. They still haven't left the office, which means we have another half hour at least. We're taking a break, both shirtless and laid out on his bed. Chris is a cuddler, so even when we're not making out, he likes to be touching.

"Tell me about the first time you knew you had feelings for me," Chris says with his face buried in my neck, one arm draped across my chest and his other hand nestled in my hair.

I think back to about a year ago, when we were surfing down at the pier. Chris fell asleep on a beach towel, and I was lying beside him on my own towel with my sunglasses on, trying to appear to be napping, but really I was watching him sleep, like a complete weirdo. I remind him of that day, then admit, "You were getting a hard-on, and I was imagining sucking you off."

"Really?" His eyebrows shoot up as he assesses me. "The first thought you had about me was a blowjob? That's so... advanced."

"I've always been at the head of the class. How about you?"

"There was no first time for me," he says, nosing my shoulder. "Remember when you were helping me out with geometry?"

"Yeah."

"I actually didn't need that much help. I just missed us not being at the same school. And when you'd be figuring out a problem, you'd get this cute little wrinkle on your forehead." He kisses the center of my brow. "Or you'd, like, gaze off at nothing, and I'd think about kissing you."

I shake my head at that, even though there's a smile on my face. "I still can't believe you knew for *so long*."

He sighs. "I did and I didn't. I wasn't sure if I was just in love with you as a friend or if there was something sexual behind it. When I got back from California and saw you, I knew it was physical too. It was like, *rawr*." His *rawr* is a deep growl that turns me on like nothing else.

"Rawr to you too." I roll onto my side to kiss him. Our lips and tongues get lost in each other, a dizzying dance where I lose all sense of time or place. Our chests press together, and he rolls me over so I'm on top of him. I brace myself on my elbows and tangle my fingers in his hair, then work my way down his neck to his collarbone, following the line to the hollow of his throat. He bucks a little to show me how aroused he is, but I couldn't possibly miss it.

"So nice," Chris murmurs dreamily, a slow smile pouring across his face as I lazily pump my hips back and forth, feeding the mounting friction between us.

"Where are your parents now?" I ask.

Chris reaches for his phone. I lean down to kiss both of his amazing pecs. I tease one nipple with my tongue and then the other. I nuzzle his chest and inhale deeply. If I could replicate his scent, I would pour it all over everything I own.

"Still at work." He grabs my face in both hands and brings my mouth to his, kisses me deeply.

I sit back and unbutton his shorts, yank them and his underwear all the way off so he's completely naked. "I like the sound of this," he says and props himself up a little on his pillows. I grab hold of his already hard penis and stroke him a few times, admiring the tightness of his cock and balls. With my fingertip I trace the tan line across his lower abdomen, below which the sun never touches. *Mine*, I feel like growling. Chris groans and raises his hips off the bed, responsive to my touch. I scoot down so I'm kneeling between his legs, bow down, and gobble up his cock, relaxing my throat so I can take him in deep.

"Aren't we supposed to use condoms for this?" he asks.

I recall his mom's five-paragraph essay on safe sex. Dave and I used condoms in the beginning, but we got a little lazy about it toward the end. There's really no risk for Chris, but if he wants to return the favor, then I should probably wear a condom. Until I get tested, it's better safe than sorry.

"Where do you keep them?" I ask.

"Treasure chest, Goldfish bag."

I find his stash, rip open the condom, and unroll it over his thick erection. "This must be where you keep all those biscuits, Gordito," I tease him.

"Yeah, and you look hungry," Chris says with a smile.

I resume my role with plenty of slobber and enthusiasm, which I've discovered is the key to a good blowjob. Chris writhes and bucks beneath me, and I have to steady him with my hand on his chest in order to keep up a successful rhythm.

"*Ohmygodwhatareyoudoing*, yes, Theo, *yes*," he exclaims as he rises off the bed and jams his junk so far down my throat I gag a little. He pumps his hips a few more times and then floods the condom. I latch on until the last little jog.

"Sorry about that," he says afterward with a huge grin that reminds me of the look he used to get after he smoked weed.

"Feel good?" I ask as I slide off the condom.

"Felt fucking amazing. You learn that from Asshole Dave?"

"Yeah."

Chris shakes his head. "Well, at least he was good for something." Chris is completely blissed out, so I wrap the condom in a tissue a few times and deposit it in the bathroom trash. "Don't forget to take out the trash so Paloma doesn't find this."

"She won't dig that deep."

I come out of the bathroom to give him a look, "Chris, come on, don't be lazy."

He's still smiling. I don't think there's anything I could say to wipe that self-satisfied grin off his face.

"Come back. I'm lonely," he whines. Back in his bed, he drapes his thigh over my hip and asks me, "You think you could show me how to do that?"

I give him a doubtful look. "Maybe, but it's going to take a lot of practice if you hope to get as good at it as me." He shoves a pillow at me and I shove it back, which turns into a wrestling match. Chris pins me to his mattress with all his weight on top of me. I stop squirming and stare at him with abject adoration because I want to be conquered by him every which way.

"I love you, Theodore Wooten the Third," he says and rubs his naked groin against my full-bodied and clothed erection. He leans down and licks my cheek like a dog. Strangely enough, he's done that a few times, before we were even together.

"I love you too, Christian Mitcham the First."

"Muy, muy?" he asks with the bright-eyed confidence of someone who already knows the answer.

I laugh and free my arms to grapple him into a big bear hug. "Sí, Gordito, muy, muy."

# ACKNOWLEDGMENTS

First love can be both tender and terrifying. With Theo and Chris, I wanted to capture that fledgling, hopeful feeling of falling in love and discovering your best friend is the person you've been looking for all along. I also wanted to be true to the awkwardness most new relationships endure, whether you've been friends for life or have only just met.

Thank you to Ashley Pope for helping me find a bittersweet ending for Theo that honors his struggle, and that of so many LGBTQIA youth in coming out to their loved ones. Sometimes we must create support networks outside our families to find the love and acceptance we need to grow and thrive.

Thank you to AngstyG for her brilliant work on the cover. She's able to translate an entire story and mood into just one illustration. No matter what I throw at her, she exceeds my expectations every time.

Thank you to Heather Whitaker and Angele McQuade for their unwavering support in this creative endeavor and Dr. J for generously providing her lake house for so many productive writerly retreats.

Thank you to the readers, the new-to-me ones and those who keep coming back for more. Your support means everything to me!

And lastly, thank you to my darling husband, brilliant daughter, and delightful son who make me laugh and bring me joy *almost* every day.

# BOOKS BY LAURA LASCARSO

**Contemporary M/M Standalones**

Andre in Flight

When Everything Is Blue

In the Pines

A Madness Most Discreet

A Soft Touch

**Hiroku Duet**

Hiroku

The Bravest Thing

**Giovanni Duet**

Giovanni

Master's schiavo

**Mortal and Divine Trilogy**

Book of Orlando

Bloodborn Prince

Parousia

# ABOUT THE AUTHOR

Laura Lascarso wants you to stay up *way* past your bedtime reading her stories. She aims to inspire more questions than answers in her fiction and believes in the power of storytelling to heal and transform a society. When not writing, Laura can be found screaming "finish" on the soccer fields, rewatching *Avatar: The Last Airbender*, and trying to convince politicians to act on climate change. She lives in North Florida with her darling husband and two kids. She loves hearing from readers, and she'd be delighted to hear from you.

Want updates and bonus content? Sign up for her newsletter at www.lauralascarso.com or join her Facebook group.